NORTH OF
DENTON

C. J. Petit

D1444395

TABLE OF CONTENTS

PROLOGUE

Sedalia, Missouri
May 17, 1875

Matt looked across the table at his younger, but far from little brother, Mike. He was hiding something. Something big. Usually he'd come bouncing in from his daily chores babbling about anything under the sun he decreed worthy of babble, but not tonight. As they ate their dinner of beans and bacon with cornbread, they ate in silence. That was okay with Matt normally, but not when he knew that Mike was going to spring something on him and after about ten minutes of quiet, Matt had enough.

"Okay, Mike. Let's have it."

Mike looked up at him sheepishly, "What are you talking about?"

"Unless you had secretly joined a monastery, there must be a reason for your tongue taking the night off."

Mike knew he couldn't keep this kind of news from his big brother, so he sighed and said, "Well, you know Margaret Henderson? Her dad runs the hardware store in Sedalia."

"You mean Maggie? The girl you've been mooning over for the past year. That Margaret?" Matt asked as he grinned.

He knew what was coming for quite some time now as Mike had been burning that four miles of trail between their farm and Sedalia until his horse didn't need any guidance coming or going.

Mike blushed slightly as he replied, "Kinda. Well, last night I asked her to marry me and she said yes, and her father was mighty pleased, too. That surprised me 'cause I thought he'd be ready to hogtie and skin me, but it turns out her ma and pa liked me almost as much as Maggie did."

Matt stood and leaned across the small table, stuck out his huge right hand which was snatched by Mike's almost as massive right hand.

"Congratulations, Mike. I'm really happy for you," Matt said.

Mike grinned with a combination of relief and sincere appreciation for his older brother's blessing.

When they had returned to their seats, Matt brought up the obvious repercussion of Mike's announcement.

"Mike," he began, "This is going to mean some serious changes around here. I know the house has two bedrooms, but that wouldn't be right. A man and a woman need a house to themselves and can't have some grown man living under the same roof."

Mike shook his head and said, "Matt, we could build you another house nearby. We've got the room. You could build it over by the corral. That's where you spend most of your time anyway."

"No. I've been thinking about this for a while and I have a different notion."

"You have? Why?"

"Hell, Mike, anyone, including a blind man, could see what was happening between you and Maggie. I was just wondering why it took you so long. Maggie is a wonderful girl and will make you a great wife."

"So," asked Mike," what are these plans that you've come up with?"

"First, after the wedding, I'm going to spend a week away from the farm. That will give you and Maggie time to, shall we say, get acquainted. Then I'll come back for a few days to get my stuff together and I'm going to hit the trail."

"Matt! You can't do that! This is our farm. Pa left it to us. It's a good money maker and that's just not right."

"Mike, when ma died four years ago, pa left us as well. He may have been here in body, but his spirit was broken. You and I have been taking care of the place since we were no taller than a fence post and just as skinny. Pa just didn't care anymore. He was always a good man, but when any man loses interest in life his life isn't worth living. Cholera may have taken ma, but pa died from a broken heart, not pneumonia like the doc said. Since then, you've done a lot more to make the farm better. You brought in the hogs and the milk cows and chickens. You built the smokehouse and chicken coops. Hell, you do more around here than two of me."

"That's not true, and you know it. It was that herd of Morgans that pa brought out here that kept this farm together in the first place. He supplied horses to the whole area. Of course, he was lucky to hang onto one stallion and six mares during the war, but after it was done, you and pa brought that herd back. Now it's back up to forty head. You did that."

"Well, that may be, but I've always wanted to see the rest of the country, especially out west. So, look at it this way. You'll be getting what you want; a home, a wife and, unless I miss my guess, a large brood of young'uns. I'll be getting what I want, a chance to see what's out there waiting for me."

Mike examined his brother to see if there was any chance that he might be making the offer as some noble gesture, rather than the truth, but he knew that Matt never lied, and his desire to leave seemed genuine.

"Alright, Matt. If that's the way you want it. But this farm is half yours, I can't deprive you of that."

"I've already thought of that. How about this? I know that you aren't fond of the horses. Me, I'm not too keen on the hogs, for obvious

3

reasons. Now, does this work for you? I'll take the herd, leaving you with a few mares and maybe a colt if you want to start breeding again. I'll take five hundred dollars out of the bank to get me started. The rest of the money and the farm will be yours, free and clear. How's that sound?"

"What will you do with a herd of Morgans? You don't have any place to put them."

"Not yet. But land in Texas is pretty cheap right now and I plan on spending some time riding trail with one of the outfits that show up in Sedalia to drop off their herd. When I have the land, I'll come back and ship them on the railroad to my new place. That way, I won't have to wake up to the smell of those damned hog pens. But you may have to hire an extra hand for a while to mind the herd for me until I'm ready to move them."

"Actually, I won't," Mike replied, somewhat chagrined, "that was the other part of my confession that I hadn't quite gotten around to. Maggie was part of a package deal. Her younger brother, Willie, will be coming along, too. He's thirteen, but big for his age. He loves horses, too, so he'll be able to keep an eye on the herd."

Matt laughed, then said, "So, it sounds like our big plan is coming together after all. While I'm away, go ahead and sell some geldings and mares to keep the herd under sixty. I'll be taking Night with me. He's already causing some problem with Prince's ladies, and Prince isn't too happy about it. I'm sure he'll calm down once Night is out of the picture. So, when's the big day?"

"Maggie wants us to get married in two weeks, on June 11th. Is that okay?"

"Your call, podner. Or, really, it's Maggie's call, I guess. I'm flexible. There are three or four outfits in Sedalia right now and I'm sure I'll be able to tag along with one of them. I'll just need to go into town and pick up the rest of what I'll need."

"One more question, Matt. Will you be my best man?"

"I'd be insulted if you had asked anyone else," Matt answered as he smiled at his brother.

They shook hands and spent the next hour or so just talking, or rather Mike spent the next hour talking while Matt listened as he gushed about Maggie.

The next thirteen days before the wedding were busier than either had expected. Aside from the usual upkeeping chores on the farm, Matt and Mike had to go to the bank and the land office to change some records and change the account to Mike's name only and create a separate account for Matt and transfer the five hundred dollars. Matt went to Sedalia and bought a new Remington Model 1875 New Army single action revolver using the 44-40 cartridge. It wasn't as popular as the Colt Peacemaker, but he liked the feel of the gun better. He also picked up a Winchester 1873, which fired the same cartridge as the Remington, then added the accessories he'd need to ride the trail; saddlebags, bed roll, canteen, rain slicker, and a couple of nice blankets. When he slid the Remington into his new holster and added eighteen cartridges to the loops, he looked more like the cowboy he would become than the farmer he currently was.

The boys had to spend an inordinate amount of time cleaning and fixing up the house for the arrival of a woman, which included a trip to Sedalia with the wagon to pick up some new furniture. Matt suggested to Mike that he leave the fripperies like curtains and tablecloths to his new bride, as whatever they would have chosen would probably have been wrong anyway.

At last, June 11th dawned bright and warm as it should have been. Mike was nervous, but Matt was happy for his kid brother and just a bit depressed. He wouldn't miss the house or the farm, but he would miss those Morgans. He had grown up with them and they were family. He had broken most of them to the saddle using an Indian technique taught to him by an old Cherokee named Crying Wolf that had escaped the Trail of Tears as a youngster and had his own farm nearby. The method Matt used to train horses was to get them to accept his presence at an early age and gradually work them to the saddle. There were no bucking bronc exhibitions on the Little farm. When they were fully saddle broke, horse and rider were a team. Matt knew each horse by the names he had given them and would miss them until he had his own place.

But today was about Mike and Maggie. Matt had spent several hours over the past two weeks talking to Maggie and had grown very fond of her. She was a perfect fit for Mike. She was a listener, which was critical, had a wonderful sense of humor and an easy-going manner about her. The fact that she was easy on the eyes was a bonus.

When they arrived at the First Baptist Church in Sedalia, the Little boys were outfitted in their new suits. Mike's was a dark blue and Matt chose a medium gray. They stood out from the crowd of men, not because of the suits, but because of their size. Mike stood two inches above six feet and weighed just at 200 pounds. The farm work he had done over the years had filled out is frame in solid muscle. The only man in the room who was bigger than Mike was his older brother Matt. Matt had more than two inches of height and thirty pounds of weight on his brother.

The irony of their family name was that it wasn't originally their grandfather's name. When he emigrated from Quebec in 1827, he hadn't stopped in New England like most of his fellow Canadian emigres. He had continued west until he had stopped in St. Louis. There, he changed his name to Little, an abbreviated translation of their French family name which translated loosely to 'small winding river'.

So, Little, they were, but small they were not.

The wedding went without any major mistakes made, although Mike had a few transpositions when repeating his vows, causing a few quiet snickers and giggles among the guests. But none of it mattered as Mike and Maggie walked down the aisle as Mr. and Mrs. Little.

The reception at Maggie's parents' house was grand with plenty of food and drink. There was dancing, and many of the young ladies lined up to dance with Mike's older brother and many a cap was set on the large handsome young man that evening, but all were disappointed when they found he was soon leaving for Texas.

6

Matt had purchased a nice flatware set for the newlyweds, which he left at the house. His original plan of camping out for the first week proved unnecessary as Maggie's parents had arranged for the young couple to spend their honeymoon in Kansas City.

After the celebration, Matt rode his horse back to the farm, telling Willie that if he'd like to come out, he'd show him around the farm and let him meet the horses, and some of the lesser livestock.

Late the next morning, Willie arrived riding a sorry-looking beast of disreputable breeding. Luckily, it was a gelding and wouldn't cause mischief with Matt's precious herd. Matt shook his hand and spent two days getting him acquainted with his equine family. Willie seemed to take to the horses well, so Matt felt a little better about leaving them in his care. The biggest chore that needed doing was milking the two cows. Willie had never done that before, so Matt had to show him how it was done. The rest of Willie's orientation went well, and by the time Mike and Maggie were due to return, Willie had been well-established on the farm.

Mike and Maggie's wagon had barely reached the front of the house that morning when Matt and Willie bounded down the steps and greeted the newlyweds. They helped them unload the full wagon, which, in addition to all of Maggie's belongings, included the large quantity of gifts they had received.

Matt had cooked the noon meal and was cleaning the dishes, while Willie was helping Maggie move her things into the bedroom, and Matt wondered if Mike had been aware of how thoughtful their parents had been when they built the house and had the two bedrooms placed on opposite sides of the house. After lunch, Matt motioned for Mike to come over to the sink.

"Mike," he said, "I'm very happy for you and Maggie. Willie is working out great and knows how to handle the Morgans and the other livestock. So, if it's all right with you, I'll be heading out in about an hour."

Mike was a bit surprised by his announcement. "You're leaving already?"

"I think it would be good. I have my essentials packed. You and Maggie need the privacy, and I'm anxious to get started."

Mike nodded and hugged his big brother. They had been together for their entire lives and hadn't been apart for more than two days that entire time before the honeymoon.

Maggie re-entered the room and saw Mike and Matt embracing and she immediately knew that Matt was leaving.

"Matt," she said, "you're not leaving us so soon, are you?"

Matt turned to his new sister-in-law and smiled. "Yes, Maggie. I think it's time. Just like Mike and you, I'm ready to start a new direction in my life. Hopefully, just like you two, it'll be just as happy.'

Matt may not have talked as much as his brother, but when he did, he usually used the right words.

Maggie approached him and kissed him on the cheek and tried to wrap her arms around him, but barely made it to his back.

"Good luck, Matt," she whispered to him.

Matt smiled at them both and walked into what would now be Willie's room. He had already saddled Night and had his Winchester in his scabbard, then he belted on his Remington, and put on his vest and his wide-brimmed hat.

He walked back into the main room, shook Willie's hand, gave Maggie a kiss on her forehead, and then he and Mike walked out to the yard. Matt untied Night's reins and shook Mike's hand one more time, climbed into the saddle and trotted Night toward the trail to Sedalia. Before he lost sight of the house, he turned one more time, saw them standing on the porch and waved.

The sun was still high in the sky when he entered Sedalia to join his new outfit and start his new life.

CHAPTER 1

South of Denton, Texas
April 18, 1883

Will Bannister sat astride his favorite bay gelding as it trotted north, leaving a dust cloud behind him. It was a bright, early spring day and the weather was perfect. He left Fort Worth very early that morning, and was heading back to Denton and his ranch, the Box B, just north of the town. He had just arranged for the purchase of a new breeding bull, paid much less than expected, and was in a splendid mood.

He was making good time and humming 'The Eyes of Texas' when he noticed he was gaining on another rider, a smaller man dressed in corduroy pants and wearing a dark blue jacket topped off by a small hat of unusual design. The man wasn't dressed as a rancher or cowhand, and Will was intrigued, so he tapped the gelding's sides and picked up the pace a bit.

When Will was closer, he found him to be a young man in his lower twenties and seemed to have a pleasant, non-threatening face and what marked him as somewhat more remarkable was the absence of a firearm.

The young man hadn't even spotted Will as he drew to just thirty feet behind him as he seemed preoccupied, so Will needed to break him out of his reverie.

"Morning!" Will shouted.

The young man jerked slightly from his shout and then turned in the saddle, saw Will and smiled.

"Well, good morning to you, sir," he said as he slowed his horse to ride alongside Will, "My name is Elliot James."

"Will Bannister."

"As we're on the same road," said Elliot, "Can I safely assume you are heading to Denton?"

"Well, past Denton, really. I own a ranch north of Denton."

"Well, that's a coincidence. I need to find a rancher north of Denton myself. I'm not familiar with the area and could use some assistance in finding him. Do you know a man by the name of Patrick Reed?"

"Yes. I know him. He's a neighbor."

"Really? That will make my trip a lot easier. Where is his ranch?"

"I'll show you exactly where it is. Why do you need to see Mr. Reed?"

"I'm a reporter with the Fort Worth Star-Telegram and was doing some research for a different story and just happened to come across a most remarkable item involving Mr. Reed. My original story was pushed aside after my discovery and I decided to write a much better one about Mr. Reed. I'm riding there now to tell him what I found and to get his reaction. I'm sure he and his family will be shocked, but most pleasantly so."

Will Bannister was more than just mildly curious. He asked Elliot about what he had found and how it related to Mr. Reed, and the young reporter was not hesitant to answer. It was his biggest story yet and he already was bursting to let it out before he returned to his desk.

As they rode, it took Elliott almost twenty minutes to fully explain what he had uncovered and its significance. As Will Bannister listened, he recognized immediately the enormous impact that the story would have, not only on Reed, but on him and his family. He was surprised that the reporter hadn't thought of the secondary effects of his discovery, or perhaps just hadn't linked his Box B to the story.

Will asked him if he had told anyone else yet and Elliot assured him that he hadn't as he had yet to return to his office.

"I can't wait to surprise Mr. Reed," he said with a grin.

His own much bigger surprise came, when in one smooth motion, Will Bannister suddenly released his hammer loop, pulled his Colt revolver, cocked the hammer and shot Elliot through the head.

———

South of Dallas
July 7, 1883

Matt Little sat motionless on Caesar as he stood on a hill overlooking the ranch. Caesar was tall for a Morgan, the tallest on his ranch, standing almost seventeen hands, but aside from his height, Caesar was standard to the type. He was mostly black with a star on his forehead as the only marking, was five years old and had become Matt's primary mount the past year. They got along.

It was mid-morning, and it was going to be a hot one, even for early July in Texas. He removed his Stetson, wiped the sheen of sweat off his brow with his shirtsleeve and pulled it back into place.

Matt was surveying the south pastures of his modestly-sized ranch southeast of Dallas. He needed to add a third corral and was planning on using this part of his ranch because it had good water from a tributary of the Trinity River. The deep creek crossed the top of his property line and made a bow, dipping across the center of the property where he had his ranch house, which was really just a large cabin. The barn was much larger and much newer and even the bunkhouse was newer than the cabin.

As he scanned the grass-covered land, he reminisced about how he had changed since leaving Missouri. After leaving his boyhood home, Matt had accomplished almost everything that he could have hoped. He had first hooked up with a Texas outfit out of Plano, the Bar T. Although he didn't know anything about cattle, he knew a lot about horses and the crew needed a new wrangler to replace the old one who had run afoul of the law in Sedalia and would be spending the next few years as a guest of the state. So, Matt hooked up with the crew to handle the large remuda on its return to Texas. He got to know the cowhands and developed a deep appreciation of their way of life and the simple rules they lived by. He learned to handle the cattle when they needed some extra help and were willing to break in a greenhorn. Matt was well-liked, and his sheer bulk made him immune from the occasional outburst of fisticuffs.

When they arrived in Texas, Matt stayed on at the ranch and took care of the horses. He didn't make as much pay as the top hands, but he didn't need it either and pocketed most of his monthly pay in a Plano bank. When the rest of the crew went into town to celebrate payday, Matt joined them in the saloon where he would enjoy a single beer and let the other boys drink themselves into oblivion and whore themselves into one disease or the other. Matt was the rock they could count on to get them out of trouble or keep them from getting in trouble in the first place, so he was rarely teased about his failure to join in their binges.

Once each year, they'd cull the sizeable herd at the Bar T and drive them north to Sedalia. After the herds were put in their pens, Matt would ride north of town and visit Mike, Maggie and Willie. It seemed like every other time he visited there was another Little for Maggie to manage. Willie had moved into a small cabin they had constructed for him nearby and it was a happy farm. Mike added a third bedroom for the expanding family just before he arrived for his third annual visit.

His herd of Morgans had been well-maintained by Willie and had numbered seventy-two horses when he finally moved his herd from Missouri to Texas. It was more than he had told Mike to keep on hand, but they were all beautiful animals and neither Mike nor Maggie wanted to sell them. Each time a mare dropped a foal, Mike would say, "Matt will love this one!" and that would be that and another horse would be added to the herd.

On his sixth visit, just a little over two years ago, Matt had stepped up to the porch and knocked on the door. Maggie swung the door wide and greeted him with her usual great big hug, at least as far as she could get her arm around him, and a kiss, then had to ring the dinner bell to get Mike and Willie back from the fields.

When they arrived, Matt told them of his recent purchase an old ranch. It hadn't eaten into his savings as much as he had expected, but he had already fixed up the buildings and hired some hands. He was going to ship the herd there the next week but left them a colt and three young mares, so they could start their own herd. Willie was sorry to see the herd go but was pleased that he had his own seeds for a new herd that would be his. Mike was happy to get the pastures back for the farm.

So, here he was – a ranch owner. The herd currently counted over one hundred of fine Morgan stock after he'd brought in some new blood earlier in the year, so he could afford to let some go. It had been difficult to finally part with some of the animals he had known, but it was a business. He was finally making money, but more importantly, he had his herd with him again and was watching it grow.

He had three hands working for him. Rafael Silva was the most experienced with horses and could talk to them as well as Matt could. The Conger brothers, Chuck and James were good with the animals and did a lot of the routine maintenance as every ranch requires, but still needed seasoning to be able to use his method for breaking the new stock. The Congers lived at their parents' ranch three miles north of his and were more part-time than full-time help. They liked the situation because it gave them a chance to pick up odd jobs for more money.

He hadn't built a true house yet because there was no need. Rafael Silva stayed in an old bunkhouse that he had repaired before even hiring him. Matt had offered to let him stay in the cabin, but Rafael preferred the bunkhouse for some reason.

The cabin, while old, was still solid with a great fireplace and wood plank floor. It had a good stove and a full separate bedroom and had just required to have new chinking and the roof repaired. Matt couldn't see building the house until he had fulfilled the last part of his dream.

He needed to find that one woman who could make the house a true home.

He'd only been looking for the past year or so, since he had brought his ranch buildings back to a livable condition, but she wasn't as easy to find as he had thought. He'd had plenty of opportunities as he was deemed a good catch in many young ladies' eyes, but he had disappointed them all. It was just that none had seemed right, and that was probably Maggie's fault. His sister-in-law had become a standard to him without realizing it. Aside from being pretty, Maggie was a natural woman with no airs. She was confident, strong, smart and yet still fun to be around. She still had a softness about her, especially when she was with her children or Mike.

Matt wanted what Mike and Maggie had, and wasn't about to settle for less. It wouldn't be fair to the woman if he did.

But that was for another time. Now, he had to concentrate on building that new corral. The new site had to be far enough away from the other two corrals or the barn and pasture where the Morgans were. He was planning on buying some Percherons rather than more Morgans. A ranch a few miles east, the JN connected, had hit hard times because of falling cattle prices and a mild drought. The owner had decided to part with a few of his precious Percheron work horses to make up for the lost income. They were a huge breed, highly prized by freight lines and farmers and Matt had bought six of them at the bargain price of seven hundred and twenty dollars. One of them was a stallion, three were mares and the other two geldings. He'd probably use the geldings around the ranch and let the others do as nature intended and start their own herd.

He trotted Caesar down to the area he had selected for the new horses, dismounted and marked off one corner with a stake, then marched off two-hundred feet, pounded in another stake and repeated it twice. He was satisfied with his choice of location and would have Chuck and James Conger get started on the corral tomorrow. The six Percherons could stay in the holding pens until the corral was built, probably in another week or so.

When he returned to the cabin, he saw Rafael standing on the front porch talking to a man in a dark jacket which wasn't a very comfortable outfit for the middle of Texas in early summer. He was of average height with dark hair, a smattering of gray, and a pleasant face. Even from a hundred feet out, Matt could tell that he wasn't a city man. His weathered, tanned face belonged to someone who spent a lot of time outdoors.

As he approached on Caesar, he saw Rafael point him out to the man, who simply nodded.

Matt dismounted as soon as Caesar slowed down then just let his reins drop as he walked to the front of the cabin.

"Matt," said Rafael, "This is Mr. Sanderson. He came down from Denton to see you."

Matt approached Mr. Sanderson and shook hands.

"Glad to meet you, Mr. Little," he said, "Although the circumstances may be less than pleasant."

Matt wondered what this was about. If he said he was from Missouri, Matt would be seriously worried, but Denton? He didn't know anyone in that town.

"Call me Matt. Would you like to come in?" he asked as he gestured toward the cabin.

"My name is John and if you lead, I'll follow."

Matt walked into his cabin, with John Sanderson following while Rafael stayed on the porch, parking himself in Matt's rocker. Matt knew Rafael would hear everything in the cabin and expected him to.

"So, what brings you way out here from Denton, John?"

Sanderson sat down on one of the two chairs in the main room and Matt sat in the second.

15

"Do you know a man named Stephen McMillan?"

"I knew a Spike McMillan. He was a good friend, but I never heard his first name."

"That's him. He had mentioned that you didn't know his first name. Well, there's no easy way to say this, Matt, but Mr. McMillan is dead."

Matt was stunned. Spike McMillan was one of his good friends from the Bar T and they'd made the Plano-Sedalia run together six times and had probably spent as much time together as some married couples.

"How did that happen? He was only a year or so older than me. Was he sick or was it an accident?"

"No. He was hanged."

If Matt was stunned by Sanderson's first statement, he was shocked by his second.

"*Hanged? Spike?* That's insane. I've never known Spike to do anything even on the mild side of bad in all the time I knew him. He was one of the few hands on the crew that didn't see the inside of the hoosegow for some minor infraction of the law."

"The men who hanged him said that he was rebranding their cattle."

"Did they even take him into Denton and let the law handle it?"

"No. They strung him up in the nearest tree and notified the law later. The sheriff just took their word for it, and said the proof was obvious and there wasn't anything he could do about it."

Matt leaned back, astonished at the story.

After the shock finally wore off, he said, "There has to be more to it than that. I will not believe for one second that Spike would have done it."

16

"There is a lot more to it, Matt. Mr. McMillan was operating on our behalf. I own a ranch near Denton, the Rocking S, and I'm also a member of the Denton Cattleman's Association. We're a group of small ranchers in the area and had a problem with rustling. We had our suspicions but couldn't get any proof of any wrongdoing when Mr. McMillan approached us and volunteered to do some investigating."

"I know that Spike had been a deputy sheriff for a short time before joining up with our outfit in Plano, but I didn't think he did any serious law work."

"Be that as it may, he knew what we were looking for, knew who was probably doing it, and volunteered his services. After he started, he left us an envelope with instructions on what to do if anything bad were to happen to him. When we heard that he had been hanged, we read the letter which contained instructions. Inside the large envelope was a smaller envelope addressed to you."

With that, he handed Matt the envelope.

After accepting it, Matt unfolded the sheets and read:

Matt:

If you're reading this, then I screwed up. Maybe I wasn't as good as I thought I was, or they were better than I figured. I knew you had your horse ranch near Dallas, so I wrote this because you knew me better than anyone else and I can trust you.

First, I'd like to tell you how much of a friend you were over those years we were riding for the Bar T. I haven't got any family, so you're as close as I got.

I don't have much, but I want you to have it. The Colt shoots straight, but I know you like your Remington better. At least it uses the same ammunition.

I got some money in the bank. Maybe you can buy some more horses with it.

But the thing I need most is to see if you'd be willing to do what I couldn't do. I know it's asking a lot. You've got your ranch and a whole life in front of you. But over here, there are good folks getting robbed and that damned sheriff is useless. I don't know if he's in with the folks stealing the cattle or if he's just plain lazy, but there's no help there.

I only came down this way to see if I could buy my own place. The Bar T was sold to some English company last year after Jim Shelton died. They thought there were too many of us two legged critters on the place, including the overpaid ramrod. One of the boys told me that I could get a place real cheap around Denton, so I rambled this way. He was wrong, but they were having a barn dance and you know my weakness for the ladies. I met a pretty gal there, Peggy Reed, and she told me how her father was being robbed and might lose his place. I never did cotton to folks being run off their land, so I told her I could help. It made her downright grateful, too.

I met with an association of the smaller cattle ranchers in the Denton area and they hired me to find the rustlers, and figured it would be easy, but it wasn't.

My best guess is that the Box B is the outfit that's making off with the cattle. When I first started looking around, it was easy to track the Lazy R cattle to the Box B. But when I got there, I couldn't find any Lazy R animals anywhere. No signs of rebranding either. Another thing that bothers me is that some of the ranches down south aren't losing that many cattle, but none of them seemed to go to the stock pens for shipment, either. They were all moved locally and just disappeared. I couldn't find any of the missing brands on the Box B when I was sneaking around. This doesn't make much sense.

But now I'm getting a bit spooked. I've only been here a few days, but I think they spotted me looking around. Maybe I'm just nervous. This hunting rustlers is more your line of work than mine anyway.

So, if you would be willing to try to help these folks as a personal favor, I'd appreciate it.

You know, I had hoped to just get this job done and get on with my life. I wanted to find that place of my own and invite Peggy to join me.

If you're reading this, then I guess things don't always work out the way we want, but she sure is pretty.

Thanks, Matt.

Spike

Matt lowered the paper. Spike was dead. Matt didn't even know he was in Denton and now he'd lost his good friend just because he tried to help some folks and to please a pretty girl. He sighed and looked back at John Sanderson.

"Do you have anything else to add?"

Sanderson nodded, then said, "I brought Mr. McMillan's things with me. They're on the buckboard and here's the draft after we closed his account."

Sanderson handed him a draft in the amount of $643.11. It was quite a bit of money and a lot more than Matt expected Spike to have accumulated.

"It must have taken him a long time to raise this much. He was trying to reach the goal of a lot of cowpokes and own his own place."

"I was told that he was saving to buy his own ranch. I'm sorry for the loss of your friend, Matt."

"Thank you. The question is, what am I going to do about it?"

"That's up to you. If you decide to honor his request, though, you can come with me back to Denton. "

"I don't think I have much to decide, John. You can stay the night and I'll get my things together and ride out with you in the morning. Spike was a good man. One of the best. Good folk shouldn't have bad things happen to them. If I can help rectify that situation, I will."

With that he stood to his full height, towering over Mr. Sanderson, who nodded and rose.

As they walked outside to the porch, Matt glanced at Rafael who made no acknowledgment of the conversation but simply followed them down the stairs to Sanderson's buckboard. Matt yanked off the tarp covering all of Spike's earthly possessions; a saddle, bedroll, saddlebags and assorted weaponry. It took two trips to unload the wagon and move Spike McMillan's entire life into the cabin.

Once everything had been put away, Rafael finally spoke when he asked, "Do you want me to come along, boss?"

Sanderson was surprised that the Mexican knew the topic of their supposedly private conversation and was more surprised that Little seemed to have expected him to know it.

"No, Rafael. I need you here to look after the herd. I'll need the Congers to build a corral out on the south section that I just staked out, Once it's built, move the Percherons. It'll be their new home, and we'll be needing to build another barn out there as well, but that can wait until I return."

"How long are you gonna be gone?"

"I don't know. Could be a week, maybe a month or two."

Rafael nodded and left the room.

Matt then sat down with John Sanderson and had him clarify the problem and then as he cooked a quick meal, told stories about the time he'd spent with Spike on the long trail rides across the prairies.

As he spoke, Matt could envision Spike's grinning face as his hands flew emphasizing his own tall tales. It was one of the reasons that he had found his best friend in Spike as he had reminded him so much of his brother, Mike, in his talkative, outgoing love of life.

They turned in and Matt lay awake for over an hour wondering what had happened to Spike and vowing to make it right for his friend.

———

Matt normally liked to hit the road early but wanted to deposit the bank draft to his account and pick up some more blank drafts, so he'd have to delay their departure slightly to wait for his bank in Dallas to open. It would mean spending a night in camp on the road, but he was used to it, and Sanderson, as a rancher, should be as well. The empty wagon wouldn't slow them down as much once he'd decided that they'd break up the trip into two parts.

A little after eight o'clock, they were on the road, Matt hitched Caesar behind the wagon to spare the horse having to carry his weight for the trip and gave him time to become better acquainted with Mister Sanderson and the situation.

After stopping in Dallas to make the deposit, Matt and Sanderson were traveling again after a minimal delay, and Sanderson used the time to continue to fill in all of the blank spots in Matt's knowledge of the area and the situation. The more Matt heard about the problems that had plagued the small ranchers, the less he liked.

He told Matt how the smaller ranches had banded together to form their association, so they could hold their own against the four larger ranches. They had problems keeping their ranch hands first and then there was the outbreak of the mysterious rustling that had confused Spike. It was the cattle rustling which had resulted in Spike's hiring and subsequent hanging. It was a difficult and confusing situation, but Matt had made his decision and he didn't regret it. Spike's silent voice will be heard.

That evening they made camp off the road under a grove of cottonwoods and didn't bother even making a fire and set their bedrolls in the wagon's bed which was dryer and flatter than the rough ground. It was a pleasant night filled with more conversation about the situation and just getting more familiar with each other. Matt found John Sanderson to be an honest and likeable man, which was critical to the upcoming conflict, as he knew must happen. He didn't expect John or the other ranchers to get involved other than giving him information, but it was vital that he believed them.

By mid-morning the next day, they entered the streets of Denton, and as the wagon rolled past a fairly large mercantile, Sanderson asked, "Do you need to stop here for anything? We still have another five miles to go before we get to my ranch. I can have the other members of the Association come over tomorrow."

"No, I'm fine. Let's head to your ranch."

John nodded, then waved to a passing rider, before he snapped the reins and they rolled out of town heading north. Keeping a steady pace for another hour and ten minutes, they reached the arched fence gateway of Sanderson's ranch and turned down the access road after crossing under his Rocking S sign.

Matt examined the newly whitewashed ranch house another quarter mile down the access road that reflected so much of the bright Texas sun it hurt his eyes.

"Nice place," Matt commented.

"Thanks," replied Sanderson. "We like it."

As they pulled up to the house, a screen door flew open and a middle-aged woman wearing a green pin-striped apron popped out onto the porch. She was shorter than average, about five feet and three inches, had light brown hair and a smiling, oval face. She must have been quite handsome in her younger days, but the years of living in the Texas sun and working to take care of the ranch had taken its toll, yet those dancing blue eyes marked her as a lively woman and Matt liked her on sight.

"Welcome home, John!" she shouted when they were barely within shouting range.

Her husband waved at her, she waved back, and Matt had to smile as they reminded him of and older version of Mike and Maggie.

As they pulled up, Mrs. Sanderson was wiping her hands on her apron and John stepped down from the buckboard, trotted up to his wife and gave her a bear hug followed by a husbandly kiss.

Matt stepped down from the driver's seat, followed a few feet behind John, and just waited, still smiling, with his arms folded.

"Mary," he said, turning to Matt, "this is Matt Little from down south of Dallas. He's the friend of Steve McMillan that I went to see, and he's going to see if he can help with our rustling problem."

Mary stepped up to Matt, smiled and said, "Welcome, Mr. Little. Won't you come in and rest for a while? I just made some lemonade that would probably be just what you both need right now."

"Thank you, ma'am," replied Matt as he tipped his hat, "please call me Matt. And I would surely enjoy some of your lemonade, but first, I've got to see to my horse."

John said, "I've got to unhitch the team, too, Mary. We'll be in shortly."

Mary gave John another peck, smiled at Matt, then turned and jogged back up the steps and disappeared into the house.

Matt led Caesar to the corral as John Sanderson stepped back onto the wagon seat and snapped the reins, getting the two-horse team moving again. After Matt had stripped Caesar and brushed him down, he released him into the corral then helped John Sanderson roll the wagon back into the barn.

When the draft horses were in the corral, John said, "Let's go and get some of that lemonade, Matt."

"Sounds like a good idea, John."

"Oh…one more thing, Matt. Just to let you know, Mary's maiden name was O'Day."

Matt didn't understand why John had mentioned it, so he just nodded and replied, "Okay."

The two new friends stepped across the yard, then entered the still open front door. Every window was wide open as well to allow any possible breeze to pass through the house. Once inside, Matt wasn't surprised to find that it was just as well ordered as the outside. Comparing it to his own cabin he could see the presence of a woman. No man that he knew could make a house feel like a home.

They walked to the back of the house and entered the cabin where they found Mary pouring lemonade into three tall glasses.

Matt said, "You have a beautiful home, Mrs. Sanderson."

"Thank you, Matt. And call me Mary. Mrs. Sanderson is John's mother."

Matt laughed and said, "Yes, ma'am."

As they sat down with their lemonade, John turned to Matt and asked, "So, what is your plan?"

Matt had been thinking about that very question for the past day, so his answer was ready.

"Tomorrow, when I meet the other members of your Association, I'll get a better idea of the problem. My first step is to pay a visit to the Box B."

John was taken aback and asked, "Why? Those are the folks we're most concerned about."

"Well, I don't know if you've noticed or not, but I tend to stick out in a crowd. For some reason, folks remember what I look like, which makes it paramount that I visit them before word gets out of any contacts with your Association."

Mary laughed and said, "Yes, I'll admit you do have qualities that make you quite noticeable. Especially to the ladies, I would think."

Matt surprised himself as he blushed before he replied, "Well, Mary, I've been so busy setting up my ranch that I haven't had time for the ladies. To be honest, none have caught my attention, either.

I'm hoping one will soon, though. I'd hate to pass on as an old bachelor."

"I'm sure that won't happen," she said, still smiling.

John changed the direction of the dialogue abruptly, and Matt appreciated the change.

"Mary, now that you've handled the matchmaking side of the conversation, we need to get back to serious business of rustling."

Mary gave a wicked glance to her husband and said, "If you think rustling is more important than matchmaking, you'll be sorely disappointed."

With that, she finished her lemonade, stood, curtsied dramatically for effect, turned and walked out of the kitchen to the bedroom to do some sewing.

John looked at Matt and said, "Sorry about that."

Matt waved him off with a grin, as he had appreciated the repartee between the couple, knowing that they had enjoyed it themselves.

"It's quite all right, John. You and Mary seem to enjoy yourselves. Anyway, after I visit the Box B, I'll go to the other three big ranches to let them all know I'm here. I'm still trying to come up with an excuse for being here without appearing to be threatening."

"You could pretend to be a ranch hand looking for a job."

"That would be inviting trouble. First, they may offer me one and it would look bad if I turned it down. Second, my rig looks too nice for an unemployed cow hand."

"Well, you'll come up with something."

Matt nodded, finished off his lemonade and said, "Well, John, I'll be heading off. What time do you think you'll have tomorrow's meeting set up?"

"Heading off to where?" John asked with eyebrows raised.

"Denton."

"Do you think I'm going to be allowed to set foot in this house again if I let you go to Denton? Mary would make my life miserable for a month of Sundays if I let that happen."

"Yes, I would!" echoed a voice from the bedroom.

Matt had to laugh at the eavesdropping and said, "Well, I appreciate the offer of your hospitality, but I don't want it getting around that I'm staying here. I'd like to remain in the background as much as possible."

The not-so-mysterious voice from the nether regions of the house echoed again.

"Good luck with that, Mr. Little. You head back to Denton, and a man your size would start rumors that would echo back to the Box B and every other rancher before the day is out. Denton's not so big that you can hide easily."

As much as he hated to admit it, what she said made sense.

"Okay, that's probably true. It's been my curse for a while, so I'll get my gear together and move it into the barn. I'll stay in the loft if that's okay."

John just sat back in his chair, looking at Matt with a mild head shake and a knowing smile. He seemed certain of what was coming, and didn't have to wait long, either, as he and Matt heard the sudden, rapid approach of light footsteps, and here came Mary.

After stalking into the room, Mary began, "You'll do no such thing, Mr. Little! We have a spare bedroom that has never been used except for the occasional visitor, and you, sir, are an occasional visitor."

Knowing he had no chance to win this one, he grinned and replied, "Yes, ma'am, if you insist."

26

"I do," and with that she executed a perfect military about face and double-timed back down the hallway to finish her sewing.

John said nothing, knowing it would only get him in trouble, but just looked at Matt, shrugged his shoulders and smiled.

Matt just continued to grin, finally understanding John's comment about Mary's Irish roots.

"I'll go get my things out of the barn," Matt said as he stood, glancing once down the hallway, then left the house through the back door.

———

After he left to get his things, Mary returned to the kitchen to start making lunch, so by the time Matt had settled his things in the spare bedroom, Mary called both men back to the kitchen for the noon meal.

Both men dutifully entered the dining room and sat as Mary put one overloaded plate of food on the table before him and two with more reasonable helpings for her and her husband, then took a seat.

Matt was surprised that she could make this much food in such a short time, even if it was leftovers from last night's dinner.

"Mary, I have never eaten this much food," Matt commented as he stared at the giant helpings.

Mary never even glanced up as she began to eat and replied, "Then it's a miracle you're as big as you are. You need the food for all the work you'll be doing, and you'll eat everything that's before you."

He looked at those smiling blue eyes, smiled himself, then said, "Thank you, Mary," before starting attacking the avalanche of food on his plate.

John just sat eating with a small smile on his face as Matt had discovered one of what he would learn John called 'Mary's rules'.

There were quite a few, but John never bothered to write them down and would let Matt discover them on his own.

After lunch, as Matt and John sat down to outline the situation, John produced a map from the county land office showing the locations and sizes of the neighboring ranches. He then started to describe the ranches in greater detail, including the families and hands that called them home. The four largest all bordered Lake Dallas to the east.

John's hand started on his own plot of land on the map as he said, "This is the southernmost ranch and you're sitting on it now, the Rocking S. We only run a hundred and fifty head, but we have good access to water, as all of them do except for the Lazy R which borders us to the east. We let them share our water and we share costs for hired help when we need it. We never had any kids and can't really afford any full-time help and that makes us the epitome of the small-time rancher."

Now the Lazy R, is almost as small. They run about two hundred head and it's owned by Patrick and Beth Reed. They have four daughters and no sons, which was bad luck for Patrick, although he'll never admit to it. They usually get free help when cowhands come to visit their daughters, though. Their ranch borders the Box B on two sides, the east and the south."

"Right here," he pointed on the map, "is the Box B, one of the largest ranches in the county. They have a long access to Lake Dallas and run about two thousand head. Will Bannister is the owner. His wife died years ago, and he's got one son and one daughter. The son is married and lives on the ranch and they have anywhere from ten to twelve full time hands."

"Any of them handy with a gun?" Matt asked.

"Nothing to brag about, but they do have one hand, Jesse Hart, who's just plain nasty. He's not great with a six-shooter, but he'll drygulch you without a second thought."

The next ranch north of the Box B is the Star M. It's owned by John and Millie Morrow. They've got two sons and a married daughter and all of them live on the ranch. The family isn't openly hostile like the Bannisters, but they aren't overly friendly either. Their outfit runs about the same number of cattle as the Box B and keeps eight on their payroll."

The next of the big ranches is the JT connected. Jeff and Susan Thompson own that. It's a bit smaller than the Box B and Star M. They have three sons and about fifteen hundred head on the place. Their hired help varies, but generally they have eight cow hands. "

John continued along the map, tracing the ranches with his finger.

"The L Bar is about the same size. It's run by Henry and Abigail Lewis. They're almost as bad as the Reeds when it comes to lack of sons, too. They only have two daughters, though and both are unattached at the moment, although one of the hands is trying to make hay with the younger daughter. They've got around eight hundred head on the ranch and have six hands."

Then, John continued to trace along the map describing each of the other small ranches in the same way; family, size of the ranch, number of cattle and ranch hands. There were eight of the smaller ranches.

John leaned back and said, "So, that's the whole bag. What do you think?"

Matt kept examining the map and after almost a minute passed in silence, he said, "You know, John, this doesn't make any sense. Why would a big outfit like the Box B rustle cattle from smaller ranches when they really don't need them? If it's not the Box B, then why rustle from the small ranches at all? It's easier to grab a few head from a bigger outfit that may not miss them for a while, if ever. I've seen range wars before, and most of the time, water is involved, but sometimes it's disputed boundaries or fences put up that don't belong. None of those things seem to be here, or am I wrong?"

"No, you're not wrong. We've been asking those questions ourselves."

"Well, let me think about it tonight. We'll talk about it to the Association tomorrow, okay?"

"Sounds good."

Matt returned to his room and opened his saddlebags, took out his favorite book, *Caesar's Commentaries,* and stretched out on the bed. He was an avid reader because his mother had instilled the love of reading into him before he could even read himself. She told him how he could travel to exotic lands by just reading about them and letting his imagination take him there and be able to go back in time to witness great events or even read about fantasies that never happened at all. Once he started reading, he never stopped. The heaviest items in his saddlebags were always his books, and on this trip, he took Caesar and Dante's *Inferno*. Even as he began to read, the problem of the curious rustling never left the back of his mind.

After dinner, Mat decided he needed to look around, and told John that he'd be outside for a while and stepped out into the still sun-filled yard.

He walked to corral first to check on Caesar and found him content, then had his customary chat with the horse, because he usually did at that time each day. Then he patted his nose and left the corral, walking toward the Box B. He knew that it was probably a mile or so away, so it wasn't likely he was going to cross any boundaries.

As he sauntered along, he appraised the care that had obviously gone into the maintenance of the Sandersons' ranch buildings and corrals. With John's limited amount of hired help, that must take a lot of effort on his and Mary's part. He could see the cattle bunched up near a slight curve in the deep stream running across the top of the property and headed that way. As he reached the cattle, he noted that most were Rocking S brands, but some wore the Lazy R on their rumps and all of them seemed to be well fed.

After passing one small herd, he continued east to a copse of cottonwoods that stood along the bank of the stream and guessed that the pastures of the Lazy R began a few hundred feet away.

He stopped and leaned against one of the larger trees, then suddenly shivered when he realized that Spike had probably been hanged from a tree just like this nearby on the Box B. His shivers gave way to anger as he thought about the injustice done to Spike as he reinforced his determination to find the bastards who hanged his friend. What he did with them was another question altogether.

As he turned to go back to the house, he heard the unmistakable sound of approaching hooves. It sounded like two horses, he thought as he glanced around and spotted two riders approaching the trees. He didn't think he'd been seen yet, so he ducked behind the same tree he had been leaning on moments before. He knew that Pat Reed of the Lazy R didn't have any hands, so it was more likely they were from the Box B and noticed that one of them was wearing a two-gun rig. Box B hands on Lazy R property near the Rocking S made for an interesting situation, and most assuredly was trespassing. The sheer arrogance of the Box B riders to cross Lazy R property like it was their own irritated him considerably.

The two riders approached closer and stopped about thirty feet away when Matt suddenly realized that he was unarmed as he hadn't expected to run into anyone out here, much less some Box B hands. What they were doing on Lazy R land was another question, but there was nothing he could do about it now.

The two riders dismounted and squatted about twenty feet from Matt. They seemed to be looking at the Rocking S ranch house and hadn't looked in his direction, but Matt was still surprised they hadn't spotted him. He wasn't exactly petite.

"Boss said to stick to the Lazy R now. He said he wants to make somethin' happen," the older one said.

"Yeah, but we been spendin' too much time on that one. It'll look bad. We oughta get some more S stock, too," replied the one with the twin-pistol rig.

"I'm with ya. But we gotta do what he says. He knows what he's doin'."

"My Pa makes mistakes. Hell, there ain't nothin' goin' on since the hangin'."

"If you feel that way, go tell him. He'd listen to you."

"Nah. He thinks I'm nothin' but a no-account. He listens to Rachel, though. Maybe I can ask her to tell him. That might work."

"Do what you gotta do, Billie."

With that, the two mounted their horses and then wheeled them to the east and rode away.

Matt was glad he hadn't been armed after hearing that comment about the hanging, but the other information was puzzling. He'd have to ask John about it when he got back so see if he could make anything out of it.

He waited a minute to make sure they weren't going to return, and then briskly walked back to the ranch house.

As he turned the corner to the house, he saw John and Mary on the porch, rocking. John was smoking a pipe and Mary seemed to be darning something.

John saw him draw near, and asked, "Welcome back, Matt. Find anything interesting?"

"Strangely enough," Matt began before he reached the porch, "I did. And it was strange enough to add even more questions to the mix."

With that he stepped up the stairs. Mary started to get up from her rocking chair, but Matt waved her down.

He leaned against the porch support column and said, "You should hear this, too, Mary. You probably could figure this out better than I can."

Both leaned forward, the pipe and the darning momentarily forgotten.

Matt repeated what he had heard near the fence line.

Matt then summarized and said, "It sounded like one of the speakers was the owner's son. Does he have a kid named Billie and a daughter name Rachel?"

"Yup. Billie is not a chip off the old block, though. His father is ruthless, but he's no idiot. Billie tries to be ruthless, but he is an idiot and even wears a fancy two-gun rig, but I doubt he knows how to use them. Now, his sister Rachel is smart as a whip, but I don't know where she stands on all of this. I haven't seen her in two or three years."

Mary asked, "What do you think of the conversation?"

Matt paused, then replied, "It sounds like they really want the Lazy R gone and are using cattle theft as a cover."

John nodded and said, "That would make sense except the Lazy R may be the poorest ranch in the county. They have limited water and the grass isn't all that great. How they run as many cattle as they do is beyond me. Maybe because I let them graze and water on my spread."

"I saw a few Lazy R head mixed in with yours. Honestly, if it didn't make sense before, it makes less now. Well, I'm going back to reading for a while before I get some shut-eye. I'll see you in the morning."

Before he reached the door, Mary asked, "What are you reading?"

Matt answered, "Caesar's Commentaries. I've admired the man since I was just a young boy. That's why my horse is named Caesar."

John replied, "It sounds like you've been well educated."

"More than some, less than others," Matt said before he gave them a short wave and entered the house.

After he had gone, Mary looked up from her darning and said to John, "That seems like an exceptional young man."

John nodded and continued to puff on his pipe.

CHAPTER 2

Matt's eyes popped open as the morning sun flooded the room with light and was momentarily disoriented before he recalled where he was, then slid out of bed and without putting on his boots, left the room and tiptoed out to the kitchen.

After visiting the privy, he entered the washroom across from his bedroom and washed before shaving. With his morning ablutions completed, he returned to the kitchen and put wood in the stove and began the fire, then, after a short search, found the coffee pot and filled it with water from the indoor pump by the sink. As he was placing the full coffeepot on the stove, he heard the floor creak behind him and turned to see Mary stepping toward him.

"Taking my job, Matt?" she asked with her blue eyes smiling.

"No, ma'am," he replied with a matching smile, " I just thought I'd get things started and save you some time."

"Well, thank you for your consideration, but I'll take it from here."

Matt acquiesced and silently strode back to his room, finished dressing and then returned, much more noisily than before. When he reached the kitchen, John was already there.

"Morning, John."

"Morning, Matt. Sleep well?"

"Yes, sir. It must be this North Texas air."

John laughed, and said, "Right. It's much different way down south, isn't it?"

Matt smiled, sat down at the kitchen table then said, "I was doing a bit of thinking about why Bannister could possibly want the Lazy R to go away. He can't use the land, so I'm wondering if there is something on his property that's valuable, maybe a mineral."

John shook his head and replied, "There aren't any valuable minerals in these parts that I'm aware of. We can ask the Association members when they get here in a few hours, but I'll be surprised if they can come up with anything, either."

"But on the other hand, I did come up with a cover story for my being here, and when I came up with the solution, I had to smack myself in the head for not coming up with it sooner."

"And the answer is?" asked John.

"I'm making the rounds looking for a breeding stallion for my herd."

"That's right. You raise horses. I had forgotten."

"The best part about this is I won't even have to pretend anything. I am always looking for a breeding stallion to improve the herd."

"Great idea."

Mary intervened by placing plates of eggs and ham in front of them – lots of eggs and ham, then set a plateful of biscuits and a crock of butter on the table as well, refilled their coffee and sat down next to John, setting her own plate on the table.

Matt knew better than to comment on the amount of food on his plate. He'd learned the first of 'Mary's Rules' well.

After breakfast, Mary asked Matt about his family, and after he started talking about the farm, she was surprised.

"You came from Missouri?" she asked.

"Yes, ma'am. Just north of Sedalia. The Bar T ranch outside of Plano had been making drives to Sedalia for some time and I latched

36

on with them one year after my younger brother was married. They continued the drives long after everyone else was just heading to the nearest rail stockyard. The owner of the spread did it to remind him of his days on the trail when he was younger, or so I was told. He had to stop just after I left to start my horse ranch when those drives cost him too much money and probably too much of his health. He died shortly after I left, and his widow wound up selling the ranch to some British company, according to Spike's letter. But I got out in time and set up my horse ranch. I have mostly Morgans, but I'm adding some new breeds, too, including some Percherons."

Mary nodded and said, "Your Caesar is an impressive horse."

"He is. He's quick like all Morgans, but he'll run for hours if he needs to, and can cover the ground faster than most. He still can't talk, though. I'm still working on that," he said, finishing with a grin.

Mary and John laughed, and then they continued to talk about his ranch while they waited for the other small ranchers to arrive.

Before long, they heard hooves outside the house announcing the arrival of the first of them and John rose, walked to the front door and was followed by Matt. The first of the Association members to show up was Mike Wilcox of the Circle W. He was greeted by John and by Mary when she stepped out on the porch, then John introduced Matt to Mike, and before any small talk could commence, more riders appeared on the access road.

Within the next twenty minutes, all the Association had arrived and were gathered in the main room in assorted chairs as John and Matt had augmented the seating by pulling in the kitchen chairs. After they had all been seated, John introduced Matt to the others.

"Gentlemen, this is Matt Little. He owns a horse ranch south of Dallas and has offered to help us to fix our rustling problem."

The first question came from Pat Reed.

"Matt, I don't mean to sound ungrateful for what you're risking to help us, but have you had any experience in this kind of thing?"

Matt replied, "That's okay, I'm not offended. But to answer your question, I've never worn a badge, but over the years, I've had to deal with rustlers both on the trail and when I was with the Bar T and seem to have a knack for it. Jim Shelton, the owner of the Bar T, would hunt me down to track down the rustlers, but there was a lot more to it than just tracking and finding them. You had to outguess them, so you didn't run into an ambush. You had to think ahead about where they were going and what they were going to do. But the reason I decided to help was that Spike McMillan died trying to find out what was going on. I've never tolerated good folks coming to harm. Spike was a good man and a good friend and if John here is any indication, I believe you are all good men, too."

Joe Litton asked, "Matt, are you any good with your gun if it comes to that?"

"I've had to use it on occasion. I've killed two men, both after they had fired at me, but most of the cattle thieves I brought in alive. I'd rather let the law deal with them than see what some men refer to as 'frontier justice'. That's why we have laws, and why what happened to Spike should never have happened."

Tim O'Malley spoke up, "Did John tell you of our troubles with the sheriff? We've been complaining about missing cattle for months. Then when Mr. McMillan was hanged, he did nothing about it."

"John told me. Your sheriff's story isn't that unusual. It's an elected position. I'd bet that between you, your sons, and even your loyal hands you couldn't scrape together fifty votes. And you don't have any money to add to a sheriff's election fund, either. So, the sheriff wants to keep his job and throws in with where the money is. Now maybe this guy is a lot dirtier than that, I don't know. But we just ignore him. I hope to be able to find enough evidence to bring it to the attention of the U.S. Marshall's office in Fort Worth. They not only can bypass the sheriff, they can remove him from office."

That got some heads bobbing in agreement.

Matt continued, "Something came up yesterday. I was out on the east end of John's ranch and standing by that group of cottonwoods by the stream right where the Lazy R land begins, when I heard some horses. Turns out it was Billie Bannister and one of his hands. They didn't see me because their attention was on the ranch house. Billie wanted to go after some of John's cattle, but the cow hand reminded him that his father wouldn't like it, and that they had to concentrate on the Lazy R. Billie then said, and I'll try to be exact. He said 'we've been spending too much time on that one. It'll look bad'. It sounds like they were taking cattle from the other spreads just to hide the fact they were taking more from the Lazy R. Does that make any sense to anyone? Mr. Reed, do you have anything valuable on your ranch, like gold or silver, that would make them want to drive you off?"

Pat Reed laughed, then said, "Gold or silver? I can't even find enough grass to feed those damned critters. No, I can't think of any reason at all. But it gets my temper up to hear they were on my ranch again. Those bastards treat my property like it was part of their ranch."

Matt said, "We couldn't come up with a reason, either. What I need to know is how many cattle each of you have lost and how many you could afford to lose before it really hurt you financially. When did all this start, exactly? I mean, was Bannister this way since he arrived? Or has he changed?"

After hearing each rancher's accounting, he found that each had lost fewer than twenty head except for Pat Reed, who had already lost more than seventy. Not only that, his operating margin was so low that he couldn't afford to lose many more. His cash reserves were at a minimum and he had a family to feed. As to the question of Bannister's behavior, they all agreed that until spring, he'd been stand-offish, but not hostile. That changed suddenly, and he became more reclusive and the rustling began in May.

"Okay," Matt said. "It looks pretty obvious that Bannister wants the Lazy R. If anyone can come up with a plausible explanation, let's have it. Other than that, the next thing we need to do is protect Mr. Reed's herd. Now I'm planning on visiting each ranch, including the Association ranches. I'll say the reason for my showing up will be to possibly purchase a breeding stallion. I need to visit all the ranches to make my story more plausible and intend to start with the Box B because it's the highest risk with possibly the greatest reward. Then, I'll move to the Lazy R and go clockwise."

There were a lot of questions and few answers. They talked through a quick lunch and onto the early afternoon, and as the conversations finally began to wind down, it was Pat Reed who brought up one question no one had asked.

"How much is your help going to cost us, Matt?"

Matt looked at each in turn before he said, "Spike McMillan already paid in full."

Each rancher came up to Matt to shake his hand and to wish him well. How many expected him to succeed and how many thought he'd suffer a similar fate to Spike was open to debate.

As they were getting ready to depart, Joe Litton looked up at Matt's towering frame and said, "You've got to be the biggest Little I've ever seen."

There was general laughter which lightened the air of desperation.

They all left in a better mood as they made their way outside to their waiting horses.

Matt and John finally relaxed and before they knew it, Mary had one of her enormous dinners on the table. Matt commented that he'd outweigh Caesar by the time he returned to his ranch, and Mary took it as a compliment, as it was intended.

After dinner, Matt turned in early. He read for a while, then just lay stretched out and thought about what he would be doing for the next few days. He eventually had his plan set in his mind and fell off to sleep.

————

Matt breakfasted with John and Mary and then went out to get Caesar ready, which began when talked to his horse for a few minutes before he even touched his tack. Caesar seemed to understand, but probably didn't, or at least he didn't reply. Matt saddled his big black, put on his saddlebags, slid his Winchester into the scabbard, then he led Caesar out of the barn and into the bright sunlight. He looked into the cloudless sky and thought it was going to be a another hot one, which was a useless thing to even bring up in Texas in July.

Matt mounted Caesar and headed him down the road leading out of the ranch, and when he reached the main road, he turned left to head him to the Box B.

Twenty minutes later, Matt and Caesar were trotting toward a large ranch house that was part adobe and part framed wood. It was a handsome structure and could see some ranch hands moving about near the large barn a hundred yards to the right of the house. One of them must have seen him coming because Matt heard a shout that was directed to another hand, and when he got within fifty yards of the porch, a young man with a two-gun rig stepped out of the house and onto the porch. Matt was sure that he was looking at Billie Bannister. Billie assumed an arrogant position, with his legs spread and his arms folded as he watched Matt approach.

"Morning," Matt called as he drew within thirty yards.

He stayed in his saddle waiting for Billie's response. Aside from the Western etiquette that made it impolite to step down from your horse unless invited to do so, Matt thought it would be wiser if he needed to beat a hasty retreat.

"What do you want?" Billie finally asked in a surly tone.

"Names Matt Little. Do you own this spread?"

"Now, what business is that of yours? I asked you what you wanted, mister. If you don't want to talk to me, then I suggest you turn that nag of yours around and head back where you came from."

Matt tilted the brim of his Stetson back on his head and replied, "Well, I don't mind you being a tad abrupt this morning, but I don't

41

appreciate your insult to Caesar. He's a stud stallion and could probably outrun anything in the county and stay at it all day."

Billie was preparing another rejoinder or maybe a threat, but as his mouth opened, the screen door behind him opened, and out stepped a tall, dark-haired young woman; the kind of woman that turns heads wherever she passes. She took one look at Matt astride his magnificent Morgan stallion and broke into a welcoming smile, then reached out and put her hand on Billie's shoulder.

"Now, Billie, that's no way to treat a stranger. Why don't you go back in and finish your coffee?"

Billie had noticeably tightened up when he had felt his sister's hand on his shoulder, then tightened up more when she took control and ordered him back into the house. His manliness challenged, he came up wanting as he turned and stomped back into the house, slamming the door behind him in a weak attempt to regain face.

"Good morning," she said as she looked up at Matt, "my name is Rachel Bannister. Won't you step down?"

"Thank you, ma'am," Matt replied as he stepped down, then threw a loop of Caesar's reins around the hitching rail and stepped up to the porch.

Rachel may have been tall for a woman, but Matt towered over her and it made her just a little uncomfortable but a lot thrilled.

"What can I do for you, Mr. Little?" she asked as she looked up at him with her dark brown eyes.

Those eyes would make most men shiver under their Stetsons, and Matt wasn't totally immune, but he could see past their desired effect.

"Well, ma'am, I need to speak to the owner. I'm in the horse business, mostly Morgans, like Caesar here. But I need to bring some new blood into the herd, so I'm hunting for another Morgan stallion. I was told that someone north of Denton had a good-sized Morgan herd and would be willing to part with one."

"I'm not sure who gave you that information, but as far as I know, the ranches in this area are almost exclusively cattle. Each ranch has its own string of horses, of course, but I doubt if anyone has a Morgan stallion."

"That's bad news. I may go check with a couple of other ranches anyway, as long as I'm up this way."

"Would you like to come in for some coffee?"

"That would be appreciated. Thank you, ma'am."

"Come on in. And stop calling me ma'am. Call me Rachel," she said as she flashed him another dazzling smile.

"Thank you for that as well, Rachel. Call me Matt."

"I will do that," she replied as they walked into a well-appointed main room. Billie was nowhere to be seen, Matt noticed.

Rachel walked before him toward the kitchen rather than waiting for him, probably for show as walking was just a mild description of her manner of personal conveyance. Rachel moved in a combination of a strut and a sashay that was designed to let every man within sight know that this was all woman in front of him and Matt wasn't about to argue the point.

She stepped into the kitchen and took two cups from a cupboard and set them on the table, then picked up the still hot coffee pot with a towel and filled the cups.

"Sugar or cream, or are you like most men around these parts and drink it black?"

"Black is fine," Matt answered.

As she and Matt took their seats, Rachel asked, "So, what is the name of your ranch?"

"It's a small spread southeast of Dallas called the Double M. I don't need a lot of range to run my three herds."

"You have three herds of Morgans?"

"Well, kind of. I have two of Morgans and I just started a third of Percherons."

"That's a bit of a change, from a Morgan to a Percheron."

"An opportunity arose that I couldn't pass up, so I branched off into a totally different breed."

Matt thought he'd do a bit of fishing, and asked, "How is the cattle business these days? I know the market is a bit depressed. Are you running longhorns or some of the short horns or Herefords?"

Rachel looked at him curiously, but answered, "You're right about the market, but we're doing fine. We can handle a down market better than most. We still have some longhorns around but most of our stock is of the new breeds."

"I worked with cattle for seven years, but I've always been a horse man, myself. I know every animal on my ranch by name. It makes it hard when it comes time to sell them, but each one is a registered Morgan and they bring a good price. I won't sell to just anyone, either. If I'm not sure they'll treat the horse right, I won't sell. It's cost me a few sales the past couple of years, but I wouldn't do it any other way."

"That's what makes it easier to run cows. They come and they go and they're never more than dumb old beef critters," Rachel said.

Matt laughed lightly then said, "I guess that makes it less difficult if some get stolen as well. I had one young mare get rustled about a year ago and it took me almost two weeks to hunt the thief down, but I caught him and brought my mare back home."

44

"Did you hang him?" she asked.

"No, I turned him over to the law. He was sentenced to twenty years."

Matt noticed she didn't say anything about the hanging on her own ranch just two weeks earlier, but she did, however, change the direction of the conversation dramatically.

"So, are you married, Matt?"

Matt smiled and said, "No. My younger brother Mike got married when we were still teenagers. He and his wife Maggie are still living on the family farm back in Missouri and have a herd of children, but I never got around to it."

"I'm not married either," she replied with a seductive edge.

"I'm a bit surprised, Rachel. You're a very beautiful woman and your father owns a large ranch. Either one of those reasons should create a line of suitors clear to Fort Worth. Both reasons would extend it to Dallas."

She laughed, then said, "There have been a few, but my father shoos most of them away before they reach the entry road."

Matt drained his coffee cup and put it on the table.

"Well, it's been nice talking to you, Rachel, but I've got to hit the road. It's still early and I can visit another ranch or two before heading back to Denton."

Rachel stood up and offered her hand. Matt took it and was surprised by the firm handshake.

"Don't make yourself a stranger," she said, with one last devastating smile.

"I'll probably be heading back to my ranch before long, but it was nice meeting you," he said as he returned her smile.

Matt headed out the door, crossed the porch and stepped down to the ground and took Caesar's reins. Rachel had followed him out and stood watching him mount.

"Good-bye, Matt."

"Good-bye, Rachel," he replied as he wheeled Caesar and began trotting down the road.

Now that was an interesting woman, he thought as he made a wide right turn heading toward the entrance road.

Caesar was trotting toward the main roadway, and just before he reached the overhead sign, a bullet traced by his head just a few inches above his Stetson's crown, followed immediately by a rifle's report. Matt waited no time to get the stallion up to speed, as he dropped down to Caesar's neck and gave him a sharp tap. Within two seconds, the big Morgan had reached full gallop, sending clouds of dust into the air behind him. Caesar took a hard right as he hit the main road in full stride. Then there was a second shot, and where the round went was anyone's guess, but Matt saw no indication of a strike anywhere.

After a few more seconds, Matt guessed he was out of range and slowed Caesar to a walk, then stopped and looked back at where he estimated the shots had originated. There were no trees, just a few bushes on the face of a hill to the west of the entrance road but could still see a cloud hanging above the hill. It wasn't an ideal ambush location, but it was the only one available.

Matt had a passing thought about going back and seeking out the shooter but knew that those were only warning shots and they served their purpose. Matt had been warned, just maybe not the way the shooter intended, but he had no idea what that intention was.

He tapped Caesar into a slow trot and kept heading south, chewing on the visit and the parting shots. A few minutes later, he noticed a cloud of dust coming down the road in his direction. Whoever it was, he was moving fast, and the horse must have already been winded as it was slowing down.

As he drew close enough to make out the rider, Matt marked the rider as a small man with long, dark red hair and feminine features. It took him a few more seconds to realize that it wasn't a man with feminine features, it was a woman in britches and a plaid flannel shirt.

She pulled up as she saw him and stopped six feet away.

"Did you hear those shots?" she asked breathlessly.

"It would be kind of hard to miss. They were directed at me."

"Thank God!" she said, as she leaned back in the saddle.

"Well, that's not a reaction I would have expected," Matt said as he smiled.

"Oh, I'm sorry, I didn't mean that I was grateful that you were the target, I just thought my father had been shot and I was worried."

Matt noticed that although she was dressed like a man, she was as far removed from his gender as possible. She was short, no taller than five feet and four inches, slim yet well rounded where females are supposed to be. She made no pretense of being beautiful, but she was a handsome young woman anyway and was struck by her bright green eyes.

As much as he was impressed by the way she looked, he was even more approving of the way she handled the horse and her confidence and control. She was what he thought every woman should be in this hard country.

"Where did you come from?" she asked.

"I was riding out of the Box B when someone tried to drygulch me."

Her previous friendly manner evaporated, and she said in a sterner voice, "You were at the Box B? Are you planning on working there?"

Matt laughed, and replied, "Hardly. I was looking to buy a Morgan stallion and checked to see if they had one. They didn't and tried to give me some hot lead as a going away present."

She immediately returned to her smiling visage and said, "Oh. You must be Matt Little. My father said you were going to be visiting and say you were trying to buy a horse. He owns the Lazy R next door. My father is Pat Reed."

"Then you must be Peggy Reed," Matt said.

"No, she's my youngest sister. I'm Sarah. Why would you guess that I'm Peggy?"

"My good friend Spike McMillan told me in a letter that he was smitten by a pretty young lady named Peggy Reed, so I assumed you, being a Reed and being very pretty, would be Peggy."

Sarah laughed, and said, "No one calls me that. That description falls on my younger sisters. Where are you headed now?"

"Nowhere in particular. Do you mind if I join you heading back, now that you know your father's safe?"

"Not at all, come along," she replied as she wheeled her still heavily breathing gelding.

Matt pulled Caesar up alongside Sarah's horse and between his tall stallion and his foot advantage in height, he could barely see the top of her head as the two horses walked alongside each other. Matt needed to keep it slow to let her horse recover, besides, he wanted to talk to Miss Sarah Reed longer.

"That's a tall horse you have there," she said.

"He's the second Morgan stallion I've used as a primary ride. His sire was called Night, as in the opposite of day. His name is Caesar. I named him after Julius Caesar, who I admire a lot."

"So," asked Sarah, "did you meet Mr. Bannister while you were at the Box B?"

"No, he was out on the ranch somewhere. I initially had an unpleasant welcome from Billie Bannister. It could have gotten ugly when his older sister intervened, but she was much more pleasant and invited me in for coffee. We chatted for a while and then I left. I'm guessing that Billie took the opportunity to take a couple of shots at me when I left."

"He tried to kill you for just showing up?"

"I don't think he was trying to even hit me. He was firing a Henry or a Winchester rifle from less than seventy yards. Let's face it, I'm not a hard target to hit. I think he was just sending a warning not to come back. I don't know if it's because he doesn't trust me or he's trying to keep me from coming back to see his sister."

"How do you know it was a one of those rifles and not another gun?"

"They're the only two common repeaters and it had to be a repeater to get that second shot off so quickly."

"So, what did you think of Rachel? She's a beautiful woman."

"Yes, she is. And just as importantly, she knows it. I think she uses her beauty as a weapon."

"You don't care for beautiful women, then?" she asked with a slight grin.

"As a rule, no. It's just like very handsome men who know they are. You know, the lady charmers. Both men and women of that ilk are at the top of the selfish chain. They seek out mirrors to admire themselves and have little time to understand other people. I'm sure there are exceptions, but I've found that to be true more often than not."

"Well, that's an interesting observation. Do you carry a mirror with you?"

Matt really let loose with a hearty laugh with that one.

"Hardly. I'm quite removed from that end of the spectrum. Most women probably think I was the child of a grizzly bear."

"Oh, I don't know," she said as she looked up at him, "I think you're passably good looking."

"Thank you for the appraisal, but don't let anyone else know. I have a reputation to uphold."

Matt took another quick glance at Sarah. He had never met any woman that he had been so comfortable with so quickly and wondered if it was because he had met her on her horse dressed like she belonged there rather than at some barn dance. All he knew was that he was dangerously close to being smitten, a condition he had never experienced and had never thought it likely to occur.

Their easy banter carried them up to the porch of a good-sized but plain ranch house. Four women were on the porch watching them approach, and he noticed that all were wearing dresses as opposed to Sarah's manner of dress.

The older woman, obviously, her mother, shouted, "Sarah is your father all right?"

"Yes, Mama, he's fine. The shots were fired at this gentleman," she shouted back as she pointed up at Matt.

Mrs. Reed looked at Matt and asked, "And who might you be?"

Before he could answer, Sarah, who was stepping down from her horse, said, "This is Matt Little, the man papa told us about. He was leaving the Box B, and someone shot at him."

"Small wonder, going into that den of thieves. Well, come on in, young man. You can tell us what happened."

"Do you mind if I take a few minutes to take care of my horse? He had a blow a little while back and I need to rub him down. I'll take care of your horse as well while I'm at it, Miss Reed."

"Thank you, Mr. Little, the barn is around back," Sarah replied.

With that the women turned and went into the house and Matt noticed that one of them, he assumed it was Peggy, took an extra-long look at him and smiled before heading inside.

Matt dismounted from Caesar and took him and Sarah's sweatier mount to the barn. Before he reached the barn, he let them drink a short while. He knew better than let them drink as much as they wanted while they were still thirsty. After they had enough, he walked them into the barn, removed their tack, then brushed both horses down before leading them to the trough to let them drink some more. When they had their fill, he put them into the barn, not wanting Caesar to find some lonesome mare.

When he walked to the back porch, he stopped then knocked on the screen door and heard Mrs. Reed say, "Come on in, Mr. Little."

He entered the house and found the women seated at the kitchen table and found it mildly disconcerting having four sets of female eyes looking at him.

"Have a seat, Mr. Little," Mrs. Reed said before asking, "Would you like some coffee?"

Matt sat down in the only empty chair and answered, "Yes, please, ma'am."

"Black?"

"Yes, ma'am."

As she poured and then handed him a scalding hot cup, she said, "Call me Jenny. Now what happened over at the Box B?"

Matt repeated the story he had told Sarah, minus the whole beautiful woman part.

Then, he said, "Sarah mentioned that your husband was headed for Denton this morning. Do you expect him back soon?"

"I hoped that it would be shortly after noon, but you can never tell with those self-important snobs at the courthouse."

"What's he doing there, if you don't mind my asking?" Matt asked.

"I suppose it doesn't matter," Jenny answered, "everyone knows. Our taxes were due last month, and Pat convinced them into giving us an extension of thirty days, but we simply can't come up with the money, so he's going to try to get them to give us another thirty days. I don't think it's going to work this time, though."

Her face was a mixture of pain and anger as she spoke of their financial dilemma which was probably due to their rustled cattle.

"How much are the taxes?" asked Matt.

"$87.45. We can't even come up with half that," she responded miserably.

Matt saw the worry in her face and noted it in her daughters as well.

"Well, let's see what we can do about that," announced Matt and abruptly stood, then walked away from the table.

Four sets of astonished eyes followed him as he quickly strode out of the room and left the house. For two minutes, they traded glances at each other in confusion, then there was the creak of the screen door opening followed by a bang as the door slammed closed.

Matt reappeared and said to Jenny, "Jenny, do you have a pen and some ink?"

She looked at him curiously and said, "Yes," and left the table, returning shortly with a pen and a bottle of ink and set them before him.

He took out a small sheet of paper and began writing, signed his name, then picked up the paper and blew across it for a few seconds before handing it to Jenny, who, once she had it in her hands simply stared at the bank draft.

Slowly, she lifted her head and even as her hand shook as she held onto the small sheet of paper, quietly said, "Mr. Little, I can't accept this. I can't take your money."

"It's not my money," he said.

"Oh. So, this bank draft isn't any good, then?"

"No," Matt replied, "it's perfectly valid. The bank will honor it without question. When I said it wasn't my money, I was referring to the source. When my good friend Spike McMillan died on the Box B a couple of weeks ago, he had prepared for that eventuality by sending me a letter that was delivered by John Sanderson. He left me all of his things, including the money he had been saving so he could buy his own ranch. Well, he can't do that now, so the least I can do is use that money to help you keep yours. It's the right thing to do."

Jenny was stunned. Ten minutes ago, she had been worried about where she and her family would go when they lost the ranch and now, now through this stranger's generosity, they could stay in their home.

She stood slowly and walked over to Matt, her eyes glistening as she wrapped her arms around his massive shoulders and quietly said, "Thank you, Mr. Little. You have no idea what this will mean to me and my family."

Matt patted her arm and said, "Don't worry about anything, Jenny. And one more thing. I will get your cattle back."

She suddenly stood straight and looked into his eyes.

"How could you do that? Everyone looked everywhere but the stolen cattle were never found."

"I have an idea about what's going on with the cattle. I don't know why they're being stolen, and that still bothers me, but I think I know where I can find them."

Sarah, who had been staring blank-faced at the bank draft on the table, suddenly came out of her reverie and asked, "What do you think has been happening to them?"

"When Spike wrote me that letter, he mentioned that he had searched all over, including the Box B and couldn't find any of the cattle, nor any rebranded animals. It caused me to rethink the whole rustling concept. Now, the cattle stolen from the northern ranches, even though they only lost a few head, would have had to cross a lot of populated area to get to the Box B, if that's who we think is behind all this. I think that's right, by the way. So, the stolen cattle are gone. Disappeared. Vanished into thin air. At least that's what we're led to believe. Why? Because stolen cattle need to be sold to make money for the thieves. But in this case, I don't think that's the motive."

Jenny quickly said, "But if they're not stealing the cattle for money, then why are they taking them?"

"Did Pat tell you what I had heard from Billie Bannister a couple of nights ago? What he had said sounded like the purpose of the rustling was to get you off your ranch. He almost succeeded by taking away your source of income by stealing about a fourth of your herd. None of the other small ranchers have lost anywhere close to that number. I know that most cattle operations are run on a tight profit margin. Most ranchers are land rich but cash poor, especially the smaller outfits. Bannister knew this. So, if he took your cattle, but only yours, it would be easier to point the finger at him. But if he spread the theft out among all the ranches, it looks like a run of the mill rustling ring. If you lost a few more than the others, it wouldn't be that important. I'll bet when you reported it to that useless sheriff, Bannister reported he had some stolen at the same time. So, you lose a few head. So, what? Everyone is losing cattle. But when you lose less than a hundred head and you can't afford to cover your tax bill, you forfeit your ranch and

Bannister buys it at auction for next to nothing. Out of curiosity, has he offered to buy your place?"

"Yes, he did, twice. The second offer was quite generous, more than the ranch is worth, honestly, but Pat and I didn't want to sell. This is where we raised our girls. It's our home. We've been here for fifteen years."

"I'd bet that the cattle rustling started shortly after you turned down his second offer."

"You're right, it did," she answered with a surprised look now that the connection was made, "So, how does that relate to finding the missing cattle?"

"When John Sanderson was tracing the ranches for me on his copy of the county map, I was looking at the surrounding free grazing land as well. I know it's mostly empty of good grass, but I wasn't looking at it at for grazing. Once you assume that the goal is not to sell the cattle to make money, there are only two other alternatives. You can slaughter the cattle and either bury the carcasses or try to sell the meat. But that would be dangerous. A bunch of slaughtered animals is difficult to hide with the buzzards suddenly appearing in big clouds over the butchering site. That leads to only one solution. They need to hide the cattle and the question is where they put them. After we're finished here, I'd like to be shown where the cattle were taken and where the tracks lead. After that, I'll spend a few days searching, but it may not take that long."

Jenny nodded and said, "I'll have Sarah show you the location. She's familiar with it."

Then she leaned back and sighed as she said, "This has been such a day of change. When Pat left to go to Denton, our future was as dark as it's ever been. But now, things are looking much better. I can't thank you enough, Mr. Little."

"Will you please call me Matt. Every time I hear that last name of mine, I cringe."

That elicited giggles from across the table and Matt took a few seconds to examine each of the Reed women. Jenny was not as pretty as her daughters, but she was far from plain. Her hair had probably started out dark brown but was half gray now. The two middle daughters were very pretty, and Matt noted that the older was pregnant. Both had light brown hair and hazel eyes and were obviously sisters. Peggy was probably the prettiest of them all. She seemed wrapped in vitality with dancing blue eyes and an almost constant mischievous smile on her face. He could see how Spike had been smitten, but he sensed that Peggy was one of those young women who enjoyed flirting more than any serious entanglements. At least she would while she was young and vivacious.

Now Sarah was at the other end of the Peggy spectrum. It wasn't that she wasn't as pretty as the others, it was that Sarah didn't seem to dwell on her appearance. It was as if she announced to the world to take her as she was or leave her be. Those piercing green eyes were another matter and he thought they could see deep into his soul if he gave them a chance.

"Matt, I have been neglecting my host duties," Jenny said, "I haven't introduced you to my girls. Sarah you've already met, and this is Katie my second oldest, Mary, our third and Peggy the youngest."

Each young lady acknowledged her introduction with a slight bow of the head.

"Well, I'm pleased to meet each one of you," Matt said.

Leave it to Peggy to ask, "Are you married?"

Jenny seemed embarrassed by the question but probably expected it anyway.

"No, I'm not married."

"Really," Peggy continued, just short of batting her eyes, "but you must have a girlfriend!"

56

"Well, of course, I do. I have quite a few, in fact," he replied, noticing a look of disappointment on Peggy's face and a less noticeable but still present one on Sarah's.

Then Matt said, "I've known each one for some time now and I'm anxious to get back to see them as soon as I can. They enjoy it when I rub them and twist their hair. I'm sure they miss me as much as I miss them."

The women were startled by the ribald description of his physical contact with his girlfriends.

"I guess…" Peggy intoned quietly.

"But I think they might miss Caesar more."

With that answer, Sarah broke into almost hysterical laughter as the other Reed women looked at her with puzzled faces.

Finally, wiping tears from her laughing eyes, she choked out, "Caesar is his horse."

The other women finally grasped the joke and joined in the laughter.

When they had calmed down, Peggy continued, "So, no human girlfriends, then?"

"No."

Peggy wasn't finished embarrassing her mother by a long shot, and probably increased her level of anxiety.

"Why?" she asked, "Don't you like girls?"

Sarah joined her mother in a serious eye roll.

Matt just chuckled and replied, "I like girls quite a lot. It's just that I never had any desire to start a relationship unless I knew it was right. Most of the girls I knew were thinking of a permanent attachment right from the start and I knew that if I took them out for a dance or something, they might start thinking that's the way it was heading. So, I decided early not to start and risk hurting them."

"How will you know when it's right?" Peggy continued.

"I'll just know. It won't take much time to know, either, I believe."

Unintentionally, or maybe less intentionally, he glanced at Sarah and caught a glimpse into those marvelous green eyes before returning to look at Peggy.

But his answer finally settled Peggy down, so he turned to Sarah.

"Sarah, when you're ready, could you show me the place where the cattle were stolen?"

"Sure. Do you want to walk or ride?"

"If it's less than a mile, I'd rather walk. Caesar is probably enjoying his time off."

"Then, let's walk."

Matt stood, waited for Sarah to stand, and then said, "Lead the way."

Sarah was still a little bit discomfited by Matt's bulk. He was so much taller than she was, she had a hard time seeing his face, but she could sense he was behind her as they strode to the porch and then down the stairs.

Once in the yard, she turned to her left and walked between the house and the barn and Matt picked up his pace to get alongside her.

"How far do we need to go?" he asked.

"Not far, less than a mile."

———

At the Box B, Will Bannister had his son and daughter in his office and wasn't happy with either of them.

"Billie, what were you trying to prove by shooting at that man?" he asked with not a small amount of anger in his voice.

"Pa, he was a stranger. I think he was like that one we hanged. I was just tellin' him not to come around again."

"Didn't you think that it might make him a bit suspicious if someone sent a few bullets his way? What if he's a lawman? Did you even consider that?"

Billie was deeply terrified of his father and when he railed at him, he felt like he was always on the edge of peeing on himself.

All he could manage was a weak, "No."

"I didn't think so. You'd better hope he wasn't a Texas Ranger or a U.S. Marshal. Get out of here while I talk to Rachel."

Billie thought just for a moment about asking if he wanted him to grab some more Lazy R cattle, but instead just turned and left the room.

Will then turned on Rachel.

"And you, Rachel, I would have thought you'd have more sense than to invite a stranger into the house while I wasn't there. What did you talk about?"

Rachel smiled when she remembered Matt, then told him about their conversation, which had appeared completely innocent to her.

Will wondered if his story was true. He doubted it, so he'd have Jesse Holt go and see if he could find out more about the stranger.

———

Matt and Sarah walked across the dirt back yard before reaching the grassy pasture, and for the first hundred yards neither spoke.

Then Sarah broke the silence by saying, "I hope you weren't embarrassed by Peggy's questions. She tends to do things like that."

Matt laughed and said, "Not at all. I'm used to those types of questions. Most men my age are already married with three or four kids. My brother Mike, for instance. He's almost two years younger than I am and has at least three."

"You're not sure?"

"When I left Missouri the last time, he and his wife Maggie had just had their third, but they seem to be consistent about having them once every two years. It's been just over that since I've heard from them, so I wouldn't be surprised if they're up to four now. So, why are there four pretty, unattached women in one place?"

"Well, Katie, if you haven't noticed, is married. Her husband is first mate on a clipper out of New Orleans. His ship left last month for a run to China, so he sent her here to have their baby. Mary was married two years ago to a cow hand from the Star M. Around the start of the year, he just rode off. She's still upset about it, but I think she'll be okay. Peggy is still very much single."

"I noticed that you left yourself out. I know why I never married, but if you don't mind my asking a Peggy-like question, how come you never married? You're the oldest daughter, you are confident, intelligent and, without trying to embarrass you, very pretty. So, what's your story?"

She sighed, then answered, "Like you, the question comes up pretty often. Usually from my parents. I've lived here all my life. It's been a lot of hard work because my father needed a son more than four daughters. So, I feel an obligation to help. I tend cattle and do a lot of the handiwork around the ranch. So, I get treated more like a son sometimes. Not intentionally, just by happenstance. It gave my sisters more of a chance to be ladies, and in Peggy's case, more of a chance to be a flirt. I didn't mind. I really wasn't interested in the social

60

life. I enjoy working on the ranch and never needed to go to barn dances and the such. Suddenly, I was twenty-four-years-old. I never learned the frippery of being a young girl, and I'm not about to start now. Besides, look at my hands."

Sarah held her hands out in front of her and Matt could see the scars and callouses from all the hard work she had done before lowered her hands after he had examined them.

"They're good hands, Sarah. They're honest hands. You know, one of the reasons I've been kind of disappointed in the young women I've met is that they seem to place great store in how they looked and managed to maintain their smooth skin. I don't know how they ever accomplish anything if they spend all their time with creams and lotions."

Sarah finally smiled before she said, "Well, now you know why I'm the way I am."

"At least you don't sound resentful about it. A lot of women put into that position would let it ruin their lives."

"There was nothing to gain by allowing that to happen. My only concern right now is the ranch and making sure that my parents keep it. I feel a deep obligation to them and the ranch. I owe everything to them. Once I think that everything is all right, then I can go about with my own life."

"Where do you see that going?"

Sarah stopped dead in her tracks, staring straight ahead. After a lengthy pause, she said in a low voice, "I don't know. I really don't know."

"If you're waiting for your parents to have enough money to be comfortable, you know that could never happen, don't you, Sarah? Small ranches always operate so close to going under, you may never have that chance."

She sighed, then said, "I know."

Matt was about to say what a waste it would be for her to give up her future but didn't want to make her any more depressed than he already had.

They began walking again and Matt said, "Sarah, no matter what happens, no matter what the Bannisters try to do, make sure that your father does not sell the ranch. Okay?"

"Why has our ranch become so important to you? First you give us money to pay the taxes, and now you're telling me to make sure my father doesn't sell."

"The first reason is that I hate to see bad things happen to good people. The second is that I believe there is an important motive behind the Bannisters trying to get this ranch, and if I can discover what it is, it can change your lives forever, and for the better. It's nagging at me now, but I'll get there soon. The bad part is that the closer I get, the more dangerous it will become. This morning's shots were just a warning by an idiot and had nothing to do with your situation. I wouldn't be surprised if he's being read the riot act by his father and sister right now. The next time it won't be a warning but I can't let them get me. I've got to be vigilant to the point of being crazy."

"Do you really believe they'll try to kill you?"

"Uh-Uh. Look at their behavior. First, it's a very polite offer to buy your place. Then the move on to rustling your cattle to drive you off. If that fails, violence is the only other alternative. They already hanged Spike McMillan just because he was looking around. My only question is who is going to try it. John Sanderson mentioned a hand they have named Jesse Hart. Somebody like that wouldn't need direct orders. Just a suggestion by the boss that something has to be done."

"You don't think Billie would do anything?"

"Billie is a loose cannon. He's insecure and not bright. He wants to prove himself. Just like this morning. Firing two warning shots at a stranger for no real reason is just plain stupid. It just draws attention to the Box B but gains nothing. If he thinks someone is a threat, he may do something drastic. Do you know him very well?"

"Not really. A long time ago, he came calling on me. That was when I was around eighteen. We're almost the same age. He's not a bad-looking boy, but he was so empty. Why do you say he's insecure? He seems pretty sure of himself to me."

"If you saw him with Rachel, I'm sure you'd change your mind. He was being Mr. Tough Guy to me when she arrived on the porch. By just touching his shoulder and saying, 'Go finish your coffee', she totally emasculated him. If he was secure with himself, he would have told her off. I can only imagine it's worse with this father."

Sarah thought about it for a while as they approached their destination, then stopped and pointed, "That's where they rounded up the cattle."

Matt walked gingerly forward, not stepping on any of the horse tracks. After a few minutes, he said, "Three horses. One of them is carrying a very heavy rider. Does the Box B have someone who weighs more than I do?"

"How much do you weigh?"

"About two hundred and thirty pounds."

She gave him a rapid inspection and continued, "There's Mel Emerson. He probably weighs more than you by twenty or thirty pounds."

"How tall is he?"

"Shorter than you. A lot shorter. I don't think he's six feet tall."

"Fat or muscle?"

"Mostly fat, I think. Does it matter?"

"It does if I have to tangle with him."

"Oh."

"Let's follow these tracks."

The trail was easily followed, which surprised Matt a bit as it had been almost three weeks since they had been taken. But three horses and seventy head of cattle are still hard to hide. When it got to the fence line, Matt stopped and asked, "Is that Box B land over there?"

"Yes. That's where we stopped. We didn't dare enter their ranch. They take it badly. That's where your friend crossed over onto their property to look at the cattle brands."

"Well, they didn't seem to have any problem with entering your property, so I'm going to see what I can find. I want you to return to the ranch house. I'll come back as soon as I'm finished."

"No. I'll stay here. I won't be able to help if I'm down there."

"Sarah, I appreciate the offer, but I'd feel a lot better if you were far away from here. I can take care of myself and I don't want to worry about you. Okay?"

Sarah thought about arguing again but saw no reason.

"Okay, I'll head back. But please don't spend a lot of time over there."

He turned and smiled at her, before she attempted a smile then turned and began walking back to the house.

After he was sure that Sarah was on her way, he stepped between the recently mended fence and followed the trail that continued for another quarter mile. Then the Lazy R herd was swallowed by the hoof prints of a much larger herd.

Matt quickly surveyed his surroundings making sure he wasn't being watched, then stepped out into the open pasture and across the torn-up grass. He continued following the large herd, staying to the left edge, climbed a rise, then scanned the horizons and noticed he could see most of the Lazy R from his current location. Then he continued following the big herd's trail. The mass of cattle suddenly made a violent turn to the right, heading south in the direction of the ranch house.

This is what he was looking for, so he turned left and headed for the north side of the ranch. There he found a smaller herd moving to the north and they had been escorted by the same three riders, and Matt grinned in satisfaction.

He scanned all directions again and began his return at a brisk walk. He had just finished crossing the pasture when heard hooves and wasn't sure if he had been spotted, so he stopped and remained motionless as he listened for the direction of the oncoming animals.

Matt turned to the left and saw the beginning of a small bunch of cattle, but no riders yet. He knew they'd be coming, so he sprinted the last fifty yards to the fence line and stepped through. Once on the other side, he dropped to the ground and stayed low in the tall grass, listening.

Finally, he heard a voice saying, "Coulda swore I saw someone over there, Jesse."

"Ah, you're just nuts. None of them Reed girls would come over here, but I wouldn't mind if they did."

"Well, you can say what you want, but I saw somebody and it sure wasn't some skinny girl."

"You just go right on ahead and keep lookin' if you want. Me, I'm gonna run that bunch of ornery critters back and forth twice more the way we were supposed to and then I'm heading back for some chow."

Matt could hear muttering as the two cowhands swung their mounts around and began driving the cattle in a U-turn.

Matt figured this behavior out quickly enough. They were told to run more cattle across the northern edge to hide the movement of the Lazy R cattle. He wondered if he had been the cause of the sudden urge to hide three-week-old evidence. He remained deep in the grass for almost another minute and slowly raised his head. He could hear the cattle moving away, so he took a chance that they wouldn't look his way, and began sprinting across the field, hoping he didn't hit a gopher hole.

As he ran, he made some quick calculations and estimated he had another three or four minutes before they turned the small herd around and headed back. Those bovine critters don't move all that fast if they don't want to, and they usually don't want to. He figured on another two minutes after the turnaround before they crossed the rise and be able to see him.

He still had a half mile to go before they could see him but didn't slow down despite losing his wind and the sweat pouring off him in the Texas heat. He thought he should be in better shape and had spent too much time on the backs of horses and not enough on his own two feet.

Soon, he reached the forested area that covered the last half mile of the border between the two ranches and knew he couldn't be seen. It was probably all a useless exercise and they probably wouldn't have noticed him, but he wanted to delay the Box B from knowing what he was doing here for as long as possible.

He finally broke stride and began walking, taking in deep breaths letting his sweat soak his shirt, then, when he looked up, he saw all four women watching him from the back porch as he was still bent over.

Sarah stepped down and approached him as he neared the porch.

"Matt, are you okay? What happened up there? We've been watching you come sprinting down the field for more than three minutes!"

Matt put up his index finger to give him a few more seconds to recover.

Finally, he said, "Let's go inside. I'll explain in there."

Three of the ladies turned and headed back into the kitchen, but Sarah waited for him to catch up and when he did, walked beside him.

"Are you all right?"

"Fine. Just not ready for a marathon, but I had to get out of there fast."

She locked her arm through his and guided him up the stairs. Her touch was so light he almost didn't notice it – almost.

When they came to the door, Matt opened it, allowed Sarah to enter, then followed into the kitchen, then took a seat at the table. Jenny had already filled a glass with water, which Matt gratefully guzzled. After he put the glass down, he took in a deep breath and exhaled sharply.

"I trailed the missing cattle for about a quarter of a mile. Then, they got mixed with a larger herd and I lost them."

Jenny said, "So, that's why no one couldn't find them."

"Well, I wouldn't have either if I had stopped there. But I've seen that trick used before by rustlers. They move the stolen herd over the trail of a larger herd. Then, after a few miles, when they figure any posse would give up, they change to the direction they wanted to go. This time, they didn't have to go a few miles. I guess they thought that because they were on their own ranch, no one would be able to investigate very far, if at all. They knew the sheriff wasn't going to do it. So, after about another quarter of a mile, I found your stolen stock again. They moved them north."

Jesse exclaimed, "North? That doesn't seem smart. There's nothing there."

Matt shook his head slightly, then said, "Yes and no. When I was looking at John Sanderson's map, I was looking for topographic features. For the first five miles or so, there is nothing but flatland with poor grazing in that direction. No cattle could stay there very long. But if you keep going about another half mile, there's a long depression.

That big gully is more like a small valley. In that gully is a stream that flows into Lake Dallas. I'll bet there's grass there as well. I think if I head out that way tomorrow, I can get your cattle back."

Sarah said quickly, "Not by yourself!"

"Why not? It's a small herd. I've done it before for longer distances than five miles. I should be able to get out there and back with the herd in ten hours or so. There won't be anyone there, I don't believe. Once I get them here, I'll show up on your eastern border. I'll have to cut the fence, drive them through and then repair the fence, but it should be a routine job. Then you'll have your cattle back and I can spend some time figuring out the last piece of the puzzle. Why Bannister wants your ranch."

"We'll talk about it after lunch," said Jenny.

"Is that why you were running," asked Sarah, "just to tell us that news?"

"No. I sort of ran into a couple of Box B riders. Almost."

Jenny asked, "Were you going to tell us that tidbit of news, or just keep it to yourself."

"I mostly forgot about it until Sarah mentioned it. I was in the middle of the northwest pasture when I heard a bunch of hoofbeats. There was a small herd, I'm guessing less than fifty head, coming right at me. I took off on a dead run before they crested the hill and slid under the wire. I crawled into some tall grass and buried myself as much as I could. There were two riders, but neither saw me. As I laid there, I could hear them talking. They were following orders to move the herd back and forth a few times across the north fence."

"Why would they do that now instead of then?" asked Sarah.

"I asked that question myself. The only thing it could be is that I spooked them a bit when I showed up at the ranch. I think they felt safe after Spike was gone. Then a new stranger arrives, and they want to cover any loose ends."

"That's kind of frightening, Matt," said Sarah.

"It's what I expected, more or less, Sarah. And I think it's going to get worse. After Bannister finds out your taxes are up to date, he'll get angry. And if your cattle are returned, it'll set him off. His hard-worked plans will be dust. Then the gloves will come off, and we'll need to beat him to the punch."

While they were talking, Jenny had sliced some roast beef and bread and set it on the table.

"Let's not forget our stomachs," she said.

As they began making their sandwiches, the door opened, and a despondent Pat Riley came through the door, then approached his wife, not even acknowledging Matt's presence.

"I'm sorry, Jenny, but they wouldn't budge. We have ten days."

Jenny beamed at him and said, "It's no matter. Sit yourself down and have some lunch."

Pat was startled.

"Are you not understanding, woman? How can you be worrying about food when such a sharp sword is hanging over our heads?"

The daughters were stifling giggles as Jenny said, "A sword you say. I don't see a sword at all. Not with this shield in my pocket."

And with that she reached into her pocked and dramatically produced the bank draft with a flourish.

As Pat reached for it, he asked, "What's this?"

He opened the draft and read it, read it again more slowly, then he raised his eyes and looked at Matt and asked, "What's this all about? Is this good?"

Matt was still chewing, but nodded and said through a half-full mouth, "Yes, sir. Quite good. You can go to the Exchange National Bank and cash it. Then you can go to the courthouse and tell those pompous snobs to take the money and stick it up their...um...noses. Politely, of course."

Pat broke into a huge grin and stood up and between slapping Matt on the back and dancing with his wife, it was a lively few minutes.

When he finally stopped whipping Jenny around the kitchen, he turned to Matt and asked simply, "Why?"

"Jenny can answer those questions. She already knows, and I've talked too much today. I've got to be heading back to John Sanderson's to update him on everything I've found, and I also told Jenny that I should hopefully have your cattle back tomorrow afternoon."

If the bank draft had caused euphoria, announcing that his cattle were being returned spawned disbelief.

"You found them?"

"Not yet, but I'm pretty sure I know where they are. I should be able to get over there and back in ten hours."

"You'll need help. I'll come with you."

"No, Pat. I'd feel better if you were here to protect what you have. I've already turned down Sarah's offer to help, as much as I'd like to have her along. I'll give you the same reason. I can do it myself at no risk to anyone else. I've done this before, but once Bannister finds that you're out of the woods the storm will come. He'll have no other options."

Pat thought about it for a short while and then said, "Okay. I can understand it. I don't like it, but I understand it."

Matt nodded as he finished his sandwich and then emptied the glass of water.

Sarah was still thinking about Matt's comment about how he'd like to have her along. She had caught his glance before they had gone out to the pastures and thought she might have misinterpreted what she read in his eyes at the time. Now, she believed she hadn't, and it gave her a warm rush that she had never experienced before.

"Pat, how many weapons do you have in the house, and who can use them?"

"I've got a Sharps with about thirty rounds of ammunition and a twelve-gauge shotgun with two boxes of bird shot. Both Jenny and I can use them both, and Sarah is pretty good with the scattergun."

Matt looked at Sarah and grinned, "Why am I not surprised?"

Then he looked back to Pat Reed and said, "It'll do for now, but that may have to be remedied soon. I'll worry about that. But now that I've eaten and found what I needed to find, and met each of you wonderful women, I think I'll head back to the Rocking S. Can you think of anything else?"

Pat stood up and walked slowly to Matt, craned his neck, stared into his face and said, "Only this, Matt Little, you've only been here a single day and you've done more to help this family than you can imagine. We'll be forever grateful and hope you'd feel welcome as part of the family."

Matt reached over, shook Pat's hand and replied, "I'd be honored"

With that solemn statement, Matt reached across to the sideboard and took his hat, pulled it on, tipped the rim to the womenfolk and left the house.

He walked out to the barn and saddled Caesar, mounted, then walked him out of the barn, saw the Reeds on the porch and waved before heading down the long path to the main road. He was going to turn toward Sanderson's place, but instead turned south toward Denton. As he rode, he thought about those green eyes and the pleasure he had just talking to Sarah.

71

He arrived thirty minutes later and after a short search, found the gunsmith. He entered the shop and was greeted by a thin man sporting a thin mustache, mutton chop sideburns and a thick pair of glasses.

"Can I help you, sir?"

"I'm sure you can. The easy part first. I need four of boxes of .44-40 ammunition and two boxes of twelve gauge, double aught buckshot. Then I need you to show me a Winchester. Which models do you have available?"

"I have four of the 1873 models and two of the 1876 versions."

"Let me see two of the 1873's."

The gunsmith laid two new 1873 models on the counter. Matt picked up the first and after making sure the receiver and chamber were empty, cycled the gun through a dry fire and lever action. It seemed smooth and well-oiled, as did the second.

While he was checking out the rifles, the gunsmith put the requested ammunition on the counter.

"These are nice weapons. You keep your stock well maintained."

"Thank you, sir. Many of my fellows tend to ignore stock weapons. That can lead to problems later."

"Let me have one of the '76s, as well. I'll need four boxes of the .45 caliber ammunition for it, too. I've never had one, but always had a hankering to try it."

"It's more robust than the '73 model and they're already modifying some of them back in New Haven to use larger caliber cartridges. These two use the standard Winchester .45-75 center fires."

He handed the brass-plated rifle to Matt who cycled it through a few times and found it smooth, then examined the breech and noticed that it was more robust as it had to be to use the more powerful rounds.

"You're right this is a good weapon."

The gun smith smiled and set the four additional boxes of .45 cartridges onto the boxes of shotgun shells and the four boxes of .44s. This was going to be one large sale.

"Two other items I'll need if you have them. A good Army compass and a pair of field glasses."

"I've got a new compass, but the only field glasses I have are used. They're in good shape though and have cases."

Matt checked out the field glasses, which proved to be in good condition. He added both to the list.

"What's the total?"

"$106.80."

Matt pulled out five double eagles and a ten-dollar bill and handed them to the clerk who counted out his change.

Matt asked, "Do you have a large sack or something I can hold these in?"

"Yes, sir. I'll give you three, so the rifles don't get damaged banging into anything else."

"Thank you."

Matt carried his deadly bags and hooked them onto Caesar's saddle. The ammunition he stored in his saddlebags, then replaced his current Winchester with the new '76 before he mounted and started back to the Rocking S. As he was trotting along the road out of Denton, he saw a rider approaching and after another two minutes took note of the two-gun rig he was wearing.

"Surely not," he mumbled, followed quickly by, "Damned if it isn't."

It was Billie Bannister riding toward him, and Matt thought this might be interesting, but didn't expect any gunfire this time as Billie seemed to be intentionally avoiding eye contact.

Another minute later, Billie rode right past him not even acknowledging his existence. Matt suspected that Daddy Bannister had laid into his insecure son for the misdirected shooting earlier in the day, then suddenly wondered if Rachel knew beforehand about Billie's warning shots, but quickly dismissed the notion. She would have told him how stupid it was and sent him slinking off to his room, mainly because it was stupid.

He continued until he reached the Sanderson's front porch, and as Matt was dismounting, he heard the screen door open and heard, "Welcome back, Matt? Any excitement today?"

He looked up at a grinning John Sanderson with Mary alongside and answered, "Some," as he unstrapped his two weighty sacks and pulled his saddlebags from Caesar.

"What do you have there?" Mary asked.

"An arsenal," he replied tersely as he mounted the steps.

John held the door for him as he entered the house and lowered the Winchesters to the floor gently. After he had laid his saddlebags down, he opened the sacks and slid the three repeaters from the bags.

"You weren't kidding, were you?" John said after he'd whistled.

"I'll fill you in shortly. Mary, you don't have any more of your delicious lemonade, to you?"

"I most certainly do," she answered, then turned to retrieve the lemonade and some glasses.

John and Matt followed her into the kitchen and sat down at the table as Mary brought the lemonade and set two glasses down in front of the men and after placing a third glass on the table, filled all three with the lemonade and took a seat herself.

After taking a long sip, Matt began filling them in on his findings, but skipped the bank draft part as it had no impact. It took almost half an hour to complete, but when he was done, all John could do was sit back and stare at him.

"So, you've been shot at, found the missing tracks, almost get caught, and now you're planning on going after the missing cattle tomorrow, after you've armed the Reeds to the teeth. Am I missing anything?"

"No," answered Matt as he absentmindedly scratched the back of his neck, "that pretty much sums it up."

Mary added, "Surely you're not going to go and bring those cattle back on your own. You'll need someone to accompany you."

"I've gone over this argument with Pat and Sarah, both of whom offered to come along. It would be a lot better if I went alone. I'm used to this. I've done it before. They won't have anyone there, so it should be pretty easy. Then there's the other reason that I didn't mention to them."

"Which is?" asked John.

"To be very blunt, it's this. I'm the odd man out here. If something were to happen to anyone else in the group, someone else will pay the price. A ranch would be lost, or someone would lose someone very dear to them. If something happens to me, it won't impact anything at all. Now, I'm not trying to be noble here. It's just logic. To be honest, it's a logic that makes me kind of wonder what my whole life up until now has meant, but it makes perfect sense if you step away from the emotional aspect of this. Spike McMillan died on the Box B a little over two weeks ago. What effect did it have on your community? Now, John, imagine the impact if you or Pat had been hanged? Or any of the other ranchers? It would be devastating to their

75

families. That's why I decided that going alone was the only thing that made sense. That, and the other valid reasons I just outlined. So, don't argue the point. I have no intention of letting anything happen to me. I'll get out there, find those big old critters and bring them home."

"Fine. I don't like it one bit, but I'll honor your request not to argue the point. Do you think you'll find all of the missing cattle?"

"I don't think so. I'm sure I'll find most, if not all, of the Lazy R's herd. I think I'll probably find yours and maybe the Circle J's, but that's about it. Those are all the southern ranches. I think the others have all had their cattle just rebranded and driven away from their ranches and turned into little more than mavericks."

"Why?"

"They don't want the cattle. They want to act like it's nothing more than normal rustling. So, the southern cattle are driven someplace to hide. The northern cattle are simply rebranded and scattered. If they're found by their owners, it doesn't matter to them. Even yours don't matter. Only Pat Reed's cattle would be important."

"That makes sense. Well, good luck tomorrow."

"John, I appreciate your help, but after tomorrow, I think it's a good idea if I moved to Denton."

"Why? You're perfectly welcome here," argued Mary.

"A little while ago, while returning from Denton with the Winchesters, I crossed paths with Billie Bannister who was heading into Denton. I'm sure he noticed all the rifle stocks. If he goes home and tells his father, things may come to a head a bit earlier than I expected. As it is, I expect that to happen within a week anyway. I'm germinating an idea that may be the cause of this ruckus and it might bear fruit in the next couple of days or so."

"Want to give me a hint?" asked John.

"It has to do with the Lazy R deed, but I'm not sure what it is yet. It's too early to tell if it's just a stupid idea or something that will work out."

"Okay."

Mary served dinner a little while later and Matt turned in early. It was going to be a long day tomorrow and hopefully, a good one.

CHAPTER 3

Matt got up early and dressed quickly but left his boots off as he used the washroom and crept into the kitchen, started the fire and put on the coffee pot.

As the water was heating, Mary entered the kitchen. "Still trying to take over my job, are you?"

"No, ma'am. Just trying to be my usual helpful self," he replied as he grinned at her.

By the time the coffee was ready, and Mary was cooking breakfast, the sun had started to rise and so did John. They had breakfast, making small talk, leaving out the serious topic of Matt's plan for the day.

When he had finished, he thanked Mary and retrieved the two new Winchester '73s and returned them to the bags, grabbed his saddlebags and the heavy bags and left the house.

Twenty minutes later, he was turning down the access road of the Lazy R, and guessed that Pat Reed must have been waiting for him because he stepped out onto the porch as Matt approached.

As he began to step down from his horse, Pat called to him, "What do you have there, Matt?"

"I'll show you in a second, Pat."

He grabbed his saddlebags, put them over his shoulder, removed the bag with the two rifles and ammunition then entered the house. Unintentionally, the first thing he noticed were those all-seeing green eyes of Sarah which made his soul feel almost naked as if no secrets were safe, but he didn't mind one bit. He'd prefer that she know everything. Well, maybe not everything.

The whole family entered the main room as Matt unloaded the weapons.

Pat's eyes grew wide as he saw the new Winchesters and said, "Matt, those Winchesters are works of art!"

"Among other things," Matt replied, as he handed one to Pat.

"I picked these up yesterday, along with some ammunition for them and your shotgun."

"We already have ammunition for the scattergun," Pat protested.

"You have bird shot. You'd need to be pretty close to your target to do serious damage. Now, these," he continued, taking out the new shotgun shells, "are double aught buck shot. Two barrels from this at fifty feet will take care of any problem."

"These are .44-40 cartridges to fit the Winchester and this," as he pulled the boxes of cartridges then Spike's Colt Peacemaker out of his saddlebags.

As he unloaded the firearms and ammunition, the girls' eyes grew as big as silver dollars and he didn't know if it was fear or fascination.

"Now, Pat, the Winchesters should be pretty easy for you and Jenny to handle. It has a lot less kick, less punch than the Sharps, but it doesn't leave you weaponless for the five seconds it takes to reload, either. It'll handle fifteen cartridges. I'll give you a quick rundown on how to load and fire it. Cleaning it is different, but I won't have time to show you that today, but don't worry about it. You shouldn't need them for the next few days anyway. I can teach you the other stuff later."

"Matt," asked Sarah, "is it going to get that bad?"

"I'm not sure. I'd rather you were prepared if it does than to find that Bannister did get that serious and you didn't stand a chance. Ten years ago, this would have all erupted into massive gunfire by now, but the law has started having an impact, even in Texas. So, my worrying may be nothing more than that. Now the Colt is an older, used gun owned by my friend. He kept it clean and well-oiled and told me it shoots straight. Pat, have you used a pistol before?"

"Yes. But not since they've started using cartridges."

"I'll show you how to load it, which should take maybe thirty seconds. I'm going to be leaving in a few minutes, but when I get back, I can answer any serious questions about the guns, and hopefully the returned cattle."

Pat said, "Thank you again, Matt. I feel safer now."

Matt then spent over a minute, rather than thirty seconds to demonstrate how to eject brass and reload the Colt, then handed the gunbelt to Pat.

"Okay. I'm off. I'll ride out and cross over to the free range and I'll see you folks before sundown."

Without waiting for any response, Matt picked up his saddlebags which still contained one box of cartridges for his Remington and another for the new '76 Winchester in his scabbard, the compass and the field glasses, then quickly walked out the door and climbed aboard Caesar.

He wheeled the stallion around the house without looking back, his mind already working on what he needed to do and quickly angled toward the northwest corner of the ranch to the Bar S. He knew that John had a small gate on the back fence, and used it to exit the property, making sure it was secure as he left it behind. He would have to cut the Lazy R fence to get the missing cattle back in, provided he found them.

He rode for an hour at a medium trot, knowing that Caesar could handle this pace a lot longer. As he rode, he closed his eyes and recalled the map he had studied at the land office, and after reopening them to the three-dimensional world, turned to the northeast.

Another thirty minutes brought him to the beginning of the gully. He could see the stream and the beginning of a better quality and quantity of grass, then followed the stream and within ten minutes came to a crude fence set across the width of the gully. He dismounted and walked to the fence and easily removed the cross members and tossed them aside. As he was removing the obstacle, he could hear the distinct lowing of cattle in the distance and smiled when he knew that he had found the missing cattle.

He stepped back into the saddle and removed his Winchester from the scabbard. He didn't expect any trouble, but it was better to be ready for it.

He walked Caesar forward, scanning the edges of the wide gully for any potential shooters. The gully was so wide that it would be a tough shot from the twenty-foot high banks, or at least he hoped so. As he rounded a curve in the gully, he was greeted by a welcome sight when he saw what appeared to be a herd of around a hundred critters, and they were an unhappy bunch, too. He could see that the grass, which may have been plentiful when they were first brought here, had been cropped to almost dirt. The good news was that hungry cattle like to be pushed to someplace where there was food and water, so this job may be easier than he hoped.

He walked Caesar through the displeased bovines, noting that almost all the brands were Lazy R, with a scattering of Rocking S and Circle J, verifying his theory of their purpose. As he passed them, he sang to them to get them ready to move and swatted his Stetson on his thigh making a popping noise.

The cattle slowly began to acknowledge his presence and lift their heads, and by the time he reached the far end of the cattle, he found another makeshift fence, then turned Caesar around, and being the well-trained Morgan that he was, began to herd the cattle. They responded and began moving, picking up others as they went. It took almost an hour for Matt to get the entire group moving and after found a mossy horn bull that seemed to be the leader, he directed him out of the gully, passing the downed fence posts.

The herd was moving at a solid pace now as the sun rose to mid-day, and as the lone drover, kept Caesar busy running around the herd to make sure they all kept up and didn't stray. Luckily, they were all well-watered from the stream, so they were easily maneuvered away from the water to the southwest. Matt was finding himself busier as the cows entered the open flatlands as they were tending to spread, but the stallion kept them from wandering too far.

It was getting on to late afternoon, and Matt suddenly felt like an idiot. He had neglected to bring any food, opting for ammunition instead. Now he wished he had brought something to quell his growling stomach and was concentrating on his stomach so much he almost missed it.

As he turned Caesar north again to push the cattle together, he caught a flash out of the corner of his eye, immediately snatching his full attention. If it was a gunsight reflection, he could be shot in a second. But the distance was too great, unless the shooter had a Sharps. The shallow hill where he had seen the flash was a good six hundred yards away, and the dust from the cattle would cause problems with sighting even if he was using the long-range rifle.

Quickly, he brought Caesar to a stop, pulled the field glasses from the saddlebag and looked at the hill and caught movement near the top. Someone was mounting a horse and heading away from him. Damn! He'd been spotted, *but by whom?* It had to be someone from the Box B because no one else knew the cattle were there. *But how had they known he was moving them?* He answered the question a moment later. It was that damned dust cloud! A hundred cattle crossing a dry plain in the summer in Texas created an enormous dust cloud. He may as well fly a great big flag announcing his plans. He should have waited until after dark to move them. Of course, that may have presented its own problems, but there was nothing he could do about it now. He had been seen and the Bannisters would know it soon enough.

As the sun almost touched the horizon, Matt reached the edge of the Lazy R. He couldn't get the cattle through the small gate that he had used to exit, so he used the fence tool he had brought along and opened a thirty-foot-wide gap to let the cattle in. As they eagerly ran to the smell of the fresh grass and water, he sat on Caesar, getting a closer count of the animals moving past. When the last slowpoke had entered the Lazy R pasture, he had counted one-hundred and twenty-seven cattle. Once they were all inside, he figured he'd let the owners sort them out, then spent another ten minutes repairing the fence before he remounted and turned Caesar back to the ranch house.

There was little sun as he approached the barn. His first thought was to get Caesar watered, unsaddled, brushed down and then put away to rest after his long day's work.

After a short stop at the trough, he walked his Morgan into the barn, dismounted and began stripping his friend of his tack. He didn't think anyone noticed his arrival but was wrong in that assumption.

He was pulling off the saddle blanket when he heard a light voice from behind him say, "Welcome back, Matt,"

He smiled, but didn't turn as he replied, "Hello, Sarah. Been waiting long?"

"Not long. A couple of hours maybe. How did it go."

"Good and bad. I'll tell you about it when we get inside. Okay?"

"That's fine. I can wait. I'm just happy you got back all in one piece."

"So am I," Matt replied.

She waited for him to brush Caeser, then as Matt began walking from the barn, fell in step next to him as they stepped to the house. No sooner had his feet hit the first step when he hear, rather than saw, Pat as he was coming out the door.

"Matt, you're back! How'd it go?"

"I'll let everyone know in a minute. I'm dragging a bit."

"Of course, of course, come on in."

Matt walked through the door and sat down so abruptly that it was a wonder the chair survived. The sudden exhaustion surprised him.

All he said was, "One-hundred and twenty-seven."

Pat understood but still asked, "You brought back one-hundred and twenty-seven head?"

Matt nodded and replied, "There are some Rocking S and Circle J stock in there for sure. There may be some others, but none that I noticed. They're a little on the thin side. They probably wouldn't have lasted another week in this heat. They had eaten every blade of grass in that gully. When they got close to home, they raced in. You'll probably have to send some over to John's place to fatten up, though."

Pat was grinning from ear-to-ear, but Matt didn't notice. He was so completely exhausted that had even forgotten his empty stomach.

Sarah asked quietly, "Matt, when I first saw you, you mentioned that there was something bad that happened. What was it?"

He glanced at her and shook his head to clear the cobwebs that were being spun rapidly inside.

"I'm sorry, Sarah. I forgot. As I as about two-thirds of the way back, I saw a flash behind me. At first, I thought it might be the sun's reflection off a gunsight, but when I scanned the hill with my field glasses, I saw a man mounting his horse and setting off to the southwest. What I must have seen was the lenses of a pair of field glasses. At first, I couldn't figure out how they could have known that I was moving the cattle, but it was pretty obvious. That dust cloud I was leaving could have been seen in Dallas. I screwed up. I should have moved them at night like they did. I don't know how I made such a stupid mistake. So now Bannister knows you have your cattle back. I was hoping for a week, or at least a few days before he found out, but now he knows. And he knows that I brought them back. So much for not being noticed."

Matt managed a weak laugh at his own expense.

Jenny asked, "Matt, have you had anything to eat today?"

Matt snickered and answered, "I missed that little item, too. I was concentrating so hard on having the right equipment, I forgot the basics. At least I remembered my canteen."

Matt slowly rose and said, "Well, as much as I'd like to stay and chat, I've got to go and let John know what's going on. I'll stop by in the morning and make sure everything is okay."

He grabbed his Stetson and headed for the door, then exited the house, crossed the small back porch, then walked unsteadily toward the barn and began setting up Caesar after having just unsaddled him minutes before. He got as far as the saddle blanket and realized he wasn't going to make it. He turned to the back of the barn and found a pile of hay and just laid down. A few minutes is all I need, he thought, just a few minutes, he kept thinking as he closed his eyes. He was sound asleep in seconds.

———

"He was a big guy, boss. He was the only one who drove 'em outta the gully."

Will Bannister was seething. *Who was this man?* He was sure it was the same one that Billie had shot at and had visited with Rachel, *but what was his interest? Was he the law?* He didn't think so. He was probably another amateur hired by that damned Association of theirs.

"Did he see you?"

"No, sir. I got out of there right fast and I was pretty far out."

"All right. There's nothing we can do about the cattle now, but we've got to look at other methods now. I need to come up with something."

———

Sarah sat on a hay bale as the morning sun filtered through the cracks in the barn's wall and examined the sleeping giant. She'd only known him for a few days and was already fully aware of the impact he had on her. She still wore her trousers and wool shirts, but he didn't seem to mind. He even saw her rough hands and seemed to like them, too. She knew that she was just as pretty as Peggy, but never bothered to let that control who she was. She wanted her own life, but she also knew that, just as she had told Matt yesterday, she needed to help her parents. *How could she do both?* Her parents had told her many times that she should marry and start her own family, but it had never been an issue until Matt Little entered her life. Now, it was a gigantic issue. She so much wanted to have him be part of her life as she was reasonably sure he wanted her in his, whether he realized it or not.

Suddenly, his eyes popped open. *Where was he? What time of day was it? Why was it even the daytime?*

"I'm in a barn?" he mumbled, not noticing Sarah seated on her hay bale just six feet away.

Then he remembered where he was and how he got there. Then he had a terrible thought. *What if the Bannisters sent someone to the Lazy R while he slept?*

He shot up and reached to check his pistol, then heard female laughter to his left.

"Good morning, Mr. Sunshine. Have a good night's sleep?"

He turned to see Sarah's smiling face, and asked in a scratchy, thick voice, "What time is it?"

"Almost ten o'clock. You know, if you weren't such a load, we could have carried you inside, but that was out of the question."

"I imagine," he said.

"Matt Little," Sarah said, "you must be the most stubborn man I've ever met, and most men are stubborn to begin with."

86

"Stubborn? Me?" he asked, then paused and said, "Well, maybe on occasion."

Sarah laughed again, as Matt shook his head and rubbed his eyes.

"Have the Bannisters done anything?" he asked, his voice sounding more normal.

"No. Everything is quiet. My father rode over to the Rocking S this morning to tell John about your recovering the lost cattle. John and Mary had been worried when you didn't return last night, but John was very happy to get his cattle back."

"That's good."

"And where do you think you'll be going?"

"I'm not sure. I told John and Mary that I'd be moving to Denton, so the Bannisters wouldn't know that I had thrown in with your lot. Did I mention that I passed Billie Bannister on my way back from Denton the day before yesterday?"

"No, you skipped that part when you practically ran from the house yesterday morning to find the cattle. You didn't even give anyone a chance to say good luck."

"Sorry. I didn't want to stretch it any longer than I had to. Anyway, he was riding into Denton as I was riding out. He rode right past me without even looking at me. I think Daddy and Big Sis let him have it for the shooting incident."

"That sounds right. So, now that they know who you are, what are you going to do?"

"I'm still thinking. Right now, I've got to get cleaned up."

Sarah laughed and said, "I imagine you're covered in straw in places that you didn't know existed."

"I'm sure you're right. But before I do that, can I ask you a question?"

"Certainly."

"Now, before I ask, I want your assurance that no matter what your answer is, you won't hold it against me. Okay?"

She had a curious look on her face, wondering what kind of confession was forthcoming, and said slowly, "Okay. This sounds serious."

Matt drew in a deep breath. This was going to be difficult because he'd never done it before and a lot hung on her answer.

"After this is all over. Would it be okay if I began calling on you? You know, really calling on you?" he asked then grimaced as if he had overstepped a boundary.

Her face opened up to the biggest smile he'd yet seen on her pretty face.

"Matt Little, why do you need permission for such a thing? I had the impression that you had been calling on me since the first day you arrived."

"So, you're not angry?"

"Hardly. I think the only one who may not be happy about it is Peggy. She's been eyeing you up since she first saw you."

"Speaking of Peggy. Can you come over here and sit closer, so I don't have to say this loudly?"

Sarah panicked a bit inside. Was this going to be some form of confession of stolen kisses or something. That would be surprising if nothing else because she didn't recall any time that he had been alone with her sister. She slowly sat down near Matt and looked up at him.

"This is going to be hard because she's your sister, and I'm sure you love her very much. But I need to tell you this, so you can be ready for it in case she ever finds out something. It has the potential to devastate her."

Sarah was really worried now. *Where was Matt going and how could he have found the time to be with Peggy?*

Matt continued, saying, "We both know that Peggy is a flirt. She enjoys making young men go into a tizzy over her. She doesn't do it maliciously. She's just a young girl enjoying the power she has. She's not like Rachel, who uses her beauty to get what she wants and then tosses them aside without a bit of emotion."

"You read that in her already?"

"It was very simple, really. Remember I told you on the first day we talked in the road how most beautiful people are so enamored with themselves there's no room for anyone else, well Rachel fit that pattern exactly. Peggy's not like that. She enjoys the attention, but she's too young to realize the damage she can do."

"Matt, I understand that, but what has Peggy done that could cause her problems in her future."

"Remember I told you that I came here because I had received a letter from a good friend, the man who was hanged by the Bannisters?"

"Yes, I remember. I met him, too."

"Well, in his letter he wrote that the reason he decided to stay and help with the rustling problem is because he met a pretty girl at a barn dance, and she told him about her family's troubles, and he said he'd help. Then he said when he got his place, he'd ask Peggy to marry him. If he hadn't met Peggy, he probably would have just ridden away."

Sarah sat wide-eyed with her hand covering her mouth.

"Sarah," Matt continued, "Peggy didn't even remember that she met him. If she ever finds out that she was the reason he stayed, it could crush her spirit. She wouldn't be Peggy any more. If she does find out, it won't be from me, but Spike may have mentioned it to someone else in the area, a cowhand or a son of one of the other ranchers. I'm just telling you this so you know that it's possible. I don't think you should tell anyone else in your family. I believe it would only cause heartache and animosity that would be unnecessary."

"Matt, why did you tell me this?"

"Because I think you are the strongest person in the family. You can know without being judgmental toward your little sister. I'm trusting your good judgment and big heart to understand her and to be ready to help her if she needs it."

"Thank you for telling me, Matt. You are a wonderful man, and I'm very happy to have you call on me, whether it's before, after or during what's happening."

"I will be very happy to," he smiled with relief. He had broached two difficult subjects and had survived.

"But first, Mr. Little. You need to get cleaned up and then get into the house. My mother is planning on feeding you until it comes out your ears."

She stood up and Matt watched her walk away with a great deal of interest. Men's clothing or not, Sarah was undeniably a woman.

He slowly rose from his ad hoc bed and stretched. He was still sore from all his riding yesterday combined with his awkward sleep. He walked over to Caesar and rubbed his nose. "Well, Julius, we seemed to have survived a few tests in the past day. Let's see what today brings."

He then hustled quickly to the privy, and then when he was relieved, he walked to the back of the house, took off his shirt and splashed cool water over his face and cleaned himself as best he could. He didn't realize he was providing the young female members of the household with unexpected entertainment, as they stood behind the kitchen window. They didn't get to see such an exhibit very often and Sarah was not immune from the show, in fact, she may have been more affected than even Peggy. Matt was calling on her, after all. A fact she hadn't told any of her family yet and wasn't sure when or even if she would. Many things could happen over the next few days that might make a courtship impossible.

After he was finished, he dried himself with the towel hung on a rack hear the sink and donned his shirt.

As he walked into the kitchen he was greeted by assorted giggles and smiles and hadn't a clue what initiated such behavior, so he turned around to see if there was something amusing behind him. Seeing an empty room, he realized that he was the cause, though he still couldn't fathom why.

"Have a seat, young man," said Jenny.

"Yes, ma'am."

She put a plate filled with scrambled eggs, bacon and biscuits in front of him and didn't need any incentive to start loading food into his demanding stomach.

After a few bites, however, he stopped in mid shovel and turned to the ladies who were still standing there watching him and asked, "Aren't you going to sit down and at least have some coffee?"

There was renewed giggling as they seated themselves, but Matt paid little attention as he cleaned his plate.

"Jenny, where is Pat?" he asked between bites.

"He's still out in the pastures with John counting cattle and checking brands."

"Well, if no one minds, I'll head out there and join them and let you ladies continue enjoying whatever you're enjoying."

Peggy's response of, "Not if you're out there," brought renewed hilarity.

Matt thought it had something to do with sleeping in the barn, so he just smiled and rose from the table to get Caesar ready for the short ride.

As he headed for the door, Peggy asked, "Matt, are you going to go to the church social tonight?"

He stopped and turned, asking, "Sarah, will you be attending?"

Sarah was obviously taken by surprise. She had never attended a dance or a social and Peggy was almost as surprised by Matt's question.

"I hadn't thought about it."

Matt thought he'd really bring the pressure when he said, "Well, if Sarah is going, I'll go, too."

Jenny turned to her oldest daughter and said, "It would be good for you to get out and enjoy yourself, Sarah. I think we should all go."

Jenny had understood the reason for Matt's question even if Peggy obviously hadn't.

With that, Sarah grudgingly acquiesced with a tentative nod, but wasn't even sure she had a dress.

Matt smiled and said, "Great! So, do I meet you here, so you can show me where it is?"

Peggy, still wondering about Sarah's role in this, said, "Yes, of course. Be here at six o'clock, and we'll all go in together."

Matt responded with a resonant, "I'll be here," then left the house.

He had Caesar saddled and mounted in less than fifteen minutes and headed for the northeast pasture, thinking that's where he could find Pat and John and spotted them just three minutes later. They saw him riding toward them and waved him over.

"Find something odd?" he asked as he approached.

"I'm not sure," said John. "Look at this steer. That's a brand I've never seen before."

Matt stepped down and examined the steer, and didn't take him long to see the rebranding.

"This steer has been rebranded. That makes no sense at all. Why rebrand cattle you're just going to hold? These guys are acting stranger by the day. John, have you heard any rumblings from the Box B about the return of the missing herd?"

"Not a peep. I think they're just standing pat until they see if anything comes of it. I believe they'll just let everything cool down for a while."

"I hope you're right, John," said Matt, then added, "Oh, by the way, Pat, I've been roped into going to the church social tonight."

Pat started laughing at his plight, until Matt mentioned that he was going as well. Matt just smiled at his discomfort before looking at John Sanderson.

"John, I have to go into Denton to get some clothes to wear. I didn't exactly pack for a church social when I left my ranch. I should be back by dinner. Do you mind if I continue staying at your place now that the Bannisters know I'm helping the Association?"

"Mary will be happy to have you, Matt. She says you keep her entertained."

Matt snickered, then climbed back aboard Caesar and turned him back toward the house, giving John and Pat a wave as he departed.

He trotted past the house without notice. A relief, considering the last time he had been with the ladies as he'd finally figured out what had them all so titillated and didn't want to get them started again.

Matt made it to Denton just half an hour later and found a clothing store and was surprised to find one in a town the size of Denton but was glad it was there. His size made it difficult to find anything in a general store. As it was, the selection was still limited because of his bulk, but he did find a nice pair of slacks, an almost matching jacket that wasn't too tight, and some shirts. He wasn't about to buy a tie. That would be going too far. He paid for his purchases, stepped outside to mount Caesar, and noticed a man wearing a bright white Stetson giving him the once-over. Matt wasn't in the mood for trouble, so after stepping into the saddle, he wheeled the stallion down the street, allowing him to get a better look at the man as he passed. Except for a long scar from the outside of his right eye extending almost to his upper lip, he was non-descript. The man continued to glare at him without concern of being noticed as Matt trotted past and half expected to be shot until he was well beyond pistol range. He wondered if the watcher was the Jesse Holt that John had mentioned.

He returned to the Rocking S just before dinnertime, rode into the barn, dismounted, then set his bag down and unsaddled Caesar and gave him a quick brush down.

He took his packages inside without knocking as Mary had threatened him with unspecified punishment if she heard him set knuckle to door and was greeted by Mary and John.

Mary was smiling as she said, "I hear you're going to the church social tonight."

"That's the rumor," he replied with his own smile.

"I've been trying to get John to take me, but he says he has nothing to wear."

"He should have said something, I would have picked him up something appropriate at the clothing store."

94

"You bought some new clothes?" she asked.

"Yes, ma'am," he replied as he showed her his packages.

"Well, this will never do. Give them to me and I'll iron them. You'd look like you'd just rolled out of bed."

"Thank you, Mary," said Matt as he handed the packages to her.

Then he turned to John and said, "John, let me ask you something. You mentioned a hand on the Box B named Jesse Holt, the one who's supposed to be a bad seed. Does he wear a white Stetson and have a long scar on the right side of his face?"

"I don't know about the hat, but the scar sure marks him as Holt. Why? Did you run into him?"

"Not so much. He was standing on the boardwalk in Denton just staring me down. He didn't care if I knew it, either."

"Well, if I were you, I'd watch my back."

————

"You sure it was him?" asked Will Bannister.

"C'mon, boss, he kinda sticks out. It was him," replied Jesse.

"Did you find out what he bought at the store?"

"He got a new jacket, some trousers and some shirts. Sounds like he's gonna be goin' to that church social."

Will Bannister was already ahead of Jesse. Ever since the cattle had been returned, he'd been waiting for a chance and this was it. There was even a full moon which would make the shot possible.

He outlined what he wanted Jesse to do, while Jesse just stood there, listened and smiled. This was right up his alley.

95

When Will Bannister was finished, he told Jesse as he was leaving, "Send Rachel to see me."

Jesse nodded and left his office.

———

After dinner, Matt dressed for the social. He contemplated wearing his Remington but had a suspicion that it would be frowned upon to walk into a dance armed for a gun battle. Nonetheless, he kept looking at the rig. Finally, he slid the gun belt from the bedpost and carried it out to the barn, saddled Caesar, putting his old Winchester '73 in its scabbard. Then he spread out his bedroll on the barn floor, laid his pistol and belt on the fabric and rolled it back into an almost normal looking bedroll shape then tied it on the back of the saddle, making sure that the weapon was centered between the ties and wouldn't fall out of the bedroll as he rode to the church social. He then led Caesar to the front of the ranch house and tied him to the post loosely.

Matt entered the main room and walked into the spare bedroom, opened a fresh box of .44-40 cartridges and dropped six into each jacket pocket. He inspected the jacket to make sure that the ammunition wasn't noticeable. It was why he was taking the '73 Winchester rather than the '76. It and the Remington shared ammunition.

"Expecting trouble?" John asked as he watched him put the cartridges into his pockets.

"Just a feeling. Hart watching me in town has me on edge. He'd be able to find out what I bought and the only reason I'd have to buy it is to go to the social. Maybe nothing will happen at all. But for the same reason I brought those Winchesters to the Reeds, I'm making sure I'm ready for whatever the Bannisters are plotting."

"Well, hopefully, it's nothing more than a friendly dance," John said as he swatted him on his shoulder.

"Don't wait up for me," he said as he ambled to the door.

He mounted Caesar and sat for a few seconds. Even if it was a peaceful evening, he thought the social event could prove interesting, if for no other reason, he'd be able to dance with Sarah. He swung the tall black stallion and walked him down the road to the Lazy R.

When he arrived, he noticed that the family wagon had been outfitted with hand-made seats that slid on the buckboards, providing comfortable seating for four. Matt imagined they had been in use quite a few times over the years.

He dismounted and walked up the steps. He was a few minutes early, but it was better than being late.

He was preparing to knock on the door when Jenny appeared, dressed in her Sunday's finest.

"Good evening, Matt, and don't you look dashing," she said as she surveyed his new outfit.

"Thank you, Jenny. Why, you look like just another of the pretty Reed sisters," he said as he smiled at her.

"Be careful what you say, young man, Pat can have quite the temper when he gets jealous," she replied with a smile.

As he entered, he saw Katie, Mary and Peggy watching him as he entered. They were all seated in various chairs in the main room, and each wore a ribbon of a different color in her hair and had a light application of rouge and lipstick. Just enough to accent their normally pretty faces.

"Good evening, ladies. I see you're all prepared to make all those young men swoon. Except for Katie, who will just make them all jealous that she's spoken for."

There was a mixture of smiles, blushes and giggles, but before any of them could reply, Pat interrupted.

"We're ready to leave, Sarah," he said loudly as he looked down the hallway.

97

A bedroom door opened, and Sarah stepped out. She wasn't wearing any rouge or lipstick, nor did she have a ribbon in her hair. Her dress was a light green affair with a white sash, but Matt was taken aback. He had been telling her that she wasn't beautiful, just very pretty, but now he wasn't sure he should have passed on that assessment. As she entered the room, her smile was part grimace.

"Hello, Matt," she said.

Matt gazed at her green eyes and said, "Sarah, you look spectacular."

She smiled more openly, but Matt thought that she believed he was just passing an idle compliment, but he wasn't.

Pat interrupted any more talk by announcing that it was time to load up the wagon and head to Denton.

Matt followed the Reeds outside, closing the main door on the way out. As the women were being seated in the wagon, he mounted Caesar, then let the wagon go first and followed behind and off to the right to minimize the accumulation of dust on his new, freshly pressed clothes.

It was a pleasant ride, and Matt could hear the family chatting amiably as the horses plodded along as he settled into a pattern of scanning the surrounding hills and holding his scan on Sarah for a few heartbeats when his eyes passed the wagon. Sarah seemed to be talking to her sisters, but not as animated as they were and had all the appearance of being in a prison wagon being taken to the gallows.

By the time they reached Denton, Matt had marked any location along the way that he thought would be good for an ambush, but there weren't many.

Pat drove the wagon through the streets of Denton and turned left on Bolivar Street. Before they reached the Presbyterian Church, Matt could see groups of well-dressed people entering the church basement. Pat turned the wagon into the adjoining field and hitched the team. Matt stopped behind the wagon and looped his reins around the right rear wheel, then he loosened Caesar's cinch before he began helping the Reed daughters down from the wagon as Pat assisted Jenny. Matt did take a little longer holding Sarah's hand as she stepped to the ground but wasn't sure she noticed as she seemed to be distracted by the crowd and the upcoming event.

The Reed family plus one followed the folks entering the church basement, and once inside, Matt was impressed with the effort that must have gone into its preparation. There were tables around the perimeter of the large room, buntings hanging under the windows and a large table with punch bowls and glasses placed on the far side of the room. It was a well thought out setup, probably because they had been doing it for years.

Pat had found a table for his family by the time Matt had finished examining the surroundings. The seats were filling up rapidly by the time the band arrived and began setting up their instruments. The size of the group surprised Matt as well. He'd expected a few fiddles and maybe a jug and a drum, but this was a real band of sixteen musicians that had sheets of music.

The minister said a few words welcoming everyone and wishing them all a good time. The band began to play, and the young people began mixing.

Before the music had started, Mary and Peggy had been surrounded by anxious young males. Even Katie, in her motherly condition was invited to dance. A few young men had approached Sarah, including Billie Bannister, but her obviously uncomfortable manner and terse refusals quickly resulted in a virtual vacuum around her.

As Matt was walking to sit by her side, he felt a quick tap on his left shoulder, turned and was greeted by the flawlessly made up face of Rachel Bannister. She was wearing a brilliant dark green silk dress with a low scooped neckline revealing a bit more of her shapely breasts than most would consider correct at a church social, but no one commented, unless it was the admiring crowd of young men that could be seen staring at her, even those currently leading their partners on the dance floor.

"Good evening, Mr. Little. I see you've decided to attend our soiree. Would you care to escort me to the dance floor?" she asked.

Matt bowed, took her waist and swept her across the floor to Strauss' 'Blue Danube' and was grateful for the dance lessons his mother had given him and Mike when they were still youngsters.

"I hear that you've become a famous finder of lost cattle, Mr. Little," she said as they turned to the waltz.

"When I was in the process of trying to purchase that Morgan stud, which, as you correctly pointed out to me, didn't exist, some of the local ranchers mentioned that they had lost some cattle. It seems that they must have wandered off. As I happened to be quite good at finding lost cattle, I offered to hunt for them and they were very happy with my success," he answered, deciding to play her little game.

"Well, congratulations. I'm sure that you've made many friends. Will you be returning to your ranch now?"

"Perhaps. I may spend a few more days in the area. It's such a peaceful location."

"It has been, but that may be changing, I'm afraid."

"What would cause such a change?" Matt asked almost stunned into a missed step by her openness.

This was getting interesting.

"Let's just say that it might have been better if you had stayed with your horses."

Matt smiled at her incredible face and said, "Ah, but then, how would I ever have met you, Rachel?"

She gave him a dazzling smile and answered, "The one highlight of your most boring trip, I'm afraid."

The band played the last notes of the waltz and the couples separated. Off in the corner, Sarah sat, having never taken her eyes from Matt as he slid across the floor with his hand on Rachel's waist.

Matt said, "Thank you for the dance, Miss Bannister. I hope the rest of your evening is enjoyable."

She presented her most charming smile for effect and floated back to her table, pursued by a number of young gentlemen hoping to be blessed to be given the rare opportunity to dance with her. Matt could see her brother Billie standing next to a gray-haired man of medium height with long muttonchop sideburns. Billie was glaring at him with murderous intent, while his father just studied him. Matt smiled at them, then gave a slight wave before turning around and heading back.

The band had struck up another tune that Matt could not recognize, and the dance floor was full as he zig-zagged his way through the dancers. When he finally made it to the Reed table, he was greeted by the sight of a lonely Reed girl sitting silently watching everyone having a good time.

Matt sighed and walked to the table and sat down next to Sarah.

"Miss Reed, may I have the honor of the next dance?" he asked, smiling at her.

"No," was her terse reply, "I can't dance. Besides, I believe you already have a dance partner."

"Sarah," he said softly, "she asked me to dance, not the other way around. I wanted to see what she really wanted, so I agreed. Did you want to know what she said?"

Sarah was torn between curiosity and seething jealousy, an emotion completely foreign to her.

"Okay," she finally admitted.

"Her first comment was meant to put me off balance. She told me that she heard I had become a famous finder of cattle. It was her way of letting me know that the Bannisters were aware of my part in returning the herd to your father. Then, she mentioned that the peaceful atmosphere is about to change. She finished by effectively telling me to get out of town and go back to my ranch. It was a threat, pure and simple."

Sarah stared at Matt in surprise and asked, "She said all that?"

"And one other thing that points to her personality more than anything."

"What was that?"

"After she said I would have been better off if I had never left my ranch, I responded by telling her that if I had stayed there, then I would have never had the pleasure of meeting her."

Sarah slipped back into an intense frame of jealousy and asked, "Why did you say such a thing? Did you mean it?"

"Of course, not. I said it to see what kind of response I would get. Most women, when getting a comment like that would smile and say, 'thank you' or come back with an equally insipid comment like 'no, it is I who am fortunate, sir'."

"What did she say?"

"She said, and I quote 'the highlight of your most boring trip, I'm afraid."

Sarah's eyes grew wide as she asked, "She said *that*?"

"Uh-Uh. It surprised even me. I thought she would try to throw some more feminine charm, but she couldn't do it. She had to let her real personality take over. It was an astonishing display of hubris. Now, what about you. Why won't you dance with me?"

"I really can't dance. I never have. I've never been to a church social or a barn dance before. I don't belong here. I belong out in the pastures. I can't even remember the last time I wore a dress. Look at Rachel out there on the dance floor. Every man in the place, even the preacher is watching her. She's like a swan. I'm a...a...damn, I don't know what I am!"

Matt couldn't put up with it any more. He stood up and put out his hand. "Come with me, Sarah."

She stared up at him, her emotions were smashing themselves into fragments in her heart.

"I told you, I can't dance," she snapped.

"We're not going to the dance floor. So, come with me, or I'll pick you up and carry you kicking and screaming. You know I could do it and will if I have to."

She knew that he could and probably would, so she stood and took his hand. He led her around the dance floor, no one paying them any mind. He crossed over behind the band, Sarah trying to keep up with him.

He entered a medium sized room whose purpose was unknown to him, then, after she entered, he closed the door. He then shocked her when he picked her up by the waist and sat her down on a large chest along the wall near the door that put her at his eye level.

"Now, Miss Reed. I have had enough of your whining! There is no reason for it, and I want it stopped."

Sarah had no response. She simply looked at Matt and gaped. She was unused to seeing him face to face, and even more unused to having him talk to her like this.

"I'm not whining," she finally blurted out, "it's all the truth."

"You haven't said one word of truth since you've been here, except maybe that you've never been to a social or barn dance before. That nonsense about Rachel being a swan and you are an unknown nothing is beyond contempt. Have you ever been with a swan? They are just so beautiful as they gracefully glide along the water. Such beauty! Such grace! But they are vicious birds and the last thing you ever want to do is turn your back on one. They'll bite your rear end before you know they're there."

The mental image elicited a giggle from Sarah as Matt continued his chastisement.

"Sarah, you are the most remarkable woman I have ever met. You're intelligent, confident, have a great sense of humor and a solid moral compass. And, I may add, you're as beautiful inside as you are outside. I will never hear you selling yourself short ever again, Miss Reed. Rachel Bannister can't hold a candle to you. And one other thing you'll learn about me if you keep me around long enough; I never say anything I don't mean. When I told you that you looked spectacular tonight, I meant it. So, no more feeling bad about yourself. There is no reason for you to take second spot to any woman. As for your dancing shortcoming, we can remedy that right now."

The music was wafting through the closed door as Matt reached out and lifted Sarah by the waist from the cabinet and gently lowered her to the floor.

"This is another waltz," he said, "now, hold my left hand and place your left hand on my shoulder."

She was still processing all that Matt had said, but she did as he directed.

"Now, the waltz is very simple. It goes 1,2,3, 1,2,3. I'll lead, so all you do is follow my steps. I'll guide you with my right hand."

They paused, waiting for the right moment, but until then, they just gazed into each other's eyes for ten seconds, saying nothing but understanding everything.

The short reverie was ended when the new movement began, and Matt said, "Now," then took her hand and gently pulled her across the floor. For the first minute or so, she was a bit awkward, but soon had the rhythm and the feel for the music and the motion. By the time the waltz finished she had a genuine smile on her face and a genuine warmth in her heart for the giant of a man guiding her. She didn't even feel the floor under her feet any longer as she floated and spun with Matt's large hand on her waist. When the music stopped, they stayed in motion as if the notes were continuing and finally just slowed to a stop, assuming their earlier, almost statue-like pose, barely breathing.

"Thank you for a wonderful dance, Miss Reed," whispered Matt.

Sarah almost didn't hear him, she was so overwhelmed. But then she finally replied.

"I didn't think I'd like it as much as I did," answered Sarah in a soft voice, "But I don't think I'm ready to do it in public yet. Is that all right?"

"Quite all right, Sarah. I really do understand how you feel. I just needed to let you know that you have qualities that make these other women, including Rachel, maybe especially Rachel, pale in comparison. One of them, I haven't told you before are those eyes of yours. The first time I saw them I felt that you could use them to see into my soul. It made me a bit nervous to tell you the truth."

Sarah laughed, finally letting the moment live only in her memory.

"Only if you have something to hide, Matt."

"Shall we return now?" he asked, his eyes still on hers.

Sarah sighed then answered, "I suppose we have to go back."

Matt opened the door and led an exultant Sarah behind the band and around to the main floor. They stayed on the right side of the dance floor to avoid the crowd but had to pass in front of the Bannister table, and suddenly Rachel was standing right in front of him. Sarah could sense confrontation and stepped back a few feet.

Rachel stepped even closer to Matt and looked up at him, and Matt caught the stares of Billie and his father out of the corner of his eye.

"You know, Matt," she began quietly, "If you take me into the storeroom, I have a lot more to offer than that little friend of yours."

"Oh, she's not my little friend," Matt replied.

"I must have misunderstood, then. So, this should be an easy decision for you."

"It is definitely an easy decision for me. You see, Rachel, Miss Sarah Reed is much more than just my friend, although she will continue to be my friend for the rest of my life. If everything works out, I intend to court Miss Reed. Hopefully, when I return to my ranch, I'll be bringing my little friend with me as my wife."

He had barely finished when Rachel's eyes flared, and she hauled back her right hand and slapped him across his left cheek while at the same time shouting loudly, "How dare you, sir! You have insulted me!"

The crack of the slap and Rachel's loud accusation floated across the suddenly silent room. Even the musicians stopped playing.

The slap surprised Matt, but the phony allegation did not. Nor did her ploy to bring embarrassment to him and to the Reed family. He anticipated something, so his response was loud enough for everyone in the room to hear.

His deep bass voice echoed, "On the contrary, Miss Bannister, it is you who have thrown the insult. You insulted Miss Reed in a most reprehensible fashion and then instituted this vulgar display to minimize your own poor behavior."

Miss Bannister, you are a very beautiful woman. Perhaps the most beautiful in the room. I'm sure you believe that as well. I also believe you easily dismiss the other women here as easily as you had Miss Reed. Yes, you are very beautiful, and yet every one of these women," Matt continued as he slowly swept his hand across the room, "that you so casually dismiss as your inferiors has more beauty in her soul than you could ever hope for. It is that beauty that their husbands and boyfriends cherish. It is a beauty that can be shared with those they love. You probably have never had a genuine boyfriend, and you may never have a genuine husband because you have nothing to share. So, don't view them as lessers, see them as models to aspire to. Your beauty is all on the outside, Miss Bannister, but your inside, your soul, is empty. And that, Rachel, is a genuine tragedy."

The entire room was quiet as Matt, turned to Sarah, offered his hand and asked, "Would you care for some punch, Miss Reed?"

Sarah took his hand then led her to the refreshment table. Before they reached it, the band began to play again, and some dancers took to the floor, but most stayed at their tables buzzing about the shocking event.

Rachel stood standing in the same place for almost a minute. Nothing had gone right. She had done exactly as her father had suggested but had been humiliated instead. She should have been furious, but she simply stood there. Matt's comments had hurt her worse than a shotgun blast as she realized that she had never had a real boyfriend, not even when she was a young girl. She was always popular with the boys, but never really liked any of them. Not one of them ever wanted to just talk to her, or to even less to listen to her.

She was still deep into self-examination when she felt a hand on her shoulder and the voice of her father telling her, "Come, Rachel, I think it's time to leave."

She nodded and walked unseeing with her father toward the door, still deep in thought and replaying each syllable of what Matt Little had said.

The reaction she had expected to have, the fury, was filling her brother. Billie wanted to shoot that bastard, but guns were not permitted in the social. He'd make him pay for what he did to embarrass the family name, sooner rather than later. He should have shot him when he had the chance.

Sarah and Matt walked back to the Reed table and Sarah noticed that almost all the women were watching them and assumed it was Matt they were watching, and she understood. She was very proud of him, but unlike the other women in the room, she was the one that Matt would be courting.

They sat down, and Pat and Jenny leaned over.

Pat said, "You'll have to tell me what that was all about."

"That was round two. I'll fill you in when we get back."

Pat nodded as Jenny just smiled broadly at Matt. Then the girls started arriving. Matt spent the rest of the evening dancing with women of all ages and sizes. Almost universally, they thanked him for what he had said. Matt made sure he squeezed in a dance with Peggy, who relished every second.

As the social was coming to a close, Matt sat in the pew next to Sarah and she surprised him when she slid her hand over his. He looked into those green eyes and smiled.

She returned his smile and said, "Thank you for a wonderful evening, Matt. I thought it was going to be horrible, but you made it one of the best nights of my life. I'll never forget it, nor will I ever forget what you said to Rachel. I don't think any of the other women in the church will forget it either."

Matt replied, "It had to be said. She's young enough and intelligent enough to change. It will be hard, but she can make a better life for herself if she tries. You, on the other hand, don't have to change a thing. You are perfect the way you are."

Sarah blushed and was only able to mouth a thank you.

Matt then turned to Pat and said, "Pat, I'm going to get the horses ready for the trip back. You can escort the ladies out when everyone is ready."

Pat nodded as Matt stood up and walked to the door.

It was dark, and it took a few minutes to find the wagon. It was Caesar's height that let him find it as quickly as he did. Most people were still in the social, but they were town dwellers, so they could stay a little later.

He tightened Caesar's cinch and checked the harness on the wagon. Then, as a matter of habit, he pulled out his Winchester and worked the lever, waiting to catch the ejected cartridge, but nothing came out of the gun. *Someone had emptied his rifle!* He was grateful he had given in to his worries and packed the extra cartridges, which he began removing and sliding into the loading gate. When all twelve had been loaded, he cycled the lever putting a round in the chamber, then released the hammer.

He then removed his bedroll and slid his Remington and gun belt from inside, returned the bedroll to its customary location and strapped on his rig. He put it on under his jacket as he needed the dark coat to help hide his white shirt in the night and wished it was a smaller moon than the almost full disk appearing in the sky. Not even clouds were there to hide their passage.

He was still looking skyward when the Reeds walked up to the wagon.

"Stargazing are you, Matt?" laughed Pat.

Matt brought his eyes back to ground level and said to him, "Pat, come over this way for a second. I have to show you something."

Pat stepped in his direction as the women were helping each other board the wagon.

Matt walked a short distance away from the wagon, turned to Pat and said quietly, "We have problem, Pat. I think they're going to try to drygulch me on the way back to the ranch. If I was absolutely sure that it was only me that they were gunning for, I'd go on ahead by myself. But they might be gunning for you as well."

Matt left out the word 'family', although it was a real concern for him.

"What gave you the idea?" Pat asked incredulously.

"Someone unloaded my Winchester while we were in the social. I'd suggest that you and your family stay in the hotel overnight, but even then, I couldn't be sure they'd be safe."

"So, now that we're disarmed, what can we do?"

"We aren't disarmed. I reloaded the Winchester with some spare ammo I had in my pockets. I also hid my Remington in my bedroll. I just had a bad feeling all day about that Hart character. I think the safest way to approach this is for you to take the Winchester with you. Keep it on the floor nearby, or you can even let Jenny drive. I'm assuming she can do that. I'll ride about a hundred yards in front. I won't keep a straight line, and don't be embarrassed by some of the things I do. I'll be trying to draw attention to me for a reason. If there is shooting, I'm guessing it'll come from the direction of the small ranches on the left side. If you see a muzzle flash, you should be out of range, but I want you to fire three rounds about 5 seconds apart where you saw the flame to distract the shooter, and then head back toward Denton about a quarter mile. When I'm finished, I'll ride back and find you. It's the best plan I can come up with."

Pat thought for a minute, then nodded and accepted the proffered Winchester. The men headed back, and Matt mounted the stallion while Pat climbed aboard the wagon. As he passed the wagon, Matt said to Pat, "Give me about thirty seconds to get ahead of you, that should be at least a hundred yards. After that you'll be able to tell where I am and how far ahead."

Pat asked, "How's that?" and heard from a disappearing Matt, "You'll see, or rather you'll hear."

Jenny was the first to ask, "What is this all about? And why do you have Matt's rifle?"

Sarah was an eager listener as Pat explained the situation.

The few lights of Denton had just about disappeared when the Reeds first heard Matt from the roadway ahead. A deep, rich voice was singing loudly, "I dream of Jenny with the light brown hair…"

110

Obviously, in addition to his surprisingly beautiful singing voice, his sense of humor still showed, but the voice told Pat where he was and how far ahead he was.

Matt, in addition to singing, was dancing Caesar up the road. He had the horse at a trot, but because he was changing direction and bobbing, he was keeping pace with the slower trailing wagon. If it wasn't for the tension, the Reeds could have enjoyed the traveling serenade on the way home.

They had been on the road for ten minutes, and Matt was in the second stanza of *Lorena* when the expected happened. Pat saw the flame stretch out a good foot toward the roadway in front from a hill on the left of the road, along with the report of a rifle. Jenny had the reins, so Pat wasted no time to take his first shot and quickly levering in a new round. As he was taking his second shot, he heard the pounding of Caesar's hooves crossing from the road to the shooter. Another shot came from the hill, then a third. Both were in Matt's direction as Pat fired his third shot and Jenny turned the wagon.

When that first shot was taken, Matt didn't waste time. The shooter was close, as he had to be. The moon may have helped the shooter, but it was a lot different than a bright Texas sun. He whipped Caesar to his left and raced in the direction of the sound, expecting that other shots would come his way but knew that this younker's chance of getting a bullet into him were getting lower by the second. His biggest concern was Caesar. He was worried about his stumbling into a gopher hole or some other depression or taking one of those .44s with his bigger body. But he knew the stallion's eyes were better than his, so he raced on. Neither the second nor the third shot were even close, but they sure marked where the shooter was. It took him just ten more seconds to reach the spot as Caesar raced up the hill. By then, he could see the man and his rifle running toward a tethered horse. Matt came up on him just as he was trying to reach for the saddle horn. Matt launched himself from Caesar and smashed into the shooter, and both Matt and the shooter tumbled along the dark Texas dirt.

Matt quickly got to his feet after the collision. The man's horse had spooked and was trotting away at a good pace, but the shooter

111

himself lay on the ground moaning. Matt didn't waste any time, and he placed his size fourteen boot on the small of the man's back, causing a screech of pain. Matt didn't care, but then rolled him over to see if he recognized him, not surprising to see the scarred face of Jesse Hart in the moonlight.

"Well, Jesse, it's just not your night, is it?"

Matt then undid Hart's gun belt and tossed it aside, then slipped off Hart's waist belt and then flipped him back on his stomach, grabbed each arm and used the belt to secure them tightly, then yanked Jesse to his feet as he moaned and with an occasional grunt of pain.

"So, now what am I going to do with you?"

Jesse's first words were a croaked, "I need me a doctor."

"Well, I aim to accommodate you. But first, I'll go and round up your horse."

Matt then walked over to Caesar, who was placidly watching the scene as he munched on some nearby grass and took out some pigging strings that he always kept in his saddlebag. He returned to the still-moaning Hart and tied his feet together and then sat him up against a small bush.

"Stay tight, Jesse. I'll be right back."

On his way to retrieve Jesse's horse, Matt picked up Hart's pistol belt and Winchester carbine. The horse had only wandered a hundred yards or so, so Matt returned in a few minutes. After inserting Hart's repeater in Caesar's empty scabbard and the gun belt around his saddle horn, he undid Hart's ankle bindings and let him mount his horse, then used the same pigging strings to tie his feet to the stirrups. It wasn't the most elegant trussing job, but it should work.

Matt mounted Caesar and led Hart's horse and groaning baggage back to the roadway, turned back toward Denton and had only traveled a quarter of a mile when he saw the wagonload of Reeds.

"What do you have there?" yelled Pat.

"Beats me," Matt answered, "I found this poor feller wandering around, so I thought I'd help him find the way back."

"Mighty kind of you, Matt," chuckled Pat.

When he arrived at the wagon, Matt asked, "The real question is what do we do with him? He says he needs a doctor."

"Did you shoot him?"

"Nope. Just jumped on him. I think he may have a broken rib or two."

"We could take him back to the sheriff," suggested Pat.

"I'm not sure that would help. Do you?"

"Probably not. What other options do we have?"

"Well," answered Matt, "I am seriously thinking of just cutting him loose."

With that, Hart's moaning suddenly stopped as he stared at Matt.

"What the hell for?" shouted Pat, "The man tried to kill you!"

"Yes, sir. He did just that," agreed Matt, "But I don't think he's going to be much use for a while. If you have ever had broken ribs, you'd know what I mean. I had some back at the Bar T a couple of years back. For almost a month, I couldn't rope a calf, or barely ride a horse. I think Hart's out of the game. I don't believe Bannister is going to cut him any slack, either. He screwed up and Bannister isn't the forgiving kind."

Matt turned to Bannister and asked, "It was Bannister that sent you to kill me, right?"

"Yeah," came the somber response.

"You got any cash on you?" asked Matt.

"What? Are you gonna rob me?"

"Nope. Just want to see if you have enough to get out of here."

"Yeah, I'm okay."

With that Matt dismounted and walked back to Hart's horse and cut the pigging strings. Then he undid the belt holding his hands and handed it back to him.

"What about my guns?" he demanded.

"My goodness. Set a murderer free and he makes demands," quipped Matt.

He walked back to Caesar and removed the gun belt from his saddle horn. He pulled out the Colt and emptied the chambers into his hand. Then he removed the cartridges from the gun loops and handed the useless weapon to Jesse Hart.

"What about my rifle?"

"It's a carbine, Jesse. If you're going to spend your life trying to shoot people in the back, you should know the difference. Consider that the wages of sin. Now you can head south, and I'd recommend you keep riding. You don't need a doc for those ribs, just don't do anything rough for about a month. Of course, if you think I'm lying to you, you can always try something. Your ribs will tell you to stop. Now head out of here."

With that Matt smacked the rump if Hart's horse then it and its rider disappeared into the night.

Matt walked up to the wagon and Jenny asked, "Was that wise, Matt?"

"It was the only thing we could do. Now, Bannister will probably lose his best weapon, because I was being honest with him about

114

those ribs. He's useless for a month, so his best plan is to get away from here for a while. But Bannister's going to have a couple of days wondering what happened. That's why I let him go."

Sarah asked, "But Matt, he tried to kill you. Weren't you mad?"

"To him, it was just a job. He has no feelings one way or the other. If you get angry at people like that it serves no purpose other than getting yourself into a tizzy."

Then he smiled and said, "Let's get you home."

As he turned back toward the Lazy R, he heard a female voice, unsure of whose, call out, "Are you going to serenade us for the rest of the way home?"

His laughter was met with a combination of laughter and giggles from the wagon, but Matt acquiesced anyway and began to sing as they headed back to the Lazy R.

———

Two hours later at the Box B, Will Bannister sat in his office, smoking his pipe and looking at the large wall clock. *Where was Hart?*

Upstairs, Rachel laid on her bed, her spectacular silk dress still on the floor. She stared at the ceiling, still ruminating over the night's events. No man had ever spoken to her like that before, but Rachel was honest with herself enough to realize that what he had said was true. When she had slapped Matt, exactly as her father had told her to do, she felt incredibly cheap. Matt had impressed her when he had arrived and when they had danced. She had played her role, said what she had been told to say, yet he had not only resisted her, but had turned the tables.

Now, Rachel was ashamed of her role in whatever her father was planning. She had heard whispers and rumors about the Reed's ranch that had suddenly become the focus of her father's life. She knew that he had been having his hands do things they shouldn't be doing and was ashamed that she had said nothing.

Rachel closed her eyes and continued to review her place on the Box B and her future.

CHAPTER 4

The next morning as Matt woke in his usual surroundings, the spare bedroom of John and Mary's home, he felt a sense of urgency. Last night, the confrontation with Rachel followed by the assassination attempt meant that he was running out of time to find the root cause of the Will Bannister's determination to take ownership of the Lazy R. It had to be the land itself but had no idea what it could be. The only thing he could do was to go to Austin and review the original land records. There must be something there, maybe a border problem that gave Pat Reed some of Bannister's property.

He shook his head to clear out the grogginess and dressed. After his morning cleanup and shave, he went into the kitchen finding Mary already there, cooking breakfast.

"I see you gave up your plans to take over," she said as she smiled.

"Just getting too lazy to do any good, I guess."

Matt sat down for breakfast and asked, "Where's John?"

Mary replied, "He's rounding up the other members of the Association. They'll be arriving in about an hour."

Matt simply nodded and ate his breakfast, still trying to understand Bannister's obsession with the Lazy R.

It was almost two hours when the members arrived at the ranch house. As they entered, they greeted Matt warmly as word was out of all the things he had done from paying off the Reed's tax bill, finding most of the rustled cattle, the attempted drygulching, and, of course, the confrontation with Rachel and the impressive lecture that followed. Matt wasn't aware of the spread of information but was glad to be accepted by the group.

117

Matt was questioned in depth about the shooting by Jesse Holt and his decision not to either kill him or take him to the sheriff. After his explanation, they accepted that he had made the right decision, but until Matt told them of the first conversation he had with Rachel, they hadn't known that the Bannisters had decided to increase the pressure on the Reeds. Matt also explained his theory about why none of the southern ranches had missing cattle among the herd that he had recovered.

"So," asked Henry Lewis of the L Bar, "where do we go from here?"

Matt took a deep breath and said, "I have to discover the reason for Bannister wanting the Lazy R. I'll have to leave for a day or two to see if my idea has merit. If it does, then we'll decide about what to about it. Just finding the reason won't necessarily make the problem go away, though."

"Can you tell us what you think the problem may be?" asked Ben Riordan of the Double X.

"I'd rather not. This is a real shot in the dark. I could be totally wrong, and probably am. I'll let everyone know when I return. Pat, before you go, I'd like to talk to you in private for a while if that's okay."

"From what I hear, Pat, I think Matt's going to ask you for Sarah's hand," laughed Jeff Thompson of the J-T Connected.

Matt flushed, and Pat just waved him down.

The meeting broke up a half an hour later and Pat approached Matt and the two walked out to the barn.

When they arrived, Pat said, "You know, if you are thinking about asking about Sarah, you've got to understand, it's not me you need to be asking, it's her."

Matt laughed and said, "I'm well aware of Sarah's spirit, Pat. But this is about the Lazy R. I need to know its history. Who you bought it from and how the previous owner obtained title for the land."

Pat ruminated for a few seconds and answered, "Jenny and I arrived from Louisiana fifteen years ago, right after the War Between the States. Our home had been burned, so we sold the land and moved here. We didn't have a lot of money, so we needed a bargain. A bargain with a house already on it. As it turns out, Adolf Zimmerman owned the property where the Lazy R is now. He bought it twelve years earlier from some defunct railroad company. He was going to turn it into nice ranch, but all he was ever able to do was build a small cabin. His two sons died in the war, in the same battle, I recall. His wife died shortly after and he lost the will to build anything. We bought the property at a good price and moved into his small cabin. It took us a few years to get the ranch house built. We needed the room for obvious reasons. We were the first ones in the area, and after that the other small ranchers moved in and then the big ones. The last one was the Bannisters. They got here about seven years ago. They weren't bad neighbors until earlier this year, and when they changed, they really became a problem."

Matt had been scribbling notes as Pat recited. When they finished, Matt said, "Okay. This will help a lot, Pat."

"Matt, can you at least tell me where you're headed?"

"Just between you and me, I'm going to Austin. But don't let that get out, not even to Jenny. I'm going to try to sneak out of here on the afternoon train."

Pat nodded, accepting the conditions before both men returned to the house where Pat mounted his horse and returned to the Lazy R.

Matt packed his clothes in a traveling bag that he borrowed from John. Except for Pat, no one knew of his destination.

He said good-bye to the Sandersons and rode Caesar down to Denton. There, he put Caesar up in a clean livery and headed for the depot. The train for Austin and San Antonio pulled in at two o'clock and was a six-hour trip to Austin. Matt was fidgety the entire trip. He didn't know what he would find, if anything, and if he found nothing, he would be right back where he started.

The train was early as it pulled into Austin, a very unusual occurrence. The summer sun was still in the sky when he checked into the Railway Hotel, had dinner, then returned to his room and had a good night's sleep. He'd need it for the boring job he had tomorrow.

———

The next morning, he had breakfast at the hotel and walked to the easily found state offices, checked the directory and headed for the land office.

He was greeted by a helpful clerk, which surprised him. His experience with bureaucrats wasn't good, but it took him three hours of searching through the stacks of records brought by the clerk. Eventually, he found the records he was looking for. It was the sales record and deed for the purchase of land by Adolf Zimmerman. He read the records and found absolutely nothing.

"There must be something!" he said aloud, "This can't be the end."

He read the original deed and the sales record six times, and he couldn't see what was important. The dimensions listed were the same as on the Lazy R deed he had sitting to the right, but there was one thing that bothered him about the sale to Zimmerman.

Why, if you're buying property from a bankrupt railroad venture would you choose the worst property available? If it was the same price, why not pick someplace with water? Not only that, why such an odd size? It was six thousand feet by forty three hundred feet. Why not at least make it square, like a full section?

He was just staring at the original deed when he saw it. *My God! How could he look at it so long and not see it?* He pulled out his pencil and a blank sheet of paper and began doing some calculations. This was stunning.

He then turned to Pat Reed's sales records and deeds and looked at them. If there had been a map included with the documents, he could have seen it easily, but it was only written out by the surveyors. There was no map.

He called over the clerk and asked if he could get a legal copy of the four documents. Matt was told it would be no problem, but it would take a few hours and cost three dollars. Matt told him to go ahead and said he'd be back at noon.

After returning all the documents to the clerk, he left the state office building and almost floated across the street until he found a law office. There were always law offices near a court house. He entered the largest firm, hoping he could find a real estate attorney. He did and spent a long time with him, explaining the issue, which the attorney found fascinating. The lawyer gave him his card and Matt paid the small consulting fee as he left the building.

He ate a quick lunch at a small café and returned to the state offices, hoping that the copies were done. They were ready, so Matt put them in a thick envelope and paid the small fee. *If only they had an idea what kind of an impact these documents would have!* He also wondered how Bannister could have found this information, which could be the only reason for his obsession.

He practically ran to the depot to see if he could catch the afternoon train to Fort Worth and Denton, glad he had kept the travel bag with him. His luck held out, as the train had been delayed and wouldn't be leaving for another hour. The train finally arrived, and Matt practically flew on board. As the train rolled north, Matt, having recovered from the excitement of his find, now tried to think about how to handle the aftermath. A lot would depend on Pat and Jenny Reed.

Unfortunately, it may depend on the sheriff as well.

He mulled over the problem as the train continued its relentless push north. At 9:25 that night, Matt stepped down onto the Denton platform. Even though it was late, he hurried to the livery stable, found liveryman still there, so Matt paid him and saddled Caesar. The tall stallion was ready for a good run and took off at a fast pace along the north bound road.

There were no bushwhackers this time, not that there should be. Matt made good time and arrived at John and Mary's house just around ten o'clock. He was glad to see that there were lights on, so he stabled Caesar and gave him a quick rubdown after removing his tack.

He trotted up the stairs and entered the house. John and Mary had been reading, but when they heard Caesar trot into the yard, they put down their books and waited for Matt's appearance.

"Well, did you find what you were looking for?" asked John.

"Yes, I did," Matt replied with a big grin on his face.

"Well," Mary asked, "are you going to keep us in suspense?"

"Unfortunately, yes. I need to present this to Pat and Jenny in the morning., but I'm sure they wouldn't mind you being present when I do."

"But now you understand why the Bannisters wanted the property, right?" asked John.

"Absolutely. And if I were in their position, I'd want it, too."

"Well, if you're not going to tell us, then I guess we may as well turn in."

With that, John and Mary went into their room and Matt went into his, clutching the thick envelope.

CHAPTER 5

Early the next morning, Matt rode Caesar behind John and Mary's buggy as they turned into the Lazy R entrance. Matt couldn't help looking around at the wide expanse of land and knowing what changes lay ahead.

As the buggy rolled to a stop, Matt stepped down and tied off Caesar at the hitchrail, removed the envelope from his saddlebag and turned to go to the house, suppressing the grin that kept trying to force its way to his face.

He walked up the steps with the Sandersons, still grinning, despite his efforts to straighten it out, and into the main room. It was quite crowded as everyone had rushed into the room, expecting Matt's arrival, but it was deathly quiet, with everyone's eyes on him. After John and Mary found seats, Matt took a deep breath.

Matt began, "Now, since I arrived, the one question that hung over everything is why the Bannisters were so desperate to own the Lazy R. None of the normal reasons for wanting land were there. Water, good grass, minerals. None of it. It's a small ranch, too. Pat, how big is your ranch, in acreage and dimensions?"

Pat scrunched up his face and said, "I don't know, about a full section, about six thousand feet by forty-three hundred feet, I think."

"Did you ever wonder about those dimensions? They seem a bit odd, don't you think?"

Pat said, "Well, that's why we got it so cheap."

Matt shook his head and replied, "No, you got it cheap because Adolf Zimmerman wanted to get off this place and you were the first one to offer to buy it."

Matt continued as Pat nodded.

"Now, yesterday, I went down to the state capital in Austin, and went to the land offices there rather than in the county because they go back further, and I wanted to see the originals. I have legal copies of thosee originals in my hand. I studied them for almost an hour without noticing anything myself, so I can see how the original problem occurred."

"What problem?" asked Jenny.

"The difference between a rod and a foot."

That had everyone confused.

"Okay, Matt, you've toyed with us enough," Pat pleaded, "out with it!"

"A rod is a standard measurement used by surveyors. It's the distance between established fence posts. That distance, in the United States is set at sixteen and a half feet. We don't use it very often anymore, but twenty-five years ago, a survey team hired by two would-be railroad magnates named Blackman and Cross surveyed the property they had purchased to build a new railroad. The surveyors used the rod rather than the foot as the standard of measurement in their survey. The railroad went bankrupt before a single rail was laid and the first man to buy some of that land was Mr. Adolf Zimmerman. He purchased a piece of land he thought was 6000 feet by 4300 feet and built his cabin on it. The reason he thought it was that size was that some draftsman in the land office had read the sales contract and just saw numbers, not the unit of measurement. He didn't see rods, he saw feet. Mr. Zimmerman never noticed. He could barely read, I'm guessing. On his bill of sale, he made a mark rather than a signature, so he never paid attention to the actual deed or sales contract. The difference was that the land he bought was not six thousand feet by forty-three hundred feet, but six thousand rods by forty-three hundred rods. The corner you are on, Pat, is the southwest corner of a much larger plot of land. So, instead of having the smallest ranch in Denton County, Mr. Reed, sir, you own the largest. Your property includes your ranch, the Box B, and a good-sized chunk of the Star M. You have about 169,000 acres on your ranch and the dimensions are about 18.7 miles by 13.4 miles."

Everyone was stunned, which was pretty much the impact he expected.

Matt started again.

"After I made that discovery, I visited a real estate attorney in Austin. I have his card in my pocket, explained what I had found, and he told me that any of the subsequent divisions and sales of your property had no legal standing. Just because a clerk in the land office made a transcription error before you bought the land doesn't matter. That would be considered by the courts as to be incidental because you had not caused the mistake. So, now we have a whole new problem, don't we?"

Matt waited for someone to say something, but no one made a sound and it stayed that way for almost a minute.

"What problems do you see, Matt?" asked Jenny finally.

"A lot depends on you and Pat. I know that you're both fine people and don't want to hurt anyone, even the Bannisters. I think that if you get a lawyer involved, we can avoid any violence. Can I make a recommendation?"

"Of course," answered Pat, "you're doing pretty well so far."

"If I were in your shoes, what I would do is to make the Morrows over at the Star M an offer to keep their property. You could sell them the Star M property that is included in the original deed. Now the Bannisters are a different issue, because you own all of the Box B. I believe you'd be better off cutting the Box B in half and offering to let them buy the half with their house. It would still leave them with a good-sized ranch, and it would also give you a good-sized ranch with plenty of water and good grass, and a healthy bank account. The only concern I see in this approach is that most ranchers are land rich and cash poor. If they offer you a fair price, they may not be able to come up with the cash. You may have to accept mortgages. Plus, there's one other potential problem, especially with the Bannisters, and that is their pride. They may tell you to take your offer and go to hell, and then decide to fight it out. There are a lot of potential problems out there, Pat and Jenny. But they're a lot better problems than you've been facing these past fifteen years."

Pat said, "Matt, this is so overwhelming that I can't begin to fathom the sheer enormity of it."

Matt replied, "Well, I'll leave you so you can decide what you want to do. I'd suggest contacting a local attorney. Maybe in Fort Worth."

Matt handed the envelope to Pat and walked to the back of the room near the door then watched as everyone gathered around Pat and Jenny, and then the joy hit them all. There was almost a party atmosphere with the Sandersons joining the Reeds.

Matt smiled at the happy family, but suddenly realized that he was the odd man out now. He was no longer necessary, and even Sarah was now focused on her family again. It was almost as if the last few days were just a dream and now, he was awake again.

He slipped out of the room and then left the house, walked out to the front of the house and mounted Caesar. It had been a good day, but with the problems all solved, he knew he should be getting back to his own ranch. He might have two or three more foals by now, and then there were the Percherons.

He turned the Morgan and trotted out past the house and down the entrance path onto the road. When he arrived, he realized he wasn't sure which way he wanted to go. He also had an empty feeling because he wasn't needed any more, but he felt he had fulfilled his own promise to Spike. Well, at least part of it. He had solved the problem of the missing cattle and the land, but the justice for Spike's illegal hanging still needed resolution.

As he thought of Spike McMillan, he wondered where they had buried him.

With that he turned left toward Denton and set off at a medium trot. Twenty minutes later, when he arrived in the town, he looked for the undertaker's location. It wasn't hard to find, so he walked Caesar to the entrance and stepped down, then entered the place with the same sense of foreboding that many do. A thin man in a dark suit and cravat was behind a desk when he stepped inside and Matt wondered why undertakers were universally thin and bartenders invariably fat.

"May I help you, sir?"

"Yes, a couple of weeks ago, a friend of mine was buried here, I believe. His name was Spike, er, Stephan McMillan."

"Ah, yes. I recall the sad situation. He was buried in the common cemetery."

"Does he have a headstone?"

"I believe not."

"I'd like to have one made. Can I order that here?"

"Of course, sir. Just write down what you would like it to read."

Matt used the proffered pencil and wrote on a pad, *Stephan McMillan 1856-1883 An Honest Man.*

He handed it to the undertaker who read it and said, "It is my understanding that he had been hanged for rustling cattle".

"Well," Matt replied, "it turned out that the rustlers were the ones that hanged him, trying to cover their own misdeeds."

"Oh! That does make a difference. That will be twenty-seven dollars."

Matt paid for the stone and left the building. Spike deserved better than this. The Bannisters may lose half their ranch, but they had murdered his good friend and were still walking around free. The more he thought about it, the angrier he became. If he had been a drinking man, he would have walked into the nearest bar and drank himself into oblivion and wondered if there might not be an advantage to that after all.

He sighed and stepped into Caesar's stirrup, took his seat, and turned back to the road leaving Denton. He still didn't want to be around anyone. He was miserable, which surprised him. *Why should he feel so badly? Everything was going so well.* But he still felt like he had let Spike down somehow.

Caesar kept up a steady pace and Matt had no idea where he was headed, so he let the horse choose. Soon he noticed that he was passing the Rocking S, his home for the past week. The next entrance he noticed was the Box B. When he approached the entrance road, he stopped Caesar and looked down the long road going to the big house. Part of him wanted to ride down that road, walk in the front door and empty his pistol into Will Bannister for what he did to Spike, but he knew he wouldn't do it. It wouldn't make him feel any better and it sure wouldn't help Spike.

He turned Caesar back the way he had come and rode for another mile or so and then left the road to the east, guessing this was Box B land, at least for now, but didn't care. He rode cross country for a while until he reached the shores of Lake Dallas. There he dismounted and unsaddled Caesar, removed his blanket and bridle, then let him wander where he could get some water and grass. Matt laid down next to his saddle and wondered what he would do next. It was just past noon, but he was in no mood to travel, so he laid his head on his saddle and put his Stetson over his eyes.

He had started to drift off when he was startled by the sound of horses approaching from behind, then yanked the Stetson from his head, sat up and looked for the source of the sound. Coming over a low hill were three riders, and they'd all seen him. One must be that fat man that he had asked Sarah about and another one was yanking his rifle from the scabbard. Matt didn't need any more incentive to move. He turned over and as he rolled, he withdrew his Winchester '76 from the scabbard and cocked it. Then he waited for them to start the dance, but they didn't. Instead they stopped about eighty yards out when they saw his rifle aimed in their direction.

"What are you doin' on Box B land?" shouted the fat man.

Matt shouted back, "Sleeping!"

"You're that bastard that took them cattle, ain't ya'?"

"I didn't take anything. I figure some kind soul found those wandering Lazy R and Rocking S cattle and decided to put them in a nice safe place until their owners came to claim them. So, I brought them back as a favor. You wouldn't know who those kind gents were that put them there, would you?"

"You're a regular smart mouth!" the fat man snapped back.

"Nope. It's just dumb. It only does what my brain tells it to. Now what do you boys aim to do?"

"We aim to take your hide back to Mr. Bannister, so he can teach you a lesson."

Matt asked loudly, "Would that be the same kind of lesson you gave to a very good friend of mine?"

"You mean that sorry son of a bitch we hanged by that tree over yonder?" the man asked as he threw his thumb over his shoulder at a small forest.

Then they laughed. They shouldn't have laughed, not about that.

Matt didn't wait for them to make the first move. It was move or die time.

He jerked the Winchester up to eye level and pulled the trigger at the man with the Winchester already pointed at him. Matt's .45 drilled squarely through the center of the man's chest, pulverizing his breastbone and exploding his aortic arch before stopping as it crashed into his thoracic spine. As the already dead man was tumbling off the back of his horse, he noticed the fat man pulling his revolver, so Matt cocked and fired at him, catching him just right of center mass, high in the chest, right near the neck. The slug ripped a large chunk where his neck and shoulder joined and severed his carotid artery. He grabbed his throat as he fell sideways off his horse and would live for another fifteen seconds. Matt didn't wait to see if the man was alive or dead as he levered in a third round and swung it slightly to the right at the third man, whose pistol had already cleared his holster, and fired at Matt. But firing in a panic from the back of a startled horse wasn't the same as it was in a target range, especially with a man with a rifle aiming at you. Where his round went was anyone's guess and it just didn't matter.

Matt's final shot punched into the man's gut just below the diaphragm, but with the upward angle of the trajectory, traveled through the diaphragm and into the bottom of his heart. His eyes grew wide as he felt the bullet's entry momentarily, but when his heart stopped pumping, the lights went out in his brain and he slowly rolled off to the side of his horse and flopped awkwardly to the ground.

The echoes had barely died down when Matt hopped to his feet then walked up to the bodies. He didn't need to kick them to make sure they were dead, but as he looked down at them, he felt no pity or remorse, either. He wasn't happy about it, but he knew it was either him or them.

He turned called to Caesar, who trotted back to him. After he'd saddled his Morgan, he knew that he couldn't head directly back to either ranch, the tracks would be too easy to follow. He didn't have any time to deal with the bodies either, so he just followed his own tracks until he came to the roadway, then guided Caesar to the left toward the Rocking S.

He arrived at the ranch house after leaving Caesar in the barn, knocked on the door, but there was no answer. He guessed that they were still at the Reeds, so he sat down on one of the two rockers.

Now he was the one with problems. He had just killed three men, and there were no witnesses to say that they had him under a gun or that they were threatening him, or that they had admitted to hanging Spike. Matt wondered if the Bannisters would even report it. They might, if they could prove that he had done it. He knew that Caesar's shoes had no distinguishing marks because he took care of them himself. Bringing in three dead men to the law, even a crooked sheriff, and with all of the gunshot wounds in the front would be difficult to explain. He was still deep in thought when heard the clopping of a horse's hooves, looked up and saw the Sanderson's buggy rolling up to the house.

"There you are, Matt. Everyone wondered where you went," John shouted as he pulled the buggy to a stop.

"I felt redundant. Now it's all legal stuff that Pat and Jenny can handle with a lawyer. I needed some time to think about things, anyway. But I need to tell you both something when you get a chance."

"Sure. Let me put away the horse and buggy."

Mary got out of the buggy and walked up the stairs, saw Matt's troubled face and asked, "Are you all right, Matt? You seem awfully upset for a man that's just helped a family as much as you have."

"A few hours ago, I was just empty. Now I have a serious problem that I need to talk to you about."

She nodded, then opened the door and went inside. A few minutes later John trotted up the steps and Matt rose then followed him into the house.

"So, what's this huge problem, Matt?" John asked, obviously not expecting a big issue at all. Maybe Sarah had told him she didn't want to get married or something.

"Well," he began as Mary sat down across from him, "about an hour ago, I killed three men."

There was a long pause before John finally asked, "What happened?"

Matt kept his eyes downward as he recited the story, from his departure from the Reeds to his arrival at the Sandersons' porch.

"Matt, you had no choice. If you hadn't shot them, we'd have found you hanged out there as well," said John.

"I know that, but that doesn't make it right. I could screw it up for everyone just because I wanted to be alone. That's stupid. *Damn it!* Well, I'll tell you one thing for sure. I'm moving out right now. I'm not going to put you at risk. I'm going to ride down to Fort Worth and turn myself in to the U.S. Marshal. At least I know I'll get a fair investigation from them that I wouldn't get from that sheriff."

"Matt," Mary said quietly, "you've been through a lot in this past week. You have to let things go for a while."

"No, Mary. I need to get myself cleared. I'll pack my things and head out."

With that pronouncement, Matt rose and went into his temporary home, quickly packed his few belongings and returned to the main room. Mary had red eyes when he arrived, and Matt walked up to Mary and gave her a soft kiss on the cheek, then shook John's hand and said, "I'd like to thank you both for being such good friends."

Then he quickly strode out the front door and trotted to the barn. He had Caesar saddled and ready in just a few minutes and was on the road to Denton just a minute later. It was early in the afternoon and it was thirty-five miles to Fort Worth, so he wouldn't get there before the offices were closed, so he decided to stop in Denton and get something to eat and pick up some food for the trip.

Less than an hour later, he was riding out of Denton at a slow trot. Just before the sun set, he looked for a place to sleep for the night and located a nice site with some trees and a small pond. He unsaddled Caesar and let him drink and graze, while he had a sandwich he had prepared at the café in Denton before he left.

He thought he'd have trouble sleeping, but he didn't, and woke up refreshed, which surprised him even more. After washing in the pond and shaving, he saddled Caesar and set out to complete his journey, arriving in Fort Worth in mid-morning. He had to stop in a mercantile to ask for the location of the U.S. Marshal's office, finding it was only two streets over, so he walked his stallion to the office, dismounted and tied him outside.

He took a deep breath and entered the brick building, and once inside he noticed how neat everything was. It was a far cry from most law enforcement facilities he'd seen, and he'd seen many of them when he was riding with the Bar T and bailing his friends out of jails.

"Can I help you, big fella?" asked a friendly voice.

Matt had to turn to see the speaker at his left. The man was almost six feet tall and wiry and sported a Deputy U.S. Marshal's badge.

"I hope so. Mind if I sit down?" Matt asked.

"Go ahead."

"My name's Matt Little. I own a horse ranch about ten miles southeast of Dallas. Yesterday, I killed three men and I came to turn myself in."

Up to this point the deputy was treating the conversation like a routine question-and-answer situation and that changed when Matt made his calm confession to murder.

"Hold on, I think we need to have my boss listen in. Okay?"

"That would be a good idea," Matt said.

The deputy marshal rose and stepped into an office just down the hallway and not even thirty seconds later, he exited the office followed by another man, about the same height but heavier. He was not much older than Matt, about thirty or so.

He sat on the corner of the desk next to Matt and reached out a hand which Matt shook. He combined the handshake with, "Howdy. I'm U.S. Marshal Jake Flowers. Deputy Harper informs me that you told him that you killed three men yesterday and want to turn yourself in. Is that right?"

"Yes, sir. It's a long story. It'll probably take twenty minutes or so."

"We have the time. Would you rather come in the back to my office? It's more comfortable."

Matt nodded, then stood and all three men walked into Marshal Flowers' office and the marshal parked himself in his upholstered chair behind the desk.

"Before you start, Matt. Let me tell you something. In my twelve years in law enforcement, I've never had anyone walk into my office and tell me he did something. We always need to chase them down and then when we catch up with the crooks, they deny it right up till the time the noose breaks their necks. That, and you don't seem the murdering kind. Now, that being said, go ahead with your story."

The lawmen were good listeners and didn't interrupt until Matt finished his story. At one point, in telling his story, he showed them Spike's letter, the spark for his current situation. When he reached its completion, they sat still for a second and exchanged glances.

"Matt," said the marshal, "I have to tell you that's the best confession I've ever heard. Unfortunately, I don't think it's a confession at all. If what you say is true, and I'm pretty sure it is because I know Harry Avery, the sheriff in Denton, and you would have been a fool to trust him to do an investigation. But ignoring a hanging and not investigating rustling cattle are worse than usual, even for Avery. Here's what I want to do. I want to get a couple of my deputies to ride up to Denton with you. I'm going to appoint you as a temporary U.S. Deputy Marshal. You have a better handle on the situation than they do, and it sounds like you did a pretty good job, all things considered. You'll be able to fill them in as you ride up there. When you get there, follow their orders explicitly. Do you understand? I don't care if he tells you to stand on your head, you do it. Okay?"

"Yes, sir. And Marshal Flowers?"

"Yes?"

"May I compliment you on having the neatest law enforcement office I have ever seen?"

Both lawmen guffawed like mules until the marshal simply said, "You'll do, Matt."

They shook his hand and asked if he had eaten yet. When they found out he hadn't even had breakfast, they took him across the street to a nice café and treated him to a filling meal and continued to talk about the situation. The story of the initial boundary mistake was something that neither of them had ever heard before.

When they returned to the office, the two deputy marshals that were being assigned to the case were there. The marshal introduced them as deputy U.S. Marshals Hannity and Croft. Hannity was shorter than the others, about five feet and eight inches, but built like a bull. Croft was just under six feet and of medium build but was noticeable for a crop of bright red hair. Both men were about Matt's age. The marshal briefed them quickly about Matt's situation and told them that Matt would give them the full story during their trip to Denton. He then administered an oath to Matt and gave him his temporary U.S. Marshall badge.

The three men walked out of the office, and as Matt untied Caesar, both men were impressed with his black Morgan stallion, and talked about the horse as Matt led him to the livery stable where the marshals' horses were stabled. Their necessaries were already packed in their saddlebags and Matt still had the supplies he had bought the day before, so without wasting any more time, they all mounted and headed out for Denton.

CHAPTER 6

They arrived in Denton just before eight o'clock that evening. There was still light in the sky, and Matt suggested that they head for the Rocking S, just a few minutes away so they could meet John Sanderson.

Matt had filled them in on most of the details of the previous week, with the exceptions of his paying off the Reed's taxes and his infatuation with Sarah. They were impressed with his detective work in finding the lost cattle and especially in tracking down the land problem.

Matt pointed at the entrance to the Rocking S and they turned down the access road and Matt was relieved to see the lamps lit inside and reined in Caesar before the house. The marshals dismounted and waited near the porch as Matt stepped up to the door.

Matt knocked and heard John's voice from the other side of the door.

"Who is it?"

Matt was puzzled by the challenge and John's reluctance to open the door.

"John, it's me. Matt," he replied loudly.

Matt heard hurried footsteps before the door was quickly yanked open and John Sanderson's anxious face looked at him.

"Matt, you've got to get out of here. There are reward posters out for you. Dead or alive. Sheriff Avery has formed a posse and they're out hunting you. We thought you were Avery's crowd."

"Mind if I invite my friends in, John?" Matt replied casually.

"Friends? What's going on with you, Matt? Didn't you hear me? They're hunting for you!"

While John was talking, Matt waved his traveling companions to the porch.

"John, I'd like you to meet my new friends, Deputy United States Marshals Sam Croft and Jim Hannity. Now, may we come in, please?"

"U.S. Marshals? Are you serious? Oh, yes, come in. Please," John said as he opened the door wide to admit Matt and the marshals.

Mary walked into the main room as they entered and appeared nervous as she spotted him with the two lawmen.

"Matt, are you under arrest?"

Matt laughed and said, "No, Mary. You can stop worrying."

Then he showed her his temporary U.S. Deputy Marshal's badge.

"Now, why don't you and John tell us what's been happening these past two days."

John blinked after seeing the badge, then said, "After you left, without so much as a wave, I might add, Bannister got a hold of that damned sheriff and told him you had drygulched three of his men. Avery then put out a reward poster for five hundred dollars, dead or alive, then formed a posse, all of them Bannister's men, of course. They've been riding herd on the small ranchers, accusing us of hiding you. They got on Pat the worst, though. They searched his house and broke almost all of his furniture."

Matt interrupted, his anger rising as he asked, "Did they hurt anyone?"

"No, but they said they'd be back."

"How many in their so-called posse?" asked Deputy Croft.

"Eight, plus the sheriff. They're probably back at the Bannisters now."

Hannity snorted, "This got bad fast, just like you warned us, Matt."

Matt said, "Guys, if it's okay with you, I'd like to check on the Reeds. They're really good people."

Croft replied, "I don't know Matt. We might be better to wait until morning."

"There are two reasons to go over there tonight," Matt said, "one, I believe that tomorrow morning that posse is going to pay them another visit. Remember, Bannister wants that land."

"And what's the second?"

Matt smiled, then replied, "Pat has four young pretty daughters."

Hannity wasted no time as he exclaimed, "Let's go!"

"Hold on for a second, Jim," Matt said, then he turned to the Sandersons, and asked, "Does Bannister know that Pat has the deed?"

"No, I don't think so," answered John.

"Okay, gentlemen, shall we go?"

The two permanent lawmen joined their temporary comrade, left the room and were shortly heading down the access road. Ten minutes later, they turned onto the Lazy R in the fading light.

The ranch house was dark, and Matt was worried as he slowed Caesar to a stop and dismounted, as did the others.

Matt quietly approached the house, stepped quietly onto the porch, and when he was close to the door, he called out, "Pat? Jenny?"

There was a delay of a few seconds and then he heard a woman's voice from deep in the house, "Matt?"

Matt waved Hannity and Croft back and walked up to the door and slowly swung it open, then took one step into the main room.

He asked softly, "Sarah?"

No one responded, but out of the dark, he heard the rush of footsteps and saw a flying shape that almost crashed into him. Suddenly, Sarah was in his arms and kissing him like they were newlyweds as tears raced across her face. As he held her in his arms, he heard more rustling from in front of him.

"Pat? Can you get some light on in here?" he asked.

"No, Matt. That's not a good idea. You've got to get out of here now. They'll get you and kill you."

Before he could answer, he heard Sarah whisper in his ear, "Matt, you left and didn't even say goodbye."

"Pat, light a lamp. There's nothing to worry about. I have two United States Deputy Marshals with me. I'm a temporary U.S. Deputy Marshal. We're going to clean this mess up once and for all and do it legally."

Matt could feel Sarah's head jerk up from his chest. "Matt, is it real? You aren't going to be arrested?"

"No, ma'am," he said quietly, "we're going to be doing the arresting. U.S. Marshal Flowers in Fort Worth listened to my story and said I was justified in my actions and that Sheriff Avery will be removed and probably arrested. Hopefully, in a short time this will all be a bad memory."

The last word was barely out of his mouth when lamps began spreading light across the devastation that used to be a neat and tidy room. As he looked around at the destruction caused by the posse, he finally noticed that the rest of the Reeds were staring at him with Sarah still firmly attached to his chest.

"Should I let you down now, Sarah?" he asked softly, "Although I'm very fond of the current situation."

"I suppose you'll have to," she said as she smiled up at him.

Regretfully, he lowered her to the floor.

"Pat and Jenny, I'd like you to introduce you to United States Deputy Marshals Jim Hannity and Sam Croft. Gentlemen, this is Pat Reed, his lovely wife Jenny, his oldest daughter, Sarah, who I'm very attached to. Then we have Katie, Mary, and the youngest, their firecracker Peggy."

The three younger women all smiled at deputies, who appreciated the wisdom of the late ride, but Sarah only had eyes for Matt.

"Now, Pat," Matt began, "fill us in on what happened here. I already know about Bannister and Avery's crowd and the reward poster, so we just need to know what happened here."

"Okay, Matt," Pat replied, "After Avery got his posse together, they began running roughshod over small ranchers, supposedly looking for you. But we really think that it's just retribution for finding out about their little plot. Late this morning, the nine of them rode in. They walked right in the house without knocking or even announcing what they were doing. They just went from room to room destroying or taking everything. They were laughing and telling us what they were going to do to us when they got back, especially to the girls."

"What happened to the guns?"

"They took them. We never even had a chance to get anywhere near them. Sorry, Matt."

"Don't worry, we'll get them back and they'll pay for the damage they did. It was probably better that you didn't have them, not with nine of them. Now, I'll defer to Deputy Marshals Croft and Hannity about what we'll do about them tomorrow. Personally, I think the smartest thing to do is for me to stay out of sight, probably in the barn, until they show up. If they're greeted by two U.S. deputy marshals, it should defang them. They can strip Avery of his badge on the spot. If I'm in the loft, I can keep a rifle on them just for backup in case they try anything. But I'll do whatever they think is best."

Hannity spoke up, asking Pat, "I've got to ask, Mr. Reed, is Matt always this big of a smart aleck?"

Pat chuckled, then replied, "Usually. But we like to keep him around anyway."

"Well," Hannity went on, "his plan is pretty much what I would have recommended. Any idea when they'll stop by?"

Pat replied, "I'd guess earlier than nine o'clock. They're all over at the Box B right now and it's not a very long ride."

Matt asked, "Did they leave you enough food to get by until tomorrow, Pat?"

"Yes, they didn't bother with the food. So, we'll be okay."

"Fine. We'll be outside setting up."

Matt smiled at Sarah, who returned it with a bigger one of her own, before the three men turned and headed to the porch.

Matt asked, "What's the plan for tonight?"

"Are you sure you want us to do something?" responded Croft with a smile.

"Well, I'll sure as hell need you in the morning," Matt replied.

Croft said, "Why don't we all sleep in the barn? It's close enough to the house so we'll be able to hear any arrivals, especially a group of horses. If we wake up earlier, we can position ourselves on the porch with our badges shining in the sunshine. With you in the loft watching our backs, Matt, we should be able to defuse the situation without bloodshed. But if one of those idiots goes for his gun don't hesitate to let him know you're there."

"Count on it, Jim," said Matt. "I'll go tell the Reeds what we're going to do."

"Fine," grinned Sam Croft, as he said, "and you can say good night to your girlfriend while you're at it. Oh, by the way, I loved your 'attached' line. I'm still laughing inside."

Matt just grinned and walked back to the house, knocked on the door jamb, and Jenny said, "Come in, Matt, you don't have to knock. You're family."

Matt replied, "I just thought I'd tell you what's going to happen in the morning. We're going to sleep in the barn, so we can hear them coming if they make an earlier than expected arrival. If they do, the deputy marshals will call to them from the barn door. Either way, I'll be up in the loft with my Winchester in case they don't behave. I want you all to stay in a back room without an outside entrance. Pat, I want you to take my pistol to protect your family if something inconceivable happens. I won't need it in this situation."

With that, Matt handed his revolver to Pat.

"Matt," asked Sarah, "can you take a minute to tell us what happened when you left? We were crushed that you didn't stay."

Matt sighed and lowered his head in embarrassment as he told her why he had felt the urge to leave and what had happened.

When he had finished, he looked up and said, "It was stupid and thoughtless. But we'll try to make everything right tomorrow."

Sarah didn't know what to think, but he had been right, after he had given the deed to her father, no one had thought to include him in the celebration. She was ashamed to admit that none of them, including her, had even noticed he was gone for almost twenty minutes.

Matt straightened up and walked out to the barn. Telling the story to the Reeds didn't make him feel any better, but they deserved to know.

As he entered the barn, Croft asked if he had told his girlfriend good night and Matt just said, "They asked why I had left so suddenly and what happened after I had gone. It wasn't very much fun, to be honest."

Jim and Sam knew when to drop the joshing.

"Let's get stretched out. Should be an exciting day tomorrow," said Sam.

Matt nodded before each man unraveled his bedroll and kicked off their boots with the understanding that it was probably going to be an interesting day in a few hours.

———

The sun wasn't up yet when Matt awakened, slid out of his bedroll and turned his boots upside down and shook them to empty out any critters that had crawled in during the night. Then he pulled on his boots and went outside, Winchester in hand as the predawn sky was getting brighter. Matt put the time at just before five o'clock. After a quick visit behind the barn rather than the more distant privy, he returned, leaned against the barn door and waited for the deputy marshals, thinking about the future, not only the next few hours, but the days and weeks after, even the years, and they all revolved around that green-eyed woman in the house.

As the first part of the sun's disk broke the horizon, Matt heard stirring behind him and turned to see Jim shedding his bedroll then kicking Sam as he did so. Soon both lawmen were up and pulling on their boots.

Like Matt, they opted for the short trip around the side of the barn before returning to the barn doors.

"Sure, could use a cup of coffee," Sam mumbled before he yawned.

Right on cue, the screen door slammed, and four pretty Reed girls stepped off the porch bearing gifts of coffee and food.

"Wow!" exclaimed Jim, "Now this is what I call room service!"

Peggy brought the coffee pot, Mary had the mugs, plates and silverware, Katie had a serving plate with bacon and biscuits and Sarah had a pan filled with scrambled eggs.

"Good morning, ladies," said Matt, "You are a sight to behold."

They smiled as they distributed the plates of food and mugs of black, steaming coffee, and the men took little time in devouring the food. Partly because they were hungry, but mostly because they knew they could be called to action at any moment.

Sarah stood next to Matt as he ate, and whispered into his ear, "Never do that again, Matt. Never leave me for any reason."

Matt stopped with his fork covered in scrambled eggs two inches from his mouth, then put it back on the plate and stared into those amazing green eyes and simply said, "I promise, Sarah. Never again."

She smiled and said, "Now finish that food. We're under Mama Reed's orders to deliver it and get back quickly."

Matt returned the smile and told her, "Your mother is right, Sarah. We've got to get ready."

He took his last bite of eggs and grabbed a strip of bacon as he rose.

The deputy marshals were finishing their breakfasts as well and handed the plates and other hardware back to the women, thanking them profusely. They were rewarded with big smiles, but Matt didn't notice as he was just swimming in Sarah's remarkable green eyes.

When Mary said, "We've got to go," Matt broke contact, reached out and softly ran his fingertips across Sarah's cheek. She smiled at him and turned to join her sisters.

After the women were gone and safely in the house, the lawmen decided it was time to set up for the expected arrival of the posse. The two deputy marshals trotted to the front porch as Matt climbed the ladder to the loft. After he reached the front of the loft, he swung the doors open wide, checked the load on his Winchester and set the extra box of cartridges on the floor, just in case things went badly wrong, but even he couldn't imagine having to expend more than a few rounds if at all.

Jim and Sam were in the rockers on the porch, and it was over an hour before they picked up the dust cloud on the road and heard the approach of a large group of horses. Matt positioned himself with a good line of fire in front of the marshals, who had left the rocking chairs and were standing at the leading edge of the porch, their badges prominently displayed.

The posse entered the access road and thundered toward the ranch house at a fast trot followed by large clouds of dust. When they saw the two lawmen, the posse slowed to a walk and then stopped a hundred feet in front of the house before Sheriff Avery walked his horse forward.

"Who are you and what are you doing here?" he shouted defiantly.

"Sheriff Avery, step down and come forward. We are Deputy United States Marshals Croft and Hannity out of Fort Worth," shouted Sam Croft.

"This here is my jurisdiction, so you boys get your asses back to Fort Worth where you belong. I have legal business here."

"Avery, you're even dumber than Marshal Flowers said you were, and I thought that was impossible. You are being suspended from duty effective immediately pending investigation for malfeasance and accessory to murder. Step forward and hand me your badge," yelled Sam so everyone else could hear.

"Boys," the sheriff shouted as he turned in his saddle to the Bannister posse, "these guys don't have no authority to do no such thing. If they won't leave, we'll make 'em leave."

"Gentlemen," Jim Hannity spoke loudly to the horsemen behind Avery, "I doubt if you are aware of the heap of trouble you are being asked to step into. We are United States Deputy Marshals. We have jurisdiction anywhere in this country. We have the authority to remove local law enforcement for incompetence or malfeasance. Now your sheriff, here, is guilty of both. If you want to make an issue of it, well we can do that too. How many of you are good with those hoglegs? Now Sam and I both qualified as expert marksmen and together we have shot and killed twelve men."

He paused as Sam held up three fingers, then continued, saying, "I stand corrected, thirteen men. As an added incentive, we have another Deputy Marshal up in the loft with a Winchester aimed this way. Right now, I imagine his sight is right on your chest, Avery. Is that right, Marshal?', he yelled.

Matt didn't want to give away his identity by shouting, so he quickly cycled his Winchester. The loud metallic sound was unmistakable and drew the attention of the sitting posse.

Hannity continued as he said, "Now boys, there is another problem we need to resolve. After we remove Mr. Avery from office, we're going to ride over to the Box B and have a little chat with Mr. Bannister. There was a hanging on that ranch about three weeks ago of an innocent man. Now, in our books that qualifies as first-degree murder. I know you understand what the end results would be if you're found guilty of that crime."

There was also some rustling of stock from neighboring ranches to investigate. That's also a hanging offense. If I were you boys and had anything to do with either of those crimes, or even knew that they had happened and didn't tell the law, you wouldn't be too popular with our Federal judge. But I'll tell you what I'm gonna do. You fellas look like a bunch of hands that just got caught up in a bad situation. So, here's the deal. We're gonna take care of Mr. Avery, here. While we're doing that, it'll give you gents about five minutes to high-tail it outta here.

Now I don't want to be surprised by a shotgun wielding Will Bannister when we arrive at his doorstep, so we're going to watch which direction you take at the end of that access road. If you head left, that'll take you to Denton, Fort Worth, and eventually Mexico. If you turn right, that'll take you to the Box B, and that would be interfering with a Federal investigation. Well, make your decisions, boys. Time's a wastin'."

It wasn't a tough decision for the Box B riders. Most felt uncomfortable doing those things that they felt they hadn't been hired for, and those that didn't really mind doing them could see the obvious. Once the first one wheeled his horse toward the road, the others followed before any dust was raised and when they reached the end of the access road, they all turned left, leaving the sheriff on his own.

After they'd ridden about a mile down the road, one rider, Miles Hanson, who had been the one to put the rope around Spike McMillan's neck, held back. As the others rode on, he turned to his left and crossed back onto Lazy R property, then trotted his horse east until he had gone almost a mile and then headed north toward the Box B.

Back at the Lazy R, soon-to-be ex-Sheriff Avery faced the two marshals, who were still on the porch.

"Drop your gun belt, Avery," ordered Croft, "And then step forward three steps."

"You ain't got no right!" shouted Avery.

Matt kept his rifle aimed at the sheriff as a few drops of sweat trickled down his back in the increasing Texas heat. Then he saw the almost imperceptible motion of Avery's right hand toward his Colt.

"Well," thought Matt, "you may not be a coward, but you sure are stupid."

He didn't hesitate, but slightly lowered the site of the Winchester and fired.

The load crack of the repeater arriving at almost the same instant that a large plume of dirt exploded just to the right of his left boot changed Avery's mind.

He swiftly jerked both hands straight up into the air.

"I wasn't gonna do nothin'!" he protested.

"I'm sure," drawled Jim, "You're just lucky our friend saw you reaching for that hogleg before we could both draw and empty a bunch of lead into that belly of yours. He saved your hide, Avery. Now with only your left hand, undo that gun belt."

Avery complied, alternating glances at the two marshals in front of him and the one in the loft, the smoke from the shot still drifted into the air.

After he dropped his rig to the dirt, Jim and Sam stepped down from the porch. As they did, Matt snatched up his spare box of cartridges, walked to the back of the loft, climbed down the ladder, then stepped out of the barn and quickly walked toward them taking long strides.

Avery took one look at Matt and threw out his right hand, pointing at him and yelled, "There he is! He's the murderer we're chasin'. You gotta arrest him. But I get the reward. I saw him first."

Sam Croft glanced at Matt and shouted, "Deputy Marshal Little, do you know what this idiot is talking about?"

If Sheriff Avery's world had been turned upside down by the appearance of the two U.S. deputy marshals, it was shattered with that title used to address the murderer.

Matt strode close to the porch and replied, "Nope. The only murderers that I've run across recently were those three miscreants who confessed to the murder and then tried to do the same to me."

As Avery kept shifting his wide-eyed face back and forth, Jim Hannity pulled his hands behind his back and slapped on a pair of handcuffs. Matt walked up the steps and into the house.

"Pat? Jenny? It's all right. You can come back out now."

The lone male of the Reed household was the first to step into the main room.

"I heard the marshals talking and then heard a rifle shot. Was that you? Did you shoot Avery?"

"No. I just warned him not to pull his Colt like he was getting ready to do. It was the dumbest thing I've ever seen anyone do. He was facing two U.S. Deputy Marshals alone and had a rifle pointed at him and he went for his gun."

"No one ever accused him of being overly bright," Pat said.

He handed the Remington back to Matt, who dropped it into its holster.

"So, is it finally over?" asked Jenny as she walked into the room.

"We're headed over to the Box B now. I think the marshals will arrest him using a John Doe warrant. They didn't have time to get a specific warrant issued. Once that is done, all that will be left is for the lawyers. And Pat, I would change my recommendation that, if Bannister is convicted and sent to prison or hanged, you keep the Box B and sell the Star M's land back to them. It'll give you a nice cash reserve."

"Always thinking, aren't you, Matt?" Pat asked as he smiled.

Matt smiled back and said, "Better than not. We need to get going before Bannister gets wind of what's going on."

Sarah walked up to him, put her hand on his arm and said, "Stay safe, Matt."

"I will," as he gave one more glance into Sarah's concerned green eyes, then turned and stepped out onto the porch.

The marshals had escorted Avery to the barn and lashed him in a sitting position to a support pole. They told him to be still and they'd be back shortly. He whined about the lack of food and water, but they ignored him as they left.

They met Matt coming down the stairs, and Matt asked, "How do you want to approach this? If they see me coming, and that could be a good half mile away, it would give them warning. If you two ride up there with your badges showing, he'll more than likely think you're there to help him. I could go cross-country and keep an eye on the back of the house and assist if it becomes necessary."

Hannity commented drily, "You've got to stop doing this. You're supposed to be listening, not telling. But as usual, you're right. We'll take the road. How long will that take us?"

"About fifteen minutes. I'll come with you to the road and as soon as we reach Box B land, which won't be long, I'll cut in and come up around back. I'll have to move a little faster than you, so don't go too fast."

"Sounds good. Let's go visit the Bannisters."

The three men mounted their horses and turned toward the main roadway and when they reached the road, headed north. After they had passed the fence marking the ranch boundary, Matt angled Caesar east onto the Box B.

At the Box B, Miles Hanson was ruining the marshals' plans. Will Bannister, Rachel and Billie listened as Hanson told of the disbanding of the posse and the flight of the Box B hands. He spoke of the pending arrival of the U.S. Marshals to arrest him for the hanging and the rustling of the other ranches' cattle and as soon as he finished, Billie was the first to speak.

"We can take them, Pop! We know they're comin'."

Will Bannister said nothing, but walked into his library and went to the far wall. There was a rack of rifles from an old Hawken to the latest Winchester. He took down his favored Henry. He wasn't aware that it was the same weapon that Billie had used a few weeks earlier to try to scare off Matt.

While he had gone, Rachel stood motionless in a state of shock. Her father was about to be arrested for murder! Suddenly, all those things that she had been hearing and suspecting for the past few months came alive.

She wandered into the kitchen, poured a cup of coffee and sat down at the table.

Will Bannister carried his Henry into the living room and Billie was still fired up and wanted action, while Miles was itching to leave now that he felt he had fulfilled his obligation. He only stayed because he expected a reward.

Will decided that he would call their bluff. With all his hands dispersed, there were no witnesses against him and he knew that he could handle himself in any court and hire the best lawyers.

"Billie go outside and cool off. Stay off the front porch. In fact, why don't you take a ride or something, but don't take the access road. Those marshals will be riding here soon."

Then Will glanced over at Miles Hanson, knew what he was waiting for, then reached into his pocket and pulled out three double eagle gold pieces and handed them to him.

"I appreciate you're coming back to warn me, Miles. This is all I have. Now get out of here and ride cross-country. Head north for a while to avoid those lawmen."

Hanson didn't need to be prodded. He snatched the offered money and ran out back to his waiting horse, mounted and headed north, not happy with the measly sixty dollars he had been given. He had expected more – much more.

Billie had already left the house and gone to the barn to collect his horse, madder than he had ever been in his life, and that was plenty mad. He wanted vengeance. If he couldn't kill those lawmen, he'd do something. After he had saddled his horse, he rode out into the pastures heading south.

Those lawmen he wanted to kill were just turning onto the access road to the Box B. As they trotted toward the house, Matt was crossing across the Box B's broad pasture land while Billie was going in the opposite direction almost a mile west. They never saw each other. After a few minutes of riding on Box B land, Matt headed toward the ranch house.

Their timing was excellent, especially considering Matt's roundabout path. Matt reached the back door of the ranch house and dismounted just as the deputy marshals arrived at the front porch.

On the front side of the expansive dwelling, Will Bannister sat on the porch, rocking back and forth in his oak rocker, the Henry across his lap. As Hannity and Croft approached, they knew that Bannister was aware of their arrival. Someone had doubled back.

"Mr. Bannister," shouted Sam, "I'm United States Deputy Marshal Sam Croft and this is United States Deputy Marshal Jim Hannity. We're investigating some crimes in the area and would like to talk to you."

"I know why you're here. I haven't done anything wrong, and I suggest you return to your office and let it go," shouted Will Bannister.

Both marshals had already slipped their hammer loops off their pistols and were ready for the expected confrontation.

"We're just doing our jobs, Mr. Bannister. If you're innocent, as you claim to be, then you'll be back here soon and can go about your business."

Bannister rethought his decision to bluff his way out. They wouldn't be here unless that damned Matt Little had gone to Fort Worth. If they were here, then they had at least given his story some credence, and that meant he needed to make a new decision and make it soon.

While the front porch drama was being played out, Matt quietly stepped onto the back porch and headed for the back door. He had his pistol in his hand, not knowing what to expect as he slowly opened the door and stepped into the kitchen. What he hadn't expected to see was Rachel sitting there with a cup of coffee at her lips.

If he hadn't expected to see her, she was shocked to see him enter the house, and adding to the effect was seeing the shiny United States Deputy Marshal badge on his massive chest.

Simultaneously, they said, "Rachel!" "Matt!"

Matt lowered his Remington but Rachel spoke first.

"Matt, I'm sorry. I really am. I didn't know. I knew deep down that things weren't right, but I didn't think it was that bad. And that man they hanged. He was your friend? And he was innocent?"

"Yes, to both. Spike was a good friend, one of the best. And he was a good man, he never did anything wrong since I knew him."

Rachel started shaking, as she said, "I feel so dirty. Matt, I've lived such a shameful life. What I did to you at the church social was despicable. I am so sorry for what I did. Slapping you like that and saying what I did in front of all those people just because my father told me it was necessary to get you out of the area. I am really sorry."

"I'm glad to hear it, Rachel. Understanding that is the first step to becoming a good human being. You have it in there, Rachel."

Before either could say another word, there was the unmistakable roar of multiple pistol shots and a rifle shot from the front porch.

Rachel and Matt bolted in that direction.

A few seconds earlier, Will Bannister had come to a decision. It was truly his final decision. He would make his stand here on his land, and he would make it now.

He had simply stood and swung the barrel of the Henry toward the marshals, who both drew as he raised it to fire. Their bullets struck him as his Henry jerked skyward, going off in the process. Jim and Sam were already dismounting as Bannister hit the wood of the porch. The front door opened and Matt, followed closely by Rachel stepped out and stared down at the bloody, prostrate body of Will Bannister.

Matt expected Rachel to react with either anger or sadness, but did neither, which surprised him. Matt squatted down next to her father and checked his pulse on his neck, knowing it was a useless exercise.

Matt stood and said to the marshals, "This is Rachel Bannister. She wasn't aware of any of her father's activities."

Finally, Rachel muttered, "It was all about land. He wanted to make the ranch bigger. I have no idea why."

Matt replied, "That's the worst part of it, Rachel. It wasn't even his ranch. This property belongs to Pat Reed."

Rachel should have been shocked, but instead she continued looking at her dead father and simply asked, "How is that possible?"

"Last week I found the original deed and sales receipt. There had been a mistake made over twenty years ago that shrunk the size of the Lazy R by over ninety percent. Your father must have found out about it somehow at the beginning of the year and tried to gain control of the Lazy R before Pat discovered the error."

Her head suddenly jerked up and she said one word, "Billie!"

The marshals looked up with quizzical looks but Matt knew exactly the ramifications of that single expletive.

He shot a look toward Rachel and said, "Where did he go, Rachel?"

"I don't know. He was so mad, and father told him to get out of the house and just ride away. I've never seen him so angry."

Matt looked at Jim and Sam. "We've got to get back to the Lazy R. Billie is her younger brother. He's a loose cannon and capable of anything when he's upset, and he's probably well past upset now. I think he'd head that way to pay the Reeds back for what he sees as their fault. You guys take the road, I'm going to cut across the property, I think I can go faster on Caesar, but you wouldn't be able to keep up. Let's go!"

Without any argument, the marshals ran to their horses as Matt cut through the house at a sprint, blasting through the kitchen door and barely touching the back step. Within seconds, he was on Caesar and had him charging across the Box B heading toward the Lazy R. It was a good three-mile ride, including that forested strip between the two ranches.

After seven minutes of hard riding, including the dodging through the trees, he saw the fence coming. He knew Caesar had cleared that height before, but this was even more critical to make the jump and slowed the stallion down to a mere fast run. Caesar saw the fence coming and already had begun to match his pace to where he knew he'd have to bunch his haunches into a jump.

Matt held on as Caesar left the ground, felt the back hoof snap the barbed wire, making a loud twanging noise, but the Morgan stallion never even broke stride. As he landed on Lazy R land, Matt urged him on to his top speed and knew that he was asking a lot of the big horse, but Caesar seemed to sense the urgency. Matt angled to his right to bring him in line with the ranch house and hoped he was wrong and that Billie had simply left the area. But he understood Billie well enough to know that he'd want payback.

When the ranch house came into view, he slowed Caesar to a normal run, spotted another horse standing untethered near the porch and was sure that it was Billie's.

His Morgan stallion was lathered and breathing heavily, but Matt knew he had to go all out for the distance. Matt really owed him for this one as he approached the barn. Everything was quiet as he slowed Caesar down, dismounted and left Caesar to wander to the trough. Before he started walking though, he took a few seconds to say, "Thank you, Julius. You're the best."

He pulled his Remington and began walking to the house, and as he drew near, the quiet was suddenly broken by the loud report of a pistol shot indoors, so Matt charged to the front porch, but slowed when he got to the porch and slowly walked up the stairs and approached the front door.

He stepped inside as quietly as he could then heard voices, frightened voices, coming from one of the bedrooms.

Then he heard Billie shouting, "I don't care what you say. It ain't so, Reed. You ain't got no paper. You're lyin'!"

Pat had obviously told him about the deed and Matt knew if he walked down that hallway Billie would do something he didn't want to contemplate.

He decided he'd see if he could talk Billie out.

"He's not lying, Billie," Matt said in a loud voice.

There was silence for a few seconds before Billie shouted back, "That you, Little?"

"Yes. I found that deed and title a week ago in Austin. He's telling you the truth, so there's no reason to hurt anyone. Just come on out and we'll talk."

"I heard them marshals was going to arrest my father, and now this bastard is going to take the Box B away."

"No one's taking anything away, Billie. The marshals are just investigating the rustling. Whoever told you that they were arresting him is lying. I was just there. He was sitting on the porch talking while Rachel was making coffee. It's not what you think, Billie."

After another pause, Billie was using his limited brain power to see if it made sense. Maybe Little was right as he recalled Rachel making coffee and his father going to the front porch.

Then he said, "How'd you get here so fast, if you was over there with them marshals?"

"Rachel said you had left and were really mad, so I thought you'd come here. I rode cross country as fast as I could to keep you from doing anything that you'd regret later. Caesar is a fast horse and even had to jump that barbed wire fence, but he made it. I'm glad he did, too. This needs to stop, Billie. Your father said he needs you."

Now Billie was confused. *What if he was right?* He pointed at Sarah.

"Sarah! You're his girlfriend. Come here!"

Sarah stood up and slowly walked toward Billie. When she got within a few feet, he reached out and took a fistful of her dark red hair in his left hand. She grimaced but didn't make a sound as he pulled her in front of him.

"All right, Little. I got your pretty little girlfriend here. Now, you come down here where I can see you. I want to look at your face when you tell me that my father is okay. I'll be able to tell if you're lying."

Matt was surprised. For Billie, it wasn't a bad plan. He slid his Remington into his holster and lowered his gun belt to the floor. With so many innocents there, he wouldn't be able to use his gun in that room anyway.

"I'm coming in Billie. I'm unarmed, so don't do anything rash."

Matt slowly stepped down the narrow hallway until he saw the open door, then turned into the doorway, stopped and presented himself at the door, just about blocking all the light.

Even in the reduced light, he could see the Reed women huddled in a corner of the room. Pat was off to the side, bleeding from his left

"Matt," said Sam Croft slowly, "did you not know that you've been shot in the chest?"

Matt looked down at his blood covered shirt. The one with the hole in it just below his collar bone. It was bubbling blood.

All he could manage was, "Oh," which was followed by a totally inexplicable, "I'm sorry."

He walked out of the bedroom, down the hall and out to the front porch. By then Mary and Katie rode up in the wagon. The bed of the buckboard covered in blankets.

Neither Sam nor Jim could believe what they were witnessing. Matt Little had taken a close-range bullet from a .44 in the chest and acted like it was a splinter, but they knew he had to get to a doctor quickly. He had already lost a lot of blood and couldn't afford to lose much more.

Pat walked out assisted by Jenny, then they stepped down from the porch and Jenny and Mary helped him into the wagon.

Sarah stepped close to Matt, her face blanched in terror.

"Matt. Matt," she said, her voice rising, "we need to get you to a doctor, but first we need to slow down the bleeding."

Matt just looked at her with glossy eyes and said, "I understand, Sarah. I'll be okay."

He staggered to the wagon and crawled into the bed next to Pat, knowing that it would be difficult to lift him. After he laid down on his back, he felt hurried hands ripping open his shirt, then wipe down his chest with something wet and put something hard on the entrance wound, felt a hand on his chest and then passed out.

After another pause, Billie was using his limited brain power to see if it made sense. Maybe Little was right as he recalled Rachel making coffee and his father going to the front porch.

Then he said, "How'd you get here so fast, if you was over there with them marshals?"

"Rachel said you had left and were really mad, so I thought you'd come here. I rode cross country as fast as I could to keep you from doing anything that you'd regret later. Caesar is a fast horse and even had to jump that barbed wire fence, but he made it. I'm glad he did, too. This needs to stop, Billie. Your father said he needs you."

Now Billie was confused. *What if he was right?* He pointed at Sarah.

"Sarah! You're his girlfriend. Come here!"

Sarah stood up and slowly walked toward Billie. When she got within a few feet, he reached out and took a fistful of her dark red hair in his left hand. She grimaced but didn't make a sound as he pulled her in front of him.

"All right, Little. I got your pretty little girlfriend here. Now, you come down here where I can see you. I want to look at your face when you tell me that my father is okay. I'll be able to tell if you're lying."

Matt was surprised. For Billie, it wasn't a bad plan. He slid his Remington into his holster and lowered his gun belt to the floor. With so many innocents there, he wouldn't be able to use his gun in that room anyway.

"I'm coming in Billie. I'm unarmed, so don't do anything rash."

Matt slowly stepped down the narrow hallway until he saw the open door, then turned into the doorway, stopped and presented himself at the door, just about blocking all the light.

Even in the reduced light, he could see the Reed women huddled in a corner of the room. Pat was off to the side, bleeding from his left

157

"Matt," said Sam Croft slowly, "did you not know that you've been shot in the chest?"

Matt looked down at his blood covered shirt. The one with the hole in it just below his collar bone. It was bubbling blood.

All he could manage was, "Oh," which was followed by a totally inexplicable, "I'm sorry."

He walked out of the bedroom, down the hall and out to the front porch. By then Mary and Katie rode up in the wagon. The bed of the buckboard covered in blankets.

Neither Sam nor Jim could believe what they were witnessing. Matt Little had taken a close-range bullet from a .44 in the chest and acted like it was a splinter, but they knew he had to get to a doctor quickly. He had already lost a lot of blood and couldn't afford to lose much more.

Pat walked out assisted by Jenny, then they stepped down from the porch and Jenny and Mary helped him into the wagon.

Sarah stepped close to Matt, her face blanched in terror.

"Matt. Matt," she said, her voice rising, "we need to get you to a doctor, but first we need to slow down the bleeding."

Matt just looked at her with glossy eyes and said, "I understand, Sarah. I'll be okay."

He staggered to the wagon and crawled into the bed next to Pat, knowing that it would be difficult to lift him. After he laid down on his back, he felt hurried hands ripping open his shirt, then wipe down his chest with something wet and put something hard on the entrance wound, felt a hand on his chest and then passed out.

After another pause, Billie was using his limited brain power to see if it made sense. Maybe Little was right as he recalled Rachel making coffee and his father going to the front porch.

Then he said, "How'd you get here so fast, if you was over there with them marshals?"

"Rachel said you had left and were really mad, so I thought you'd come here. I rode cross country as fast as I could to keep you from doing anything that you'd regret later. Caesar is a fast horse and even had to jump that barbed wire fence, but he made it. I'm glad he did, too. This needs to stop, Billie. Your father said he needs you."

Now Billie was confused. *What if he was right?* He pointed at Sarah.

"Sarah! You're his girlfriend. Come here!"

Sarah stood up and slowly walked toward Billie. When she got within a few feet, he reached out and took a fistful of her dark red hair in his left hand. She grimaced but didn't make a sound as he pulled her in front of him.

"All right, Little. I got your pretty little girlfriend here. Now, you come down here where I can see you. I want to look at your face when you tell me that my father is okay. I'll be able to tell if you're lying."

Matt was surprised. For Billie, it wasn't a bad plan. He slid his Remington into his holster and lowered his gun belt to the floor. With so many innocents there, he wouldn't be able to use his gun in that room anyway.

"I'm coming in Billie. I'm unarmed, so don't do anything rash."

Matt slowly stepped down the narrow hallway until he saw the open door, then turned into the doorway, stopped and presented himself at the door, just about blocking all the light.

Even in the reduced light, he could see the Reed women huddled in a corner of the room. Pat was off to the side, bleeding from his left arm. Billie was standing six feet away, his left hand wrapped in Sarah's hair. She showed no fear. *Lord, he was proud of that woman!*

Billie held his revolver a few inches from her right ear, the muzzle pointing in his direction.

"Now, big man, tell me that my father is okay."

Matt put on his most sincere face and said, "When I left your house, Rachel was making coffee and your father was talking to the deputy marshals. Rachel is the one that told me to come here. Your father told me that he needed your help."

Billie was about to believe Matt when the light flashed off the United States Deputy Marshal badge still pinned to his chest.

"What the hell are you wearin' a badge for? You're one of those lawmen? You're lying, Little!"

Matt screamed, "Get down, Sarah!"

The words had barely escaped his lips when he launched himself at Billie as he fired. Matt felt the bullet hit him high on the left side of his chest, but it didn't matter. He had fire in his eyes. When Billie fired, he had released Sarah, who didn't need Matt's suggestion, as she quickly dropped to the floor and rolled to her left.

Matt crashed into Billie before he could pull the hammer back for a second shot. Matt scrambled to his feet, pulled back his right fist and crushed Billie's face with a massive blow. Billie staggered and fell to the floor, unconscious from the force of the heavy hit.

Matt stood up and glanced over at Sarah, asking, "Are you all right, Sarah?"

He saw her nod then turned his attention to Pat.

Matt stepped over to him and pulled the shirt sleeve back from Pat's wound. It was still bleeding, but it hadn't broken a bone and had only sliced off a small piece of bicep. It looked ugly, but it wasn't bad.

Matt turned his head to Jenny, who, along with the other women had come to their feet.

"Jenny, we need to get Pat's wound cleaned and wrapped with a bandage. It's not bad, but he needs to get to a doctor. Mary, can you go hitch up the wagon? Katie, get some blankets to load in back to make the ride into Denton easier for him. Okay?"

Both women nodded and left the room as Matt helped Pat to his feet.

Matt heard rushing hooves outside the door and knew the deputy marshals had arrived.

As the two marshals entered the house, Matt shouted, "Back here, guys. We have a wounded man here and an unconscious Bannister. He shot Pat Reed and threatened the women."

The two lawmen walked to the room and saw Matt leaning over Pat.

Matt said, without turning, "His daughters have gone to get the wagon ready to take Pat to Denton to see the doctor."

Sarah stepped over to Matt and asked, "Matt, how could he miss you at such a close range?"

"Beats me. I just jumped at him before he could get off a second shot."

Matt stood up to face Sam and Jim and felt a bit woozy. *Now what was that all about?*

Matt asked, "Did you want to cuff Billie before he wakes up? I mean, he's still wearing his second pistol."

He looked at them, but they didn't seem to be paying attention. They were just looking at his chest.

"Matt," said Sam Croft slowly, "did you not know that you've been shot in the chest?"

Matt looked down at his blood covered shirt. The one with the hole in it just below his collar bone. It was bubbling blood.

All he could manage was, "Oh," which was followed by a totally inexplicable, "I'm sorry."

He walked out of the bedroom, down the hall and out to the front porch. By then Mary and Katie rode up in the wagon. The bed of the buckboard covered in blankets.

Neither Sam nor Jim could believe what they were witnessing. Matt Little had taken a close-range bullet from a .44 in the chest and acted like it was a splinter, but they knew he had to get to a doctor quickly. He had already lost a lot of blood and couldn't afford to lose much more.

Pat walked out assisted by Jenny, then they stepped down from the porch and Jenny and Mary helped him into the wagon.

Sarah stepped close to Matt, her face blanched in terror.

"Matt. Matt," she said, her voice rising, "we need to get you to a doctor, but first we need to slow down the bleeding."

Matt just looked at her with glossy eyes and said, "I understand, Sarah. I'll be okay."

He staggered to the wagon and crawled into the bed next to Pat, knowing that it would be difficult to lift him. After he laid down on his back, he felt hurried hands ripping open his shirt, then wipe down his chest with something wet and put something hard on the entrance wound, felt a hand on his chest and then passed out.

CHAPTER 7

Matt was cold. He thought how stupid that was when it was summer in Texas. Maybe it was already winter. That made sense. *Didn't it?*

He slowly opened his eyes, discovering he was lying in a bed. Everything seemed white, and extremely bright, too. Maybe he had died, and this was the entrance to the pearly gates, but for someone about to spend eternity in bliss, he felt sorely depressed.

The more he laid there in the bright light, the more his mood slipped into gloom. So, he thought, it was time to get moving. He started to sit up, but his chest hit him with a sharp burst of pain and he dropped back onto his back. So much for the heaven theory.

"Hello? Anyone here?" he shouted.

At least he thought he had shouted, but it had come out as a reasonably loud croak. But at least he heard footsteps, then a door open as the footsteps came closer. *Was it Sarah?* He hoped so, but it wasn't. It was some woman he had never seen before. She was in her low thirties and dressed in a gray outfit that seemed almost like a uniform.

"So," she said, "you're finally awake."

"Finally? I've only been here a few minutes," he croaked.

"No," she responded, "you arrived here more than five days ago. You had lost a lot of blood by the time you arrived and lost more when you were in surgery having that bullet removed. Your left lung had collapsed, but the doctor says it has inflated well. You'll be sore for some time, but you should be totally back to normal in a couple of months. Somehow, the bullet passed between your ribs. To be honest, when we heard the story of how you were shot and what you did afterward, we were all quite amazed that you survived. You're a very robust man, Mr. Little. That saved you, I believe."

"What time is it?"

"Almost four o'clock in the afternoon."

"Well, thank you and please thank the doctor for me. Would it be possible to get something to eat and drink?"

"You'll have to go light on the food for a day or two, but I'll see what I can bring you. By the way you've had visitors waiting to see you every day, but one young lady has barely left."

"Sarah," he whispered.

"Yes, we've talked quite a bit. She's down the hall right now. Would you like me to send her in?"

"Please. And you never did tell me your name."

"I am Nurse Elma Richards. Please call me Elma," she replied as she gave him a comforting smile.

"Call me Matt. My last name doesn't fit me anyway."

Elma laughed and left the room.

Two minutes later, the door opened again and, as before, women's steps crossed the room. Elma seemed nice, Matt thought, but he'd rather it was Sarah.

The sudden appearance of those wonderful green eyes before his face confirmed his wish.

He gazed into those eyes and said, "When I woke up, I thought I was dead, Sarah. I saw all the white and the bright light and I thought I had gone to heaven, but I felt alone and I was miserable."

Sarah tilted her head, and asked, "Why would you be sad about going to heaven?"

"Because you wouldn't be there with me. It wouldn't be heaven at all."

"Of all the wonderful things you've said to me, Matt, that is the most beautiful."

"Sarah, I really did feel that way. I was confused at first as to where I was. Then I remembered getting shot and it seemed like a minute ago. Once I came to the realization that I was dead, and probably in heaven, all I could think of was all the time I'd lose that should have been spent with you. And do you know what made it even worse?"

"No," she answered quietly.

"When I thought that more than just losing you, that you might find someone else and get married. That hurt much more than a bullet ever could."

"Well, Mr. Little, you're still with us in this world. I am here now, and I'm with you."

"Then I guess I am in heaven," he smiled.

She leaned over and kissed him gently on the lips and whispered, "I love you, Matt."

He took her hand and whispered, "And you know I've loved you from the first day I saw you. You knew that, didn't you Sarah?"

"Yes, I knew. I was afraid at first. I've never had such feelings. I had prepared my whole life for being self-sufficient. Suddenly, I didn't want that any more. That night at the church social awakened me to what we could have together. Then, when you rode off into the night after that shooter, I almost died inside and I knew I couldn't lose you. When you came back that night after the posse had raided our house, you can't imagine the relief that poured through me when I heard your voice. The same relief when I heard it in the house when Billie was there. I knew things would be all right."

Then, I watched him shoot you and was terrified. But then you stood up, and I thought you were okay. I couldn't see the blood. You acted like nothing was wrong, so I relaxed. Then when I saw the marshals staring at your chest, I knew something was wrong and I saw the blood and the hole. I felt my soul shudder. I was not going to lose you! When you laid down in the wagon and we got you cleaned up, somebody had to hold a piece of leather against your chest to keep it from bubbling, so I did that. I had to. Now, you're better and soon you'll be able to come back to us."

"Speaking of the rest of the Reeds, what has happened since I've been asleep."

"Well, the Box B has been vacated. Billie's trial was in Fort Worth yesterday. The marshals said that because you were unconscious, the only witnesses they needed were their own two deputy marshals. Rachel stopped by a couple of times. She's changed, Matt. She was very nice to me and said I was very lucky to have you and said if you weren't so attached to me, she'd be next in line. She said she owed it to you. I guess that speech you gave at the church social made her realize how bleak her future would be if she stayed the way she was."

Papa hired a lawyer in Denton. The Morrows at the Star M have talked to Papa and have come to an agreement on keeping their ranch intact. It's a combination of cattle and cash that Papa agreed to. They are happy to have settled the issue. We're in the process of moving into the big house on the Box B, and Papa's having the lawyers restructure the old Box B into the Lazy R."

Matt suddenly remembered Caesar and asked, "Sarah, I left Caesar loose behind your barn. Is he okay?"

"He's fine. I think he's even attached to two of our mares. We were in such a rush to get you and Papa to the doctor that we didn't even see him. When my parents returned with my sisters, they found him next to the corral chatting with the ladies. We took care of him, and he seemed determined to stay with the mares, so we just put him in the corral. He's very happy with himself."

Matt said hoarsely, "You wouldn't believe the ride we made getting to you. He was in a gallop all the way from the Box B ranch house and only slowed to jump the fence. I'm proud of him for getting me there in time. Wait till you see my Morgan herd. They are all beautiful horses."

"I'll look forward to that," she said.

The door opened, and Elma arrived with a plate of food and a glass of water. Sarah didn't leave, she just stepped aside and let the nurse place the food on a small tray next to the bed before Elma smiled at Sarah and left the room.

Before he tried to eat, Matt looked at Sarah and said, "Elma tells me that you've been here almost all the time, Sarah. You need to get some rest."

"You go ahead and eat. I'll wait and then we can talk about my rest."

Matt nodded and tried the food. First, though, he took a swallow of water. It was almost painful at first but felt better after the second swallow, but it soothed his throat.

The food, on the other hand, seemed almost tasteless. He hoped it wouldn't stay this way. After he had finished the small portions, he finished the water. Although it wasn't much, it satisfied his empty stomach.

"I wonder how much weight I've lost. I don't feel that weak. I wonder if they'll let me out of the doctor's place now that I'm awake," he said hopefully.

"You need to ask Nurse Elma or the doctor. Just being awake doesn't qualify for being well enough to leave."

Matt sighed and said, "I suppose, but I need to get back to my ranch. I've been gone over a month."

Nurse Elma entered the room carrying a yellow sheet of paper.

"This just arrived for you Matt," she said.

She handed him a telegram and started to leave, but Matt called to her.

"Elma, before you go, can you tell me when I'll be able to leave?"

"The doctor is going to come and examine you shortly. He'll let you know."

"Thank you, Elma," She waved and left the room.

He opened the telegram and read:

MATT LITTLE DOCTOR EMERSON MEDICAL DENTON TEXAS

BILLIE FOUND GUILTY OF ASSAULT ATTEMPTED MURDER

ASSAULT FOR SHOOTING PAT REED

SENTENCED TO THIRTY YEARS

STOP AND SEE ME ON WAY BACK TO RANCH

US MARSHAL FLOWERS FORT WORTH TEXAS

He handed the telegram to Sarah. She read it and handed it back to Matt.

"I can't say he didn't earn it. What does the marshal want to talk to you about? You can't be in trouble for anything you did, could you? You saved us all."

"I'm not sure. Maybe I broke some protocol. I didn't exactly do what Marshal Flowers said to do. He had told me to follow orders, not to

166

give them. I don't think it's a crime, but maybe he just wants to yell at me."

"He had better not," Sarah said defiantly.

Matt smiled as Doctor Emerson walked in and smiled at Sarah.

"I see all of your persistence paid off. Our patient seems to be recovering nicely."

He spent a few minutes looking at the wound and listening to Matt's chest.

When he finished his examination, he asked, "Can you sit up?"

Matt took in a breath and slowly sat up. It hurt, but not too much, and still took a few seconds, but eventually he made it to an upright sitting position.

"That's quite remarkable, Mr. Little. Patients with sucking chest wounds rarely survive. From what I hear, you functioned normally for some minutes after the wound and then survived a thirty-minute wagon ride all the way down here. Now, you're able to sit up straight within an hour of waking. Amazing. You must have the constitution of a longhorn bull. Your lung sounds clear. If there was an infection, it would have shown itself already. That in itself, was amazing. You never ran any fever. All you should need now is some time to rest and recuperate. You should start feeling normal within a few weeks, but I caution you against any strenuous activities. Your wound has been sutured and bandaged. You'll need to come back in six days to have the sutures removed. The bandage must be changed daily and kept clean. If you promise me you can arrange that, I'll let you go tomorrow."

Matt slowly lowered himself back to the bed.

"Thanks, Doctor Emerson. How much do I owe you?"

"Your bill was paid by the United States Marshal Service. I understand you were acting as a deputy marshal when you were shot."

"Thanks again, Doctor."

After he had left, Matt asked, "Sarah, will you be able to come back tomorrow?"

"I intend to. I'll go back to the ranch and borrow the Sanderson's buggy. Then as soon as you're ready we can go back."

"I'd enjoy a buggy ride with you, Miss Reed."

Sarah laughed, leaned over and kissed him again and it was no swift peck this time.

The next morning, after a good night's sleep, Matt was feeling much better. His chest was still sore, but if he took it slow, it wasn't a big problem.

Around mid-morning, Sarah came in, gave him a kiss and told him the buggy was out front waiting for him. He told her that he was feeling better, but still couldn't wait to get some real food.

They had been talking for about twenty minutes when the doctor arrived and after examining his patient, was satisfied with his advanced state of healing.

"Well, Mr. Little, it appears you will be leaving us today. Remember what I told you yesterday. I've told the same thing to Miss Reed, who assures me that she will enforce the rules if you miss any."

"Thanks for all you've done, Doctor," said Matt.

The doctor waved as he left the room. Not even a minute later, the nurse arrived with his clothes, and put them on the same cart she had placed the food earlier then told him that she had taken the liberty of sending his clothes to the laundry where they had been cleaned and the bullet hole repaired.

Matt thanked her and then after he had managed to get his feet on the floor said, "Ladies, I'd like to get dressed."

Both women stood there for a few seconds looking at him like he hadn't said anything.

Sarah then said with a grin, "We're waiting."

"Please, I'd like some privacy."

"Oh, like I haven't seen you naked," laughed Elma.

"Or I won't," Sarah said with a giggle.

But they both finally left the room sufficiently entertained by his discomfort.

It took a while to get into his clothes as he was a little dizzy at first but wasn't about to say anything. He got his shirt on without problem, but his denim pants were a bit awkward, but his socks and boots presented a whole new issue. He stood and gingerly walked around, getting used to being upright again. When he was reasonably sure he wasn't going to fall flat on his face, he opened the door and found both women right by the doorway and noticed his bare feet.

"Could I get some assistance with my socks and boots, please?"

Sarah said, "I'll take care of it, Elma."

Elma nodded and headed down the hallway.

Matt stepped over and sat on the bed as Sara picked up his socks. Sarah slid on his socks without a problem, but the boots took a while. Finally, they were on his feet where they belonged, and he stood up.

He looked down at Sarah and said, "Shall we go, Miss Reed?"

169

She smiled and took him by the arm. They walked out of the doctor's medical, stepped out onto the boardwalk into the Texas sun and Matt was blinded by the sudden change.

After his pupils had contracted, Matt walked slowly to the buggy but boarded without any problem and were soon on their way. Sarah drove as Matt felt the joy of being mobile again.

Matt asked, "So where is Caesar?"

"He's still at the old Lazy R. I think you're the only one that's going to pry him away from those mares."

"Can we stop by and see him?"

"Of course, we can."

Twenty minutes later, they were turning into the old Lazy R access road. Sarah drove past the house and barn and stopped at the corral. Matt took a breath and stepped down before stepping slowly to the fencing where he found Caesar was on the opposite side of the corral nuzzling a gray dappled mare. As Matt leaned on the corral, Sarah stepped up next to him and put her hand on his arm.

"Good morning, Imperator," Matt said loudly.

Caesar forgot about the mare for the moment and quickly trotted over to Matt and brought his head within inches of Matt's. Matt stroked Caesar's muzzle and talked to him for a few minutes about his heroic run to the Lazy R and the incredible jump, then thanked him for getting him back in time to help the Reeds. Then he introduced Caesar to Sarah who reached up and rubbed his face.

"Caesar is a beautiful horse, Matt. He suits you."

Matt nodded and told Caesar he'd be back shortly.

They returned to the buggy and climbed aboard, then Sarah guided them down the road past the fence line and a few miles later, turned down the long drive to what used to be the Box B ranch house.

After pulling the buggy to a halt, Sarah stepped down, then after Matt exited the buggy, took his arm as they walked up the porch steps and crossed to the front door. She opened the door and motioned him in.

He hadn't set one foot in the door when he was engulfed in a wave of applause. Sarah walked behind him, beaming.

"What's this?" he asked her.

"Welcome home, Matt," she said.

As he walked into the great room, he recognized each of the members of the Association and their families, then turned to say something to Sarah, but she was gone. He scanned the room but couldn't find her anywhere.

He was surrounded by well-wishers who shook his hand and welcomed him back. It was a bit overwhelming. Then he saw, of all people, Rachel Bannister. She had a big, genuine smile on her beautiful lips and stepped forward and took his hands.

"Welcome back, Matt," she said, her warm, smiling face looking up at him.

He leaned down and kissed her on her cheek before he said, "You've done it, Rachel. I am happy for you. You're more beautiful than ever."

"Well, thank you, sir," she said honestly, "I'll always be grateful, Matt."

"It was always there, Rachel. All you had to do was look for it."

She gave him one more smile and left to talk to someone.

Matt found John and Mary Sanderson, then took two steps and said, "I appreciate the loan of your buggy, John and Mary. I'm not sure I'm up to riding Caesar yet."

John shook his hand and said, "Matt, we are all so proud of what you have done for the community. We just wanted you to know how much we appreciated it."

"To be honest, John, it's a bit overwhelming."

"Well, enjoy it."

He gave Mary as strong a hug as he could manage then said, "Thank you, both. You've become more than friends. You're family."

As they moved on, Matt became aware that he hadn't seen any of the Reeds.

As he inspected the large room full of people, he still couldn't see them anywhere.

But when he looked toward the corner of the room, he saw something that was very peculiar. There was a small group of musicians sitting in a tight group. As he wondered about it, he saw the trombone player look toward the other end of the room and nod. He began tapping his foot as the other musicians picked up their instruments. Others turned their face toward the group as they began the first notes of *The Blue Danube*.

When the first few notes began, everyone else in the room stepped back toward the walls, leaving Matt alone in the center of the large room. He looked at the crowd, but they weren't looking toward him anymore. He followed their eyes and saw a gap in the line of guests.

As the band continued playing, Pat and Jenny walked into the room preceding Mary, Katie and Peggy. The girls were all dressed as they had for the church social and wore gigantic smiles on their faces as the guests applauded their entrance. After Peggy had entered the room, there was a short pause and then Sarah entered. She was wearing an elegant dress that looked familiar and was stunning. She was also radiant with the kind of look rarely seen on women other than in bridal attire.

She stepped toward Matt and held out her arms. Matt took two strides toward her and placed his large hand around her waist, took her right hand in his left and, just like in the hidden room in the church, held her stationary, waiting for the right moment. And just as before, they took just a few moments to pass unspoken thoughts through their locked eyes. Then, Matt began to guide Sarah to the waltz. Soon, the applause died, and others danced as well.

Matt gazed at her, "Sarah, you made me speechless."

She said nothing but continued to look up at him as he led her across the floor.

The Strauss waltz is a lengthy piece, but it didn't seem so to Matt. It seemed that he had barely taken her hand when the musicians played the final note. Everyone gave the musicians the applause they deserved and Matt was surprised how well they had performed the waltz with so few musicians.

Matt leaned over to Sarah and said, "I was wrong, Sarah."

She tilted her head quizzically, and asked, "How?"

"When I told you that most beautiful women weren't worth my attention. You are, and have my full attention, Sarah Reed."

She blushed mildly and just said, "I'm glad that I do."

Pat and Jenny came near and Matt and Sarah turned to greet them.

Pat shook Matt's hand and said, "We've had this set for you for a few days. You had us all worried there for a while when you stayed asleep for so long, especially the Reed daughter you have on your arm. But this was her idea, so we told everyone we'd do it as soon as we got word from Sarah that you were coming home. So, welcome home, Matt."

"Thank you, Pat."

Then he looked at Jenny and said, "Jenny, if I could, I'd pick you up and hug you, but that would make the doctor and Sarah mad, and I can't have that, so," he leaned over and gave her a kiss on her forehead, before saying "thank you, Jenny. And I'd like to thank you both for raising such a perfect daughter."

There were smiles all around, and Matt made sure to dance with each of the Reed women, including Jenny. He also danced with Rachel in a much more pleasant experience than their last dance. Food was available for guests in the dining room as they enjoyed the dancing and music.

At last the evening wore down. Guests made their farewells, again thanking Matt, and returned home.

As the last guests, John and Mary Sorenson prepared to leave, Matt said, "John, can you hold up for a minute?"

John nodded as Matt sought out Pat.

"Pat, I'll be going back to the Rocking S with John and Mary. I want to thank you again for a wonderful surprise."

"Matt, why leave? We have plenty of room here. Each daughter has her own room for once, and we have two rooms to spare."

"I'm happy that the girls have so much space. It must be a welcome change. But I'll have to turn down your offer. There would be way too much temptation, and I have a reputation to uphold," he said with a smile.

Pat replied, "You know I trust you, Matt."

"I know you do, Pat. But I don't trust myself. I'll say my farewells," Matt said as he noticed that Sarah was within hearing range and was wearing a coy smile.

Pat nodded with a smile and watched as Matt said something to each of his female family members, spending more time with Sarah, of course.

Whatever he said to Sarah sure tickled her funny bone and she was still laughing when he found the Sandersons and left the house.

Matt drove the buggy back to the Rocking S, despite Matt's protest that he should drive the bumpy wagon and they take the smooth-riding buggy. At least it was a short drive.

CHAPTER 8

The next morning, Matt sat rocking in the front porch, feeling as if he were already in retirement. In a way, he was, albeit temporarily. The sun felt good, though.

Matt saw a rider approaching and it didn't take him long to recognize Sarah. Thinking back to the first time he had seen her, he was wondering how he could have possibly thought she was a small man. She waved as she saw him on the porch.

He stood up as she brought her mount to a stop and led him to the hitch rail.

When she was close, he said, "Good morning, Miss Reed. I'm pleasantly surprised to see you. I would have thought you would still be sleeping after all that dancing that we did last night."

As she climbed the steps, she replied. "I've never slept past six a.m. since I was five years old. But this just came for you, so someone had to bring it to you. Somehow, everyone thought I should be the messenger. Not that I wouldn't have volunteered."

"You know, Sarah, last night you were beautiful and elegant in that fancy dress. But to be honest, I like you better in your current outfit."

Sarah laughed and replied, "I'm happy that you do. This is much more comfortable. But I came to deliver this."

She handed Matt a telegram.

"You didn't read it?" Matt asked.

"No. I thought you'd tell me if it was serious."

Matt opened the sheet and read:

MATT LITTLE LAZY R RANCH DENTON TEXAS

TRAIN DERAILED WEST OF FORT WORTH

TRAIN TRANSPORTING EIGHT PRISONERS

TWO KILLED SIX ESCAPED INCLUDING BILLIE BANNISTER

CAUGHT TWO

BILLIE AND THREE OTHERS STILL AT LARGE

MILES HANSON ALSO ESCAPEE

TWO US DEPUTY MARSHALS ALSO KILLED

SAM CROFT ONE

CANT SPARE HELP

KEEP TEMPORARY MARSHAL BADGE

WILL NOTIFY IF CAUGHT

GOOD LUCK

US MARSHAL FLOWERS FORT WORTH TEXAS

Matt leaned against the port post, dropping his hand holding the telegram. He was stunned.

Sarah saw the look on his face and asked, "Matt! What is it?"

He handed her the telegram and waited for her reaction and didn't have to wait long.

"Surely, this can't be that bad. Can it? He was probably still shackled and wearing a prison uniform."

"No, they only issue prison uniforms after they arrive at the penitentiary. As far as the shackles, I'd imagine that in the chaos of the wreck, the prisoners could retrieve the keys from the dead marshals. Not only that, they could help themselves to weapons and money from the other dead and wounded as well. In cases like this, it's always better to accept the worst case as real."

John came out the door when he heard Sarah's voice and noted the strained look on her face and the telegram still in her hand.

"Bad news, Matt?"

Sarah gave him the telegram and after reading, he asked almost the same question to Matt that Sarah had asked and Matt gave him the same answer.

John handed the telegram back to Matt, who folded it and put it in his pocket.

Sarah then asked, "Who is Miles Hanson and why is the marshal telling you he escaped?"

"Miles Hanson was the Bannister cow hand that backtracked to their place after we let him go. He warned the Bannisters that we were coming, which is why Billie came to your house. I don't know what he did to get himself arrested and sent to prison. I doubt if he'd try to bust Billie out."

"What are we going to do, Matt?"

"The first thing, Sarah, is that I need you to get back to the Lazy R as quickly as possible and let everyone know. John, I need to get Caesar, so I'll need a ride over there and I'll need you to saddle him for me. I couldn't get that heavy saddle that high without damage."

Sarah interrupted, "I can do that, Matt."

"Sarah, I know you're an extremely capable woman, but you have some limitations. Caesar is a very tall horse. I have no problem with it because I have a long reach. But even John may have a problem, but

178

he's got a better shot at it. It's more important that you get a warning to your family, and Rachel as well. After I get Caesar, I'll be coming over."

"Okay, Matt," she said before she hopped down to the ground and quickly stepped into the saddle, then was gone in seconds.

John went around back to hitch up the wagon while Matt went inside and told Mary what was going on. By the time he had finished explaining and answering her questions, the wagon was sitting in front of the house.

Matt walked as quickly as he could to the wagon and climbed in with a slight grimace.

The ride to the old Lazy R didn't take long, a fact that Matt appreciated in the rough-riding buckboard. Matt told John that his saddle was in the barn as he walked to the corral to fetch Caesar. The huge stallion was bouncing and stroking the ground, anxious to run. Mares or no mares, he needed to stretch his legs. Matt swung the corral gate open and led him to the barn. It took longer than usual to get him saddled, but they managed it. It wasn't as hard as Matt expected to get in the saddle, and he was grateful. He knew that Caesar, for all his speed, had a smooth gait and a comfortable ride.

After he was in the saddle, Matt waved at John and trotted Caesar to the main roadway. Once there, he experimented with slowly increasing speeds to see if it caused him any problems. They didn't, so, before long, the black Morgan was eating up miles like a thoroughbred and arrived at the old Box B house in good time and climbed down.

He walked up the stairs to the door and knocked. In just seconds, the door opened, and Peggy said, "Matt, why do you insist on knocking? It's a waste of everyone's time."

"Sorry, Peggy. Old habits," he replied smiling.

"They're all in the sitting room, waiting for you," she said as she led the way, knowing he hadn't a clue to its location.

179

When he found the room, he saw that all the Reeds were present, as was Rachel. He wondered if she was still living in the house. In that odd way that brains leap to connections without being asked, he finally realized that the beautiful dress that Sarah was wearing at the welcoming was the same one worn by Rachel at the church social. It was an interesting connection, he thought.

"Good morning, everyone," Matt said.

"Have a seat, Matt," Pat said, pointing with his good arm. The chairs had all been arranged in a large circle.

After everyone had been seated, he repeated the situation that Sarah had undoubtedly already told them but could add more detail and some suppositions.

When he had finished, Jenny asked, "What do you think he will do?"

"That's a good question. If it were just Billie, it would be easier to figure. But adding Miles Hanson to the mix creates a whole new world of possibilities. Billie would just do what is easy. He'd want to get even, so he'd want to get back here. Billie doesn't plan ahead. Judging by Hanson's actions on that day last week, he's a schemer. He'd be expected to light out for Mexico, unless he has some incentive to stay with Billie. I need to take some time to examine the possibilities before I can come up with a plan. Pat, did you get those Winchesters, the shotgun and Sam's Colt back from the posse?"

"Yes, in a manner of speaking. We found them in the bunkhouse, along with the other stuff they'd stolen, including the ammunition. There were just bags of things. We brought them inside the house and have them in the pantry."

"That's a start. Rachel, are there any more weapons in the house?"

"Yes, my father kept a large gun rack and case in the library."

"Could you show me where it is?"

"Sure. Follow me."

Rachel rose and stepped into the hallway, turning right, stopped two doors down and opened the door. Matt started to go in and stopped like he had walked into a wall. Pat almost walked into him.

"Matt, what's wrong?"

Matt's eyes roved the shelves. Books. Hundreds of books. His eyes grew wide just like a six-year-old staring at a penny candy smorgasbord.

"This is extraordinary," he mumbled as he slowly walked forward, firearms forgotten.

He stepped carefully up to the closest shelf and ran his hand along the leather spines.

"Dickens. Hawthorne. Blackstone. Even the collected works of William Shakespeare. I don't believe what my eyes are telling me."

Rachel walked beside him and said, "If you'll notice, none of them have been read. My father bought them for show."

Matt croaked, "For show? There is a treasure of knowledge here. I've never seen the like."

As he spoke, he continued scanning the shelves and running his hand across the books.

Pat broke his reverie by saying loudly, "Matt! We have to check out the guns."

After shaking his head to clear his thoughts, Matt turned to the right and saw the gun rack, and below it, a gun case. He walked to the rack and noticed a Hawken, which would be useless, an old Sharps, also useless. There was a Henry and two Winchesters.

He knelt on one knee and opened the case. Inside he found two trays with handguns of various calibers. Three derringers, but one was an older cap and ball design. The other two were the popular Remington over under that used a .41 caliber cartridge. There were two .45 caliber Colts and three Webley Bull Dogs. They shot the same ammunition as his Remington and the Winchesters but had a short barrel. Underneath the trays of pistols was a shelf that contained boxes of ammunition of various calibers.

Matt closed the door and said, "Okay. Now I know that we have available. It's more than enough, but we need to be more aware than armed. We have to figure out what they might do, assuming they're staying together."

Pat, one more thing. Do you have my temporary United States Deputy Marshal badge? Marshal Flowers can't send help because he lost two deputies and the rest are scouring the county looking for the four escapees still at large."

"I gave it to John."

"Okay, let's head back to the sitting room."

They filed into the sitting room and Matt told them of the arsenal in the library.

Then he said, "I need to go to Denton to send a telegram. I'll have to wait for a reply, but it'll help me get a handle on the problem. Now the train derailment was less than two days ago. At best, they couldn't be here in three days. That's if they found horses the first day and decided to come here quickly. I'll go send the telegram and should be back by six o'clock. Until then, stay in a group. Anyone who can handle a gun needs to be armed. Use the three Webleys, the Colts, and the two cartridge derringers. Any questions?"

Sarah asked, a look of concern on her face, "Matt are you up to this? You were shot in the chest a week ago."

"As long as I don't try any sudden movements or lift anything heavy, I'll be fine. I've got to go."

Matt turned and headed for the door realizing that he was already tired. A result of having that slug in his chest less than a week ago, he was sure.

He mounted Caesar and rode toward Denton, and once he arrived, he rode to the Western Union office and hoped that Marshal Flowers was still in his office and not assisting the search.

He stepped inside and stood at the shelf stacked with blank sheets. He took a pencil and wrote:

UNITED STATES MARSHAL FLOWERS FORT WORTH TEXAS

NEED TO KNOW THE REASON HANSON WAS ARRESTED

ANY LUCK WITH SEARCH

SORRY ABOUT SAM CROFT

HE WAS A GOOD MAN

MATT LITTLE LAZY R RANCH DENTON TEXAS

He handed the telegrapher the sheet. He counted the words and said, "That'll be forty cents."

Matt paid the fee and told him that he'd be back in a while to check for replies. The telegrapher nodded before he turned and tapped out the message.

After he had left the office, he wondered what he could do to pass the time. Then he suddenly knew, mounted Caesar and headed for the common cemetery. It took him a few minutes of hunting through the surprisingly large cemetery before he found Spike's gravesite. The new headstone was in place and read as he had requested. He had worried that the undertaker would make a mistake. Matt wasn't a religious man, so he knew no formal prayers. But he removed his hat and bowed his head and spoke to God like he was just another friend and asked Him to watch over his good friend Spike, who didn't deserve his fate. He finished his conversational prayer and put his Stetson back where it belonged.

He left the cemetery and went to the café and had lunch. When he was finished, he thought he may as well head over to the Western Union office. As he walked in, the telegrapher waved him over and handed him a yellow sheet.

It read:

MATT LITTLE LAZY R RANCH DENTON TEXAS

BILLIE AND TWO OTHERS STILL AT LARGE CAUGHT ONE

MILES HANSON ARRESTED FOR ATTEMPT TO FREE BILLIE AFTER TRIAL

SHOT AND INJURED DEPUTY SHERIFF ENROUTE TO COUNTY JAIL

THIRD MAN MAY BE WITH BILLIE

NAME RAY MITCHELL CONVICTED FOR MULTIPLE RAPES AND ASSAULTS

US MARSHAL FLOWERS FORT WORTH TEXAS

So, Hanson had tried to bust Billie out of jail after all, Matt thought as he wondered about that. That means they were more likely together, but hoped that the third escapee wasn't with Billie, but if the marshal suspected he was, then it was likely. He guessed that once they were away from the train wreck they would have ridden whatever they could find, maybe even doubling up for a while.

He put the telegram in his pocket, mounted, then turned to head back to the ranch.

He rode Caesar faster than he normally would on a routine trip because he had to stop at the Rocking S and talk to John and Mary and needed to pick up his temporary badge.

He was knocking on their door thirty minutes later. Mary opened the door and smiled, "Well, about time you got here, Matt."

He smiled back at her and stepped into the room.

John was walking into the main room, drying his hands on his pants as he asked, "Howdy, Matt. What's the latest news?"

He told them about the probability that Billie was traveling with at least one partner, Miles Hanson, and maybe another prisoner.

"That makes things complicated, Matt," said John.

"Yup. But I need to figure out why Hanson tried to free Billie. He's sticking with Billie for a reason."

"You'll come up with it, if I know you."

"I hope so. While I'm here, I need to pick up my temporary marshal's badge. Marshall Flower can't send any help, so we're on our own."

Mary said, "I'll get it."

She quickly walked off to the back of the house, returning with the badge after a minute, then handed it to Matt, who pinned it to his shirt.

"Thank you, Mary. I've got to get back to the new Lazy R. I don't think you'll be in danger, but you still need to keep aware. I'm almost sure they'll be heading for the old Box B house."

John nodded, and Matt headed out the door.

The ride to the new Lazy R took almost as long as the ride from Denton to the Rocking S. After bringing Caesar to the barn and unsaddling him, which really stretched his instructions from the doctor to its limits, he strode to the house and knocked on the door.

This time the door was opened by Katie, who admonished him just as Peggy had earlier about not knocking and he gave the same weak excuse. He asked where everyone was, and she said that because he was back earlier than expected, the Reeds were scattered throughout the house and grounds. He asked Katie if they could join him in the sitting room, and by the time he asked, Sarah had already entered the room, having heard Matt's voice.

"Any news?" she asked.

Matt reached in his pocket, pulled out the telegram and handed it to her.

"Hanson tried to break Billie out of jail?" she asked incredulously.

"Kind of. He tried to ambush the deputy as Billie was being escorted back to the jail from the courtroom."

Soon, the other Reeds and Rachel trickled into the room. When all were present, Matt began.

"I sent a question to Marshal Flowers in Fort Worth and asked him why Miles Hanson had been arrested. It turns out that he tried to free Billie as he was being led back to the jail from the courthouse. He shot one deputy, but he was lucky that the deputy lived. He'd have been hanged otherwise. What this means is that Billie and Miles are probably together. The third prisoner, named Ray Mitchell, was convicted for multiple assaults and rapes and may also be with them. Initially, I thought this complicated the issue. But suddenly, I realized it was just the opposite. It makes it easier to understand."

Pat asked, "How's that, Matt?"

"There had to be a reason for Hanson to try to free Billie. It sure wasn't loyalty. Why take such a high risk to free someone that couldn't do you any favors anymore?"

Peggy popped in, "Money?"

"Exactly!" Matt said as Peggy grinned, "Money. I imagine that Billie would brag to Hanson that he could get his hands on some serious money. It's the only possible reason for Hanson to make the attempt to free Billie."

He turned to Rachel, "Rachel, did your father keep any large sums of money in the house?"

Rachel tilted her head to the side and responded, "I'm not sure. I never really paid attention. I know that Billie did, though. He was always asking my father about how much money he had. If he did have any, I'd guess that he kept it in the library. My father spent a lot of time there, and when he needed cash, he'd go there. It's possible that Billy found out about it, though."

"Thanks, Rachel. It appears we'll be heading to the library. Before we go, Pat, I'm assuming any money we find belongs to Rachel. Is that the way you look at it?"

"Of course, it belongs to her," Pat answered.

"I don't want it," Rachel said, "it's dirty money."

"Rachel," Matt replied, "it's just money. It's what it's used for that determines whether it's dirty or not. If it helps you have a brighter future, then it will be very clean money. Rachel, I need you to come along, I may need to ask you some questions. And Sarah, I'd like you to come along as well. Just because I'd like to have you come along."

She just smiled before Matt led Rachel and Sarah into the library, and when he entered was still in awe of the expanse of books.

"You know, Rachel, these books should belong to you as well."

"Matt, I'd feel a lot better if you took them. Obviously, you cherish them much more than I ever would."

"We'll talk about it later. Now if you were storing a significant amount of cash in this room, where would you put it?"

They scanned around the room, looking for potential hiding places. The obvious places, in the desk, behind the pictures, were quickly eliminated. Soon all that was left were the books. It looked like a daunting task. Rachel and Sarah sat in upholstered chairs while Matt remained standing.

"I'm going to scan the titles and see if anything sticks out. Rachel, who put the books here?"

"Father hired some librarian to place the books on the shelves, why?"

"Most people have a pattern that makes sense to them. Now, a librarian would use a standard shelving pattern like they do in a library."

With that piece of information, he began reading the titles and detected the pattern very quickly.

There were books of poetry, books of classical origins, including a fancier, leather-bound copy of Caesar's Commentaries that put his to shame. Next were many shelves of fiction. Next, he started the non-fiction. There were textbooks on engineering, geology, mathematics, and even physics, including a copy of Isaac Newton's *Principia*. Then he saw it. It was in the correct location, but the name struck him as much as its misplacement in the shelves. It was a copy of Adam Smith's, *The Wealth of Nations*. Both women suddenly paid attention as Matt withdrew the heavy volume, opened the book and was disappointed. It was just a book. He laid the book on a nearby table and reached into the cavity left by the book, then felt a hole in the back of the bookcase slightly larger than his finger. He then removed the four books to the left and the right of the cavity, and with the added light, he could see a hinged door. He inserted his finger into the hole and used it to open the door. Inside was a large leather box. He slid the box from its hiding place and walked to the desk and was followed by Sarah and Rachel.

He looked at them and said, "*The Wealth of Nations*. Kind of obvious, really."

There was no lock on the box, so Matt swung it open and even he was surprised at the amount of cash inside. He took out the paper money and handed it to Rachel, "Count this."

The rest of the money was in the form of gold double eagles. There were at least fifty. He handed a handful to Sarah and said, "You count these, and I'll handle the rest."

It didn't take long, Sarah had a total of $560. Matt counted thirty-seven double eagles for a total of $740. But Rachel had the big cache. Her total was $2,180, leaving a grand total of $3, 480.

Rachel handed the bills back to Matt with shaking hands, then added them to the two piles of gold pieces that he already had returned to the box.

"Well, Rachel. It looks like your future has become much brighter," as he smiled at her.

"No. No. It's too much. I can't take all that," she said as she kept shaking her head.

"Sit down, Rachel. Please," Matt said quietly as he gestured toward a chair next to the desk.

"Sarah, what do you think?" Matt asked, knowing what her response would be.

"I believe Rachel should take every dime. Rachel, you have a chance to make an even greater change in your life than you've done already. It's a wonderful opportunity."

Rachel continued shaking her head slowly as she said, "I don't know, Matt. It's kind of terrifying."

"Change usually is, Rachel. Look how much my life has changed in the past month since John Sanderson arrived at my ranch. It's been one series of adventures after another, if you include being shot an adventure. But it's also brought me to Sarah, so even getting shot was worth it. It'll be the same for you. Changes will come, and you'll handle them and become a better person for it."

He paused before continuing.

"Now, we need to find a place to hide this in case Billie and his partners come calling. Any ideas?"

Sarah suggested the kitchen and pointed out that men seldom spend any time there and wouldn't know what belonged there and what didn't.

"Good suggestion, Sarah. What we need to do is take the cash out of the box and return it to its hiding spot."

Rachel found an almost empty tin of pipe tobacco and Matt took the can and dumped the remaining tobacco into the fireplace. The money was put into the can and the top pushed on tightly. Matt closed the leather-bound box and reinserted it into its nook and closed the small door, then replaced the book in the same order they had been. It was unlikely that Billie would notice the difference, but Matt didn't want to take that chance. Besides, he intended that none of them would make it past an entrance door. Once everything was in place, they left the library and walked to the kitchen.

Sarah suggested burying it in the flour bin, so after they reached the kitchen, they scooped out some flour, placed the money-laden can into the white hole and covered it with the removed flour. Satisfied that the stash of money was well hidden, Matt, Sarah and Rachel returned to the sitting room.

They were greeted with eager eyes as Peggy asked, "Did you find any?"

"Yes. Over three thousand dollars," answered Matt.

His answer flattened everyone into their chairs except Sarah and Rachel.

"Where did you hide it?" asked Katie.

Matt looked over at Rachel. It was, after all, her money.

"In the flour bin," Rachel replied, "so, if you do any baking, be careful what you put in the bread."

That produced a round of much needed laughter.

Matt let the mood stay for as long as possible, then said," Now that we know the money is in the house, we can be sure that Billie does as well. It's probably the reason Hanson made his attempt to free him, and why they're probably heading here. The wild card is if the third prisoner is with them. He sounds little more than a vicious criminal. What does have me concerned is that he is a convicted multiple rapist. Every woman here needs to know that. From now on travel in pairs at least, and one of the pair needs to be armed. We have three derringers. I'll load them all. They are simple to use. Just cock the hammer and pull the trigger. Make sure the victim is less than ten feet away, so you don't miss."

Matt blew out his breath and continued, "Anyway, here's my best guess as to what they will do. If it was only Billie, he'd come in shooting everyone in sight. Hanson probably talked him out of it, because it would destroy his whole reason for coming along. So, I believe that when they get into the area, they'll stay hidden as close to the house as possible. They may already be here for all we know. They'll watch the house, seeing how many people are here. They'll want to get in, get the money and get away. Except for the lust of Ray Mitchell, the only person here who is in real danger is Rachel."

Matt was interrupted by a startled Rachel, who asked, "*Me?* Why would I be the only one in danger?"

Matt shifted his gaze to Rachel, and replied, "Billie has probably envied and hated you for years. You probably never even noticed it because it was so gradual. Now, you're living in his house with the Reeds. To Billie, that would only add to his hatred. We can't let him get close to you or find you alone."

Rachel looked confused, and asked, "Why do you think he hates me?"

Matt explained, by asking, "Remember the day I first rode up to the Box B?"

"Yes," Rachel answered, "Billie was trying to bully you into leaving and I came out and told him to get coffee. It wasn't that significant."

"But it was, Rachel. I was watching Billie. When you put your hand on his shoulder before you spoke, his face went from forceful bully to that of a kid caught stealing a cookie. Then, when you told him to go have some coffee, he just withered. He was furious, but he said nothing and just turned away. You were watching me, so you didn't see it. You had gelded Billie in front of another man. He was trying to be the big man, and suddenly, he wasn't a man at all."

I could see the hate in his eyes, but it wasn't directed at me, it was at you, Rachel. He wanted to be the big, tough man to impress his father, but you stopped him cold. He really hates and resents you. He thinks that if you weren't there, he'd be important. On that day that I was shot, I tried to talk Billie out of the room. I found that the one line that got his attention and seemed to be working, was when I told him that his father had sent word that he needed him. It might have worked if some idiot temporary U.S. Deputy Marshal had remembered to remove his badge. As soon as he saw it, he made me out as a threat, and had to kill me."

If they're already watching the house, then Billie knows you're here. It's just a question of whether Hanson can maintain enough control to keep him from charging in and trying to kill his traitorous sister. If Mitchell is with them, it'll be the same thing. Hanson's motive will be the money and nothing else. The other two have alternate goals, and it will be up to Hanson to keep them both under his thumb."

Pat asked, "If they're watching the house, why can't we just go get them? The only place that they can watch it without being seen is the stretch of woods to the south."

"I thought of that," Matt answered, "but the problem is that once we go into the woods, we become targets as well. They could stay hidden and shoot us before we knew where they were. Also, by acting like we don't know they're here, they'll feel more confident and we can set up a trap."

Jenny asked, "Do you have a plan, then?"

"A rough plan, and it's all assuming they'll be coming back here. If they run somewhere else, then it's all unnecessary and we can just go on as if nothing had happened. If they do come back here, though, I assume that they'll want to be able to access the money when no one's around. They won't come at night because Billie wouldn't be able to see well enough to find the money. So, they need to enter the house during the day when it's empty. I intend to give them that opportunity, but it needs to be believable."

Tomorrow is Sunday, so we're all going to church in Denton. Pat, you and I will ride horseback. Jenny, you'll drive the buckboard with those homemade seats in the back. Rachel, you'll sit on the front seat with Jenny and the four Reed daughters will take their accustomed positions in back. We'll leave a little after seven. The trick will be to have some weapons hidden in the wagon's foot well. Pat and I will have Winchesters in our scabbards, which won't look suspicious. We should be able to wear our gun belts under our jackets as well. We can put three more rifles in the foot well. Most importantly, I'll need to make sure the shotgun is there. It's critical. I need it loaded with the double aught shells and put a few spares in my jacket. We'll have to work out on how to get the guns there without them noticing."

Now comes the hard part. After we leave and turn on the main road, we travel south toward Denton. We'll need to go at least two or three miles to make sure they think we're gone. Pat and I will then cut into the ranch through the trees. I guess that they'll wait a good twenty to thirty minutes to make sure we're gone. We'll go in about a mile and then turn back to the ranch house. Jenny, you'll then drive the wagon to the old Lazy R ranch house. The mares are still there, and I saw saddles and gear in the barn, so I want you to saddle two of the mares. Who are the best shots among the women?"

193

Sarah spoke up, "Me and mama."

"That's what I thought. When you get dressed, either wear some riding pants underneath or carry some spare clothes and get changed in the ranch house. Do everything quickly. Rachel, you and Mary, Katie and Peggy can get the horses saddled while they're getting changed. Sarah and Jenny, each of you take a Winchester and an extra box of ammunition. Those remaining need to stay in the old ranch house and keep the other weapons ready. Make sure you have the pistols in your purses. If you hear someone coming, assume it's one of the bad guys until you hear one of us call to you."

Sarah, you and Jenny will be our backup. Ride back to the house using the road but walk the horses on the access road to keep the dust down. When you get within a quarter of a mile, tie up your horses out of sight and creep up as close as you can to the house. If any of them try to make a break for it, put a warning shot in front of them. Try to drive them back to us. If not, shoot them."

When Pat and I get near the ranch house we'll stay in the woods and see if they've shown up. If not, we wait. Once they arrive at the house, we let them go inside. Then we leave the horses and move quickly to the house. Pat, you cover the front door. Stay under cover. The trough near the entrance should work. I'll take the shotgun to the back door. That's the door I'm sure they'll use. I plan on standing off to the side until they come out. Once they do, I'll level the shotgun and get them to surrender."

That's the plan. Like most plans, there are holes that I hope you can fill in. The one thing you all must remember, it you are confronted with one of these men, they are not your friends. No matter what they say. Rachel, this goes double for you. Keep your weapon pointed at them with the hammer back. If they make any move toward you, pull the trigger and cock the hammer immediately. This is not a game. These men would hurt you without feeling a bit of remorse. I hope that I've put some fear into every one of you. Some fear is always good. It keeps you sharp and ready. You are all strong people. We'll get through this and come Monday, we'll get our lives back to normal. Now, let's discuss what we have to do."

194

A quarter of a mile from where Matt was laying out his defensive plan, Miles Hanson was trying to explain to his two dull cohorts what he expected them to do and they weren't listening.

"Look," said Billie, "I know where the stuff is, we can just go around to the side of barn down there and wait for that big bastard to show his face and take him out. The rest will be easy. There would be only one man left who probably can handle a gun anyway. The women will just scream and run around while we grab the box and get out of there."

Ray, who had been watching the house with the field glasses, didn't look away.

He just drawled, "Sounds good to me. I'm all for gettin' this over with. We haven't had a hot meal in two days. This waitin' around is stupid."

"Listen," Miles said in exasperation, "it's really simple. If we start shooting and go in there, I'd bet that some of those fillies will be armed. Billie, you told me that your father had a bunch of weapons in the house."

"So, what?" Billie exclaimed in reply, "They don't even know we're here. They've been coming and going out of the house like everything was okay."

"Maybe. But I don't want to take a chance. Once there's shooting, there's a chance that one or two of us gets shot. You told me yourself that you put a .44 slug into that big man's chest from point-blank range and he's still walking around two weeks later like it was nothing. If you shoot him, you alert everyone and more than likely, won't put him down. Just do like I said and wait. We'll get our chance."

"We'd better," growled Mitchell, "and sooner rather than later."

195

A few hours later as the sky darkened, Matt walked out onto the porch, sat in a rocking chair and scanned the trees a few hundred yards away.

"Are you there?" he asked himself.

He hated waiting. He wanted to just walk into the trees and confront the issue. But he knew how stupid it would be. His only real question now was whether they were in the trees or halfway to Mexico.

He sat in the chair for almost an hour waiting for the last light of sunset to leave, then returned to the house and sat in the chair behind the desk in the library.

Jenny, Mary and Sarah were in the kitchen putting away cleaned plates and pans after the evening meal. He had given Mary, Peggy and Katie rudimentary dry fire practice with the derringers, loaded them and given one to each. Rachel had fired a handgun before, so he gave her a loaded Webley Bull Dog. It was heavier than she thought it would be but could handle it acceptably well. He had set up Pat with Spike's Colt rig.

Now came the hard part. He had to come up with a method to invisibly transfer the Winchesters and the shotgun to the wagon. He was mulling it over when Sarah joined him and took a seat in the chair facing the desk.

"You seemed deep in thought, Matt."

"I need to get those guns to the wagons without anyone noticing. It's dark enough, so, I could probably get it done. But if I'm spotted, it'll ruin everything."

"That's because you're trying to do it in the dark of the night. We should do it in the morning."

Matt glanced at her, smiled and asked, "Sounds like you have a plan, Miss Reed. Care to elaborate?"

"We need to move three long guns and some ammunition. My mother, Rachel and I can each hide a gun under our skirts. We can put the ammunition in our purses."

"Those rifles aren't light. How could you manage to handle it?"

"It's simple, really. We just wrap a piece of cloth around our shoulder and around the gun's stock. We have enough room to let it sit by our legs as we walk. The only awkward part will be climbing on the wagon. But if we have some assistance, we can act like we're just holding our skirts while we lift the barrel. Once we get far enough away, we can just slide the guns out by slipping the cloth off our shoulders. There may be a moment or two of immodesty, but I'm sure you won't object."

Matt's eyebrows shot up as he said, "Immodest or not, it's a great idea, Sarah. I'll leave the engineering up to you."

Sarah stood up and walked to his side of the desk and sat down on his lap, which was not an easy task and barely made it, even using a short hop.

"Well, this is nice," commented Matt.

"Matt, how is your wound? The doctor said not to do anything strenuous and tomorrow sounds like it's going to be hard."

Matt has his hand around her small waist and said, "Sarah, I'm okay. When it starts to hurt, I stop what I'm doing. I do have to get those sutures removed, but we need to get this issue dealt with first. But don't worry, I've always been a fast healer."

"Have you ever been shot before?"

"No. I've had a few cuts though, including stabbing myself with a pitchfork when I was seventeen."

"I would think that in raising horses, you would have been thrown a few times as well."

"Surprisingly, I've never been thrown from a horse."

"Don't you break them?"

"I do, but I use a different method. It was shown to me by an old Cherokee. Because I raise them from the time they're foaled, I spend time with them. I talk to them. I rub them down. I'll put a rope on them when they're young, so they are used to it when they get older. I build trust between us. When they're ready for the saddle, it's just another small step instead of the big leap for most horses. They're used to being well-treated and don't object to me or Rafael, my trainer, putting on a saddle. Some of them may mildly object to my climbing on board because of my weight, but if I keep talking to them, they calm down. That's why Caesar seems more like a friend than just a mount. I've been there with him as long as he can remember."

"I'd love to see that."

"I would enjoy showing you everything, Sarah. More than just the horses or the ranch. I want to show you everything that makes this world worthwhile. I'd like to spend the rest of our lives together sharing all those wondrous things. Will you marry me, Sarah Reed?"

Sarah's green eyes filled with tears as she replied, "I was wondering how long it would take you to ask, Matt. I can think of nothing that would make me happier."

He leaned down and pulled her close and kissed her, her tears wetting his face. After they separated, Sarah, wiping her face with her fingers, said, "I suppose we have to worry about other things now."

"I'm afraid so. But those other things will be just a momentary bump in our road together, Sarah. I promise. I love you, Sarah."

"And I love you, Matt. Please stay safe tomorrow."

"I have to. I have a wedding to attend."

She sighed and slid to the floor.

After leaving Matt, Sarah gathered her sisters, mother and Rachel and told them of her idea for hiding the weapons. She also mentioned Matt's proposal, which livened the work of creating the cloth slings. They tried using the slings while wearing a dress, and it proved to be not as uncomfortable as they expected. The key was holding the skirt around the barrel.

Matt sat with Pat and reviewed tomorrow's plans and came up with some contingencies. Like most plans, there were always surprises and Matt knew that tomorrow would be no exception.

CHAPTER 9

Everyone was up early as the preparations got underway in earnest as Jenny and Sarah fixed breakfast.

After breakfast, Sarah and Jenny dressed first, hanging the Winchesters from the slings before slipping their clothing over the weapons. It was a tight fit under the bodice, but it wouldn't be for long and each of the women would all be wearing shawls to hide the bulges on the sides.

They had practiced sliding the sling over their shoulders to release the rifles last night and were confident they could handle it. Rachel then hid the shotgun for Matt's use. It was a bit bulkier, but shorter. By six-thirty, they were ready. Mary, Katie and Peggy each stored a box of ammunition in their purses next to their derringers and Rachel was loaded down with the Webley pistol. The heavily armed women then entered the sitting room.

Matt and Pat were already waiting for the women, and Matt had to make sure that Pat would be able to handle his rifle with his arm still bandaged. They had to wrap the arm with heavier cloth to act as a splint, but Pat could handle the rifle well after it was done.

Matt went out to the barn and saddled Caesar and Pat's horse. It was painful, but not as bad as expected, then he harnessed the wagon and slipped the seats onto the sides, tied the two saddled horses to the wagon and drove the combination to the front of the house.

The women exited the front door and stepped down the stairs as Matt watched to see if there was any indication of the hidden weapons and was impressed how naturally they appeared to be moving. They walked the short distance to the wagon, Pat helped Jenny up to the wagon seat as Matt assisted Rachel aboard. Sarah and Mary were assisted by Katie and Peggy, who were helped into the wagon bed by

200

Pat and Matt. Everything looked very normal, and even the men's pistols were unnoticeable.

Matt and Pat mounted their horses and the group slowly moved out of the yard.

———

Miles Hanson had the field glasses on them as they left and hadn't noticed anything out of the ordinary as they headed down the access road.

"Looks like they're going to church," he said, "Billie, did your family go to church often?"

"Sometimes, but those Reeds go every Sunday."

"Okay. Let's give them some time to get down the road. If they suspect we're here, they may be setting us up."

Billie laughed and asked, "Why the hell would they know we're here?"

Hanson didn't reply as he kept the field glasses on the departing churchgoers until they rounded a curve and were out of sight.

"Ray, get on your horse and walk him down toward the road to Denton. Stay in the trees, but I want to make sure they're really going."

Billie snapped, "Let's go, Miles! They're gone, and we're wastin' time 'cause you're actin' like an old woman."

Hanson ignored Billie and glared at Ray Mitchell waiting for him to leave.

Without comment, Ray Mitchell stood, then turned, walked to his horse and mounted. He wheeled his gelding to the west and walked his horse a half mile toward the road. He had barely reached the end of the forest when he heard the clopping of passing horses. He backed further into the protection of the trees but was still able to see Matt and Pat following the woman-laden wagon. *Those were some fine lookin' specimens of womanhood,* he thought as he waited until the wagon and riders were out of his sight, probably more than a mile away, then whipped his horse around and trotted the horse back to his two new partners.

When he reached them two minutes later, he dismounted, tied off his horse then walked up behind Hanson.

"They're gone."

"Well, I'm still going to give them another half hour or so."

"Why?" asked Hanson.

"If they are going to church, they'll be gone almost two hours at least. It won't hurt to be sure. We don't need to rush this."

Billie said, "I think we should get in there right now. We can be on the road in twenty minutes."

None of them, not even Billie, realized that for once, Billie Bannister was right. If they had followed his suggestion, they would have been in and out before anyone returned, but even that would have only worked if they had been able to find the money he'd promised was in the library.

"We wait," reinforced Hanson.

"Hey, Billie," Mitchell asked, "your paw really have ten thousand dollars in that box?"

"I told you nearly ten thousand. It may only be eight or nine thousand, but it's still a lot of money. We'll be able to go anywhere. Maybe California would be a good place to go."

Hanson broke in, saying, "After we get the money, we divvy it up and then go where we want. If you two want to hang together after we get the cash, enjoy yourselves. Me? I'm going solo."

Billie just shrugged, as they continued to wait, periodically passing off the field glasses to watch the house.

———

Two miles away, Rachel was wiggling her shoulder as she slid the sling over past her elbow, then stood up in the wagon, letting the shotgun slide to the foot well, then lifted her skirts and pulled the weapon free. Rachel handed the gun to Matt, who removed the sling then placed the shotgun in a second scabbard.

By then, Sarah and Jenny had removed their Winchesters, while Mary had given Matt a box of shotgun shells and a box of .44 cartridges. He cycled his own Winchester, ensuring a cartridge was in the breech. Pat did the same. They then released their hammers before Matt took six double-aught shells and put them in his right jacket pocket and a dozen .45 cartridges in his left. He handed some .44 cartridges to Pat who dropped them in his jacket pocket as Matt donned his temporary U.S. Deputy Marshal's badge.

The entire exercise had gone smoother than expected and took less than five minutes.

Matt leaned over and said, "Good luck, ladies. Stay safe. Sarah and Jenny, stay out of sight and only fire if you have to."

Sarah looked at Matt, and said, "Come back to me, Matt."

He just nodded and wheeled Caesar into the woods to the east, followed by Pat just a few yards behind.

Jenny got the wagon moving again at a rapid pace. They only had two miles to go to the old Lazy R ranch house and it should take them less than ten minutes.

Once they arrived, Jenny and Sarah dropped off the wagon as soon as it stopped, jogged to the house with skirts held high, entered the house, got out of their dresses, and stood in their britches as they removed the shirts they had stored in their handbags. While they were changing, Mary, Katie and Rachel were preparing two mares for their return trip.

Matt and Pat trotted about a mile into the woods, then turned north. Once they did that, they slowed their horses to a slow walk, not wanting to risk surprising their targets.

————

A half mile away, their targets were getting antsy.

Finally, ten minutes short of Hanson's dictated half hour, Billie stood up and said, "Hell with this. I'm going in. You can sit here and wait if you want."

Mitchell agreed and said, "I'm comin'."

Hanson shook his head and stood. He had thought they wouldn't have waited ten minutes, so twenty was better than he hoped for.

The three walked their horses to the ranch grounds and headed for the back door where they tied them to a porch support post, then stepped down and Billie led them into the house.

————

Matt and Pat had almost cleared the trees, and Matt could see the ranch house and the three horses tied to the back.

"Looks like you were right, Matt," Pat said.

"I wish I had been wrong, and they had gone to Mexico. But let's get at it."

They tied off their horses to hanging branches, and Pat trotted toward the front of the house, his Winchester held by his good right arm while Matt sprinted to the back of the house with the shotgun, passed behind their horses and thought about untying them, but figured it would be unnecessary and that the men in the house might hear the horses running and get spooked. He quietly climbed the

204

stairs and slid to the right of the doorway, making sure that the door would open to the opposite side. He was set in position and cocked both hammers.

Pat reached the trough and laid on the ground. Now, it was just waiting for things to happen.

Sarah and Jenny were riding hard to get into their location near the access road, so it took them just twelve minutes to reach the entrance to the ranch. They then slowed the horses to a walk as they entered the ranch road. They knew that the front of the ranch could be seen after the next curve, so they dismounted and led their horses into a small grove of young lone pines. Although the horses could still be seen, they weren't as noticeable it they were just standing in the field.

They took their Winchesters and walked quickly to the tall grass bordering the access road and each picked a spot they had seen on their departure, as Sarah went on the north side while Jenny took the south. Each was roughly fifty yards from the road where they could see the house and even make out Pat lying in behind the trough, which told the women that Billie and the others must be in the house.

Inside the house, Billie was attacking the library while the other two watched. He had yanked out *The Wealth of Nations* first, tossed it aside, and then just swatted books off the shelves letting them crash to the floor.

He saw the trap door and shouted, "There it is! Right where I told you it was!"

He smiled as he grabbed the leather-covered box from its secret compartment and the box had barely cleared the small vault when he could tell something was wrong. It was too light.

Hanson didn't wait to hear anything from Billie, and simply stepped in front of him and took the box from his hand. He didn't know how much it was supposed to weigh. It could be filled with paper currency. Mitchell just had a wild gleam in his eyes when he saw Hanson holding the box of money.

Hanson walked to the desk and slammed the box down. He opened it and saw a single sheet of paper. *There wasn't a dime!*

He was already furious as he snatched the paper from the box and read:

Welcome to the new Lazy R ranch house, boys! Sorry to disappoint you.

"It's a trap!" screamed Hanson as he stood and rushed to the doorway.

As he raced out of the room, the other two followed and all three desperate men took ran through the kitchen, opened the door and stepped out onto the porch. As they exited the house, they heard a loud, deep voice to their right.

"Stand where you are! I'm a U.S. Deputy Marshal and you are all under arrest!"

They skidded to a stop and all of the quickly looked left and found themselves staring down the menacing barrels of a cocked twelve-gauge shotgun.

Matt said loudly, "Don't even twitch, boys. I've got this scatter gun loaded with double aught shot. At this range, all of you would be cut in half. Now, slowly drop your gun belts where you stand. Use your left hand."

Billie was in front of the trio, Hanson was standing to his left and Mitchell was almost directly behind Billie, who was already unbuckling his guns. Hanson had also begun to comply.

But Mitchell lowered his left hand as if he were going to follow the directions, and as Billie's guns hit the porch floor, he suddenly slammed his left palm into Billie's back and shoved him at Matt.

The move surprised Matt who had just thought how smoothly this was going. Shotguns had a way of making even the baddest of bad guys obedient.

Billie tripped into Matt causing the shotgun to go off with a huge roar almost cutting Hanson in half. Billie took two of the large shotgun pellets to his left arm and shoulder before Matt was knocked clear off the porch, hitting the dusty ground knocking the wind out of him when his back hit the dirt. Mitchell took his chance to make his break, ran down the stairs, jumped into his saddle and took off toward the front of the house.

Pat heard the shotgun blast, popped up from behind the trough and raced to the porch, raced up the stairs and threw open the front door, his Winchester swinging left and right before he trotted down the hallway through the kitchen to the back porch and saw the remains of Hanson scattered across the floorboards. Billie was squirming on the porch grabbing his left shoulder, and then he saw Matt scrambling to his feet.

Matt quickly brushed himself off, leaving the shotgun on the ground and quickly said, "Pat, take care of Billie and then tie him up somewhere. Mitchell took off toward the road. I'll go get him!"

Even though it would have been quicker to use one of the outlaws' horses, he sprinted the short distance to Caesar. He needed a horse he could count on.

Mitchell was racing past for the access road, glancing behind him to see if Matt followed.

A few hundred yards ahead, Sarah and Jenny had heard the shotgun and saw Pat run into the house and knew there was trouble and seconds later saw Mitchell putting the spurs to his horse and riding straight at them.

Both women took aim, remembered Matt's instructions and Sarah was the first to pull her trigger, firing at the ground in front of the pounding hooves. Jenny fired a second later.

Mitchell was stunned by the gunfire in front of him and quickly turned his horse to the left and headed south, reaching the woods in a few seconds. Both Sarah and Jenny fired again as he turned to spur his departure.

He had just disappeared into the woods when Sarah spotted Matt atop Caesar racing down the road and watched as he turned his Morgan toward the forest after the outlaw before Sarah and Jenny ran back to their horses.

Mitchell glanced behind and saw Matt alter his direction, then yanked his Winchester from his scabbard, turned in the saddle and threw a round at him. Matt saw him fire and began alternating direction changes as he continued the chase. After Mitchell took another shot, he faced forward again, shoved the Winchester back into the scabbard, then rode harder as he darted deeper into the trees.

Matt had to make a speed adjustment as well, but he had to slow as he approached the trees. As he now he had to worry about bullets more than tree trunks and branches, because he wasn't sure where Mitchell was. The man could have just pulled up and was lying in wait, so he kept Caesar at a steady trot, scanning the trees for a possible ambush.

Sarah and Jenny mounted their horses and headed them back down the access road, then turned back on the road to the old Lazy R ranch house.

A few minutes later, Mitchell cleared the trees at the back end of the old Lazy R, saw the house and headed that way. Then he saw the unusually configured wagon, and the chase was forgotten, as he smiled and recalled that woman-loaded wagon. He trotted to the corral and stepped down, pulled out his Colt and let his horse wander.

Peggy stepped out onto the porch, having heard hooves, and looked down the access road, shading her eyes with her hands but couldn't see anyone.

Then she heard the terrifying nearby click of a pistol hammer being locked into position behind her, followed by a deep male voice saying, "Well, hello, you pretty thing."

She whirled around and saw a pair of hideous eyes in addition to what looked like a cannon pointed in her direction.

"Who are you? And what do you want?" she asked, trying to sound unafraid, but failing.

"Why, girlie, you know what I want, and you won't be needin' to know my name. So, why don't you just step down over here, so we can get better acquainted."

"I...I need to go back," she stammered.

"Get your ass over here, girl!" he shouted, "We're gonna go over to that barn and have ourselves a little fun."

He raised the gun to make his point and Peggy closed her eyes, simply frozen in fear.

"I said get over here!" he shouted as he stepped closer.

Peggy was beyond simple fear. She couldn't let him take her! She couldn't let that happen! Her eyes were squeezed tight, waiting for the shot she knew would come because she wasn't going to go with him.

Then it happened. The gun roared so very close and she shuddered, but there was no pain. *He missed!*

She opened her eyes, afraid of what to expect, and what her eyes told her didn't make any sense at all. She couldn't understand what had happened. The man was lying on the ground, his gun still in his hand with his eyes wide open.

She turned and saw a grim-faced Rachel standing at the door, her pistol still smoking as she held it with straight arms.

Peggy turned to Rachel and said in a strained monotone, "You killed him, Rachel."

Rachel lowered the gun slowly and stared at the dead man on the ground. Mary and Katie had appeared at the door and stood behind Rachel looking at the body, a pool of blood surrounding his head.

Then they heard more hooves and Matt roared around the back of the corral and brought his big black stallion to a crushing stop, leaving a huge cloud of dust. He jumped from the saddle and jogged to the body of Ray Mitchell and gave him a good swift kick in the ribs to make sure he was dead. The slug had penetrated the front of his neck and ripped through the right side. He then looked at the scene on the porch and could instantly see what had happened.

He stepped up to the porch and walked to Rachel who was standing like a statue beside a shaken Peggy.

He put his hand around the Webley and said softly, "I'll take the gun, Rachel."

She nodded as Matt pried the weapon from her stiff fingers, then walked to her front and wrapped her in his arms as she began to sob.

Matt leaned over to her and whispered, "It's a hard thing to kill a man, Rachel. I know. But this man was the worst sort of human being on this planet. He preyed on women. What you did was a brave and necessary thing to do. You need to let it go. Look at me, Rachel."

She tilted her head and looked into his eyes.

"I'm proud of you, Rachel."

Then she asked quietly, "Is Billie dead?"

"No. I had them under the shotgun. Billie and Hanson had already dropped their guns and were surrendering when Mitchell shoved Billie into me causing the shotgun to go off. Hanson is dead, but Billie only caught a couple of pellets in his shoulder. He'll be okay."

Rachel whispered, "That's good."

Sarah and Jenny rode to the front of the porch and quickly dismounted.

Jenny asked, "What happened?"

Peggy ran to her mother, hugged her closely and explained what happened through tear-filled eyes, and as she was telling the story, Matt led Rachel down the stairs with his arm around her shoulders, nodded to Sarah, and when she approached, Matt took his arm from Rachel and said, "Sarah is here. She'll help. Okay?"

Rachel just nodded as Sarah saw the shock and pain in her eyes and glanced at Matt and mouthed silently, "I've got this," then Matt took his arm from around Rachel and Sarah took her arm. She guided Rachel into the house and was followed by the other Reed women.

Matt watched until the women were all in the house, then walked back to Mitchell's body. He stripped his gun belt, removed the coiled rope from his horse then led the horse next to the body and tied the rope around the feet. He slid the rope across the saddle and used it to pull the body across the saddle. He knew he couldn't lift it and wasn't about to ask any of the women to help with the grisly business.

He finished tying the body down to the horse, tied it to the fence post and walked into the house and found Reed women were sitting in a circle as Rachel talked to Sarah. Rachel seemed to be better, so Matt waved Sarah over, took her arm and walked with her to the kitchen.

"Sarah, I've got to go and retrieve Hanson's body and take Billie into Denton. Then I'll wire Marshall Flowers and let him know what happened. He'll be able to suspend the search and send someone to pick up Billie. I'll leave a note telling him what happened and if he needed more information, I'll be at the Lazy R. I may not make it back tonight."

"Matt, what happened?"

"I had them, Sarah. Billie and Hanson were surrendering, but Mitchell shoved Billie into me. The shotgun went off killing Hanson and wounding Billie. I was flat on my back in the dirt when Mitchell made his break. I heard you and Jenny firing, so I knew he was there. You know the rest. How is Rachel doing?"

"She's still pretty shook up. But I think she'll be okay."

211

"How about Peggy?"

"She's better than I thought she'd be. I think it was because her eyes were closed when Rachel made the shot, so she didn't see what happened."

Matt said, "Okay. I'll need you all to stay here until I load Hanson's body and get Billie on the wagon and then get past the entrance to head to Denton. I don't want Rachel to see the bodies. Give me an hour. Okay?"

"I understand. I can see the road from here, so I'll keep a watch out and after you pass, I'll wait another fifteen minutes before we return to the big house."

He leaned over, kissed her quickly, and then told her that he was proud of all of them. She nodded and then returned to the main room and Matt followed behind her and nodded at the women as he continued to the porch.

He attached the body-laden gelding to Caesar, then mounted and headed down the access road, arriving at the big house twenty minutes later, and found Pat sitting on the front porch with Billie. His shoulder was swathed in cloth, but blood still soaked through.

"How are you holding up, Pat?"

"I'm fine. Billie here needs a doctor."

"I'm going to go around back and put Hanson's body on his horse."

"I see you caught up with Mitchell."

"No. I was too late. He got to the old ranch house and saw Peggy. He pulled his gun and was making noise about having his way with her and Rachel shot him. Killed him with one shot, too. Rachel was in shock, but she's doing better. Peggy was upset, but she'll be fine."

"Rachel did that?"

"Yes. I wish I had gotten there earlier. I can deal with it better than she can. It'll take a while for her to get over it."

Billie yelled, "Will you two stop your jabbering and get me to a doctor?"

"He's your problem for a little while, Pat. I'll bring his horse around after I get Hanson loaded."

Matt had Hanson's body tied down in less time than it took for Mitchell, so five minutes later, he returned to the front of the house where he and Pat got Billie mounted and lashed to the saddle.

Pat asked, "Do you want me to come with you, Matt?"

"No, Pat. You'll need to be here when everyone returns. You might want to throw some water over the back porch to get rid of the blood, too."

Pat nodded, and Matt led the three horses down the access road.

It took almost ninety minutes to reach Denton with the slow pace necessitated by the body-laden horses, and Billie complained the entire time, which wore thin after the first few hundred yards. When they reached Denton, it was almost two o'clock in the afternoon. Townsfolk stared at the convoy as it made its way through the town until Matt stopped at the sheriff's office. He tied Caesar to the post and untied Billie, let him step down and led him to the door.

Matt opened the door and led the complaining Billie into the room where he found a very young deputy sitting with his boots on ex-Sheriff Avery's desk. His feet quickly hit the floor and gaped as Matt entered wearing the Deputy U.S. Marshal's badge and leading a bloody Billie Bannister.

"Are you in charge?" Matt asked.

"Uh…yes, sir!"

"Well, deputy, this is Billie Bannister, an escaped prisoner. He's wounded and needs to see Doctor Emerson quickly. I also have the other two escaped prisoners' bodies stretched over their horses outside. They need to go to the undertakers. Do you have any help?"

"No, sir. I'm alone right now."

"Okay, I'll walk Billie here to the doctor's office. You can let the undertaker know he has two customers out front but tell him not to touch their possessions because they're evidence."

"Yes, sir. I'll lock up and do that."

"I'll be back shortly. I need to wire Marshal Flowers, too."

"Yes, sir."

Matt took Billie by the arm and walked him the short distance to Doctor Emerson's office, opened the door, let Billie in, and hadn't walked five feet when he heard Elma.

"Welcome back Matt. We expected to see you two days ago to get your stitches removed."

"Sorry, I've been busy, and this is one of the reasons. I brought you a new customer. He caught a few stray shotgun pellets into his shoulder."

She asked, "And can I guess that you were at the other end of the shotgun?"

"Yes, ma'am. If you can have the doctor fix him up, I'd appreciate it. I've got to send a wire. I should be back in about a half hour."

"My, my, you have been busy! When you come back, I'll have the doctor examine your wound and remove the sutures."

"Thank you, Elma. I'll be back. Oh, by the way, he's an escaped prisoner, so you may want to leave the bindings on."

Elma nodded as Matt turned and exited the house. He had to ride to the Western Union office because it was on the other side of town, and when he arrived, he dismounted, entered, stood at the shelf and wrote:

UNITED STATES MARSHAL FLOWERS FORT WORTH TEXAS

THREE ESCAPEES ATTEMPTED ROBBERY AT LAZY R

MITCHELL AND HANSON DEAD BANNISTER WOUNDED

BANNISTER CURRENTLY IN DENTON COUNTY JAIL

WILL AWAIT YOUR REPLY

MATT LITTLE LAZY R RANCH DENTON TEXAS

The telegrapher read the sheet, raised his eyebrows at Matt and said, "Really? This will be forty cents."

Matt paid the man and told him he'd check back for a reply.

He returned to the doctor's office on Caesar. When he entered, Elma said the doctor was working on Billie and should be done in about thirty minutes, and Matt told her he'd be back after he got something to eat, then walked to the café across the street and had a late lunch while he thought of all of the remarkable events since he'd been to Denton; some remarkably tragic, others remarkably uplifting.

When he was finished eating, he went back to retrieve his still whining prisoner. Before Elma would release Billie to him, she ushered him into an examination room as the good doctor wheeled into the room and without so much as a 'howdy' told him to remove his shirt. After examining the gunshot wound, he stood up and said, "This is amazing! You were right in saying you recovered quickly. The healing is well in advance of what I expected to find. Before I remove the stitches, I'd like to ask your permission to write of your case in a

215

medical journal. I'm not a religious man, but if I was, I'd be declaring this a miracle. This wound looks almost a month old. Amazing!"

The sutures were removed. Matt thanked the doctor and paid the eight dollar bill for treating Billie. He was annoyed that it was costing him money to make Billie feel better.

He marched Billie to the county jail, found that the deputy was back in the office and when he entered with his prisoner, the deputy unlocked a cell for Billie. Matt untied him as he complained about being hungry.

An overly-annoyed Matt simply said, "Oh, shut up, Billie!"

Billie did no such thing as Matt turned and left the cell and then the office.

He mounted Caesar and rode him back to the Western Union office, and as soon as he walked in, the telegrapher waved him over.

That was a fast response, Matt thought. The operator handed him the message, which read:

MATT LITTLE LAZY R RANCH DENTON TEXAS

GREAT JOB

WILL SEND A DEPUTY TO DENTON TO PICK UP BILLIE

WILL NEED A WRITTEN REPORT

NEED YOU TO COME TO OFFICE AS SOON AS POSSIBLE

US MARSHAL FLOWERS FORT WORTH TEXAS

So, now he had to go to Fort Worth. That'd have to wait a couple of days, though, and hoped that fit into Marshal Flowers' definition of as soon as possible.

He stuffed the telegram into his pocket and mounted Caesar. It was barely half past three.

He made much better time on the return, reaching the barn before four-thirty, then dismounted, unsaddled Caesar and led him to a stall, brushed him down, threw some hay in the stall and filled the feed bin with oats. He spent a few minutes thanking his favorite stallion for the magnificent job he had done that day.

When he was satisfied that the Morgan was content, he walked to the house, and as he reached up to knock on the door, he stopped and quickly withdrew his hand, remembering the last two times he had done it, then opened the door and entered the great room. No one was there, so he continued down the hallway, passing an empty library and an empty sitting room before he could hear chatter and picked up the smell of roast beef and had a good idea where everyone was.

As he turned into the dining room, the Reeds and Rachel were sitting around the table enjoying a well-deserved meal.

Jenny was the first to spot Matt and cried out, "Matt! We weren't expecting you for a while."

She began to rise so she could set a place for him at the large table.

Matt waved her down and said, "I'll get the plate and other things. You sit and eat."

He quickly went back to the kitchen and picked out what he needed and returned to the dining room. He joined in the general chatter as he ate and stole a glance at Rachel. She seemed normal, but didn't add anything to the conversation, only tersely answering questions directed at her. Peggy, he noticed was as perky as ever.

"So, Matt," asked Pat, "did everything go well in Denton?"

"Better than expected," he answered, "I went and saw Doctor McNamara with Billie and after he fixed him up, he checked on my bullet hole and was happy with the progress. He removed the stitches and asked to write up my case in the medical journals. He mumbled something about a miracle in how fast I had healed."

Sarah asked, "He said you were completely healed?"

"Not totally, just well ahead of where I should be. Oh, and Elma passed along greetings to you, Sarah."

"Anything else happen?" asked Peggy.

"After I sent a telegram to Marshal Flowers, he replied quickly. He needs me to write a report of the incident and wants me to get to Fort Worth as soon as possible. Those are the words he used. I had planned on spending a few days just relaxing in the sun, but I guess that's out. I'll leave on tomorrow's train for Fort Worth. Rachel, I think you should come along. You'll have to write your own statement, I believe. Sarah, I think it would be a good idea if you came, too. You and Rachel could chaperone me to keep me out of trouble."

That elicited a laugh from everyone, including Rachel.

Matt added, "So, ladies, pack enough clothes for a couple of days and I'll see you in the morning. The train leaves Denton at 10:15, so we'll need to be on the road by eight o'clock. Pat, we'll use your seated wagon, if that's okay. Can you drive us down to Denton?"

"Sure," replied Pat.

Tomorrow's agenda was set, so the discussions then drifted to less dramatic topics as everyone seemed to want the deadly events of the day put into the past even faster.

Despite his earlier decision to stay with John and Mary Sanderson, Matt found he was simply too exhausted to leave the house, so when it came time to turn in, he was assigned an empty room and without thinking of anything other than sleep, he entered the bedroom, undressed before he crawled under the blankets and was soon deep in slumber.

CHAPTER 10

The Denton to Fort Worth train arrived just after ten o'clock. The only problem in the trip that morning had been Rachel's continued difficulty in accepting that the money in the tobacco tin belonged to her. The immediate issue was postponed when Matt had Sarah take the tin with her in her purse as they left the ranch.

They hadn't had time in Denton to go to the bank anyway, so it took most of the trip to convince Rachel to at least deposit the money in a bank account in her name when they got to Fort Worth.

So, the first thing they did after they stepped down onto the Fort Worth platform was to hire a carriage to take them to downtown Fort Worth and Matt had the cab drop them off at the First National Bank.

After entering the impressive brick building, they found a clerk to assist them and Matt had him open an account for Rachel and suggested that she keep a hundred dollars in cash. When she asked why, he smiled and told her that she and Sarah might want to do some shopping while in the city.

Their business completed, Matt escorted the women to a small café.

After they had seated, Matt remained standing and said, "I'm going to see the marshal to make sure he's in. You have some coffee and I'll be right back."

He gave them a short wave and a smile before turning and leaving just as the waitress arrived at the table.

Matt trotted across the busy street, avoiding traffic, and walked the short distance to the United States Marshal's office, entered the office and saw the same deputy marshal sitting at the desk that he had seen the first time he had walked through the door.

"Deputy Harper, how are you?" he asked as he shook his hand.

"Fine, Matt. These stories we're getting out of Denton are keeping everyone entertained. I can't wait to read your official report."

"Is the marshal in?"

Matt didn't have to wait for a reply as United States Marshal Jake Flowers strode into the front office.

"Matt! Glad to see you," he said with a smile as he shook Matt's hand and continued, "Come on back to my office."

When they had seated, Marshal Flowers asked for a quick summation of the events as Matt handed him the report that he had written last night. The marshal set aside the official report as Matt began his narrative.

When Matt had finished, he sat back and asked, "So, Jake, how are you doing? I was really sad when I heard about Sam's death. He was a good man."

The marshal replied, "He was, and we all miss him. As far as I'm concerned, we're busy as usual. They're sending me two new deputies straight out of training. That's what I wanted to talk to you about. You've done some incredible work these past few weeks. I've never had any deputy accomplish half of what you've done and I'd like to bring you on as a Deputy Marshal."

"I'm honored, Jake. But your timing couldn't be worse. I'm getting married shortly and I still have my ranch to worry about. I'll think about it, though."

"I wish you would. I could use a man with your talents. The way you figured things out was extraordinary."

"Speaking of which. Have you had any missing persons reported about six or seven months back?"

The marshal thought for a second then replied, "We had a dance hall girl reported missing, but she turned up in Dallas a month later. We also have a missing reporter from the Fort Worth Star-Telegram. Never did find him, though. Figured he was on some story somewhere. Why?"

"One thing that's been bothering me since this thing started is how did Bannister find out about the land problem. He sure didn't find it himself. Someone must have told him about it. It wasn't anyone from the land office. If they had found the mistake, they would have notified Pat Reed, not Bannister. You may have the answer. If you do some investigating, I'll bet that reporter found out about it and Bannister got it from him. How I can't imagine. But when he did, Bannister couldn't let him publish the story, could he?"

Flowers nodded then said, "We'll check into it. Oh, and before I forget, this is yours."

He reached into his desk and pulled out a sheet of paper and slid it across to Matt.

Matt read it in shock. It was a bank draft for fifteen hundred dollars from the Missouri-Pacific Railroad.

"What's this?"

"After the derailment, the railroad put out a reward on the escaped prisoners. Something about liability. As you were only a temporary marshal, you can take reward money but the rest of us can't."

"I'll have to explain something in a minute, though. So, Jake, how are the wife and kids?"

The marshal looked at him and scratched his head before replying, "Do you know something I don't know? Last time I knew I was a confirmed bachelor."

"Just wondering. I mean, here you are a United States Marshal, not a bad-looking sort, I just assumed you'd have been tied down long ago."

"Nope. Never met a filly that I wanted to rope. What brought that on?"

"Nothing, really. Anyway, I'll be back in a little while to write out my report. As I mentioned earlier, Mitchell was shot by Rachel Bannister, not me. Technically, the reward for his demise should go to her, but she was so deeply affected by the shooting, I don't want to add to it. It took us a long time to convince her to take the three thousand dollars we found in her father's library. She didn't want it because she called it 'dirty money'. I know this would be worse, so I'll accept it for her and hold it until she can take it. I've brought Rachel with me because I told her you'd probably need a signed statement. Is that right?"

"Yes. Especially in this case."

"If you could, I'd like to bring her here, to your office. She's a plain-looking woman who's led a sheltered life under her father's thumb. I have my fiancée with her now to act as a chaperone, so if you'll stay here, I'll bring them over, okay?"

"Sorry to hear she was hurt so badly. In can be rough, shooting someone if you're not used to it. I'll treat her with kid gloves. So, she's just a spinster?"

"She's heading that way. She looks like a schoolmarm, but she's very nice. Don't go surprising her or anything, just stay here. I'll convince her that you're a good man."

"Okay, Matt."

Matt left the office, extremely pleased with himself. He didn't want Jake to be aware of Rachel's extraordinary beauty as it would upset his matchmaking plans. He never would have even given the idea a thought with the old Rachel, but the new Rachel was completely different and needed someone. He couldn't think of a better someone than Jake Flowers. Now, he needed to prime the other half of the pump and see if his devious plan worked.

He crossed the street and approached the two women who were engaged in conversation. They both glanced at him as Matt pulled out a chair and sat down.

"Are you ready, Rachel? I've talked to the marshal. His name is Jake, by the way. Don't be put off by his grizzled appearance. He's just a lonely old man ready to retire, but he's very nice and will listen to your story before you write it down, okay?"

Rachel nodded and asked, "Will this take long?"

"No, you should be done in less than thirty minutes. Then, I suggest that I rent a buggy and take you ladies shopping."

Sarah smiled, but Rachel was still nervous. Matt looked at Sarah and winked and she responded with a curious look. *What was Matt up to?*

Matt escorted them across the street and toward the marshal's office, opened the door and waved the women inside.

"Deputy Harper, this is my fiancée Sarah Reed and my good friend, Rachel Bannister. I'll be taking Rachel back to see the marshal, okay?"

Deputy Harper was struck dumb by the two women and just nodded.

Matt took Rachel by the hand and led her to Jake's office, turned the corner stuck his head in the doorway and said, "Marshal Flowers, I'd like to introduce my dear friend, Rachel Bannister."

Jake Flowers started to stand, his hand extended for a handshake and literally froze halfway.

Rachel wasn't much better. She had begun to say, "Nice to meet you," but only finished 'nice'.

Both Jake and Rachel knew that they had been had, but neither took any time to admonish Matt, their thoughts were elsewhere.

"Won't you have a seat, Miss Bannister?" Jake finally managed to ask.

"Please, call me Rachel, Marshal," she replied as she began to sit.

"Call me Jake, please, Rachel," he said, smiling as if his face would split.

"I'll just step outside with Sarah," Matt said, but neither acknowledged him.

Matt was grinning as he turned then walked back to the outer office where he found Sarah telling Matt stories to Deputy Harper. Whether he was enthralled with the stories or with Sarah was anyone's guess.

Sarah saw him approaching and asked, "So, do we wait until she's done?"

"No," replied Matt, "this may take longer than I expected. Let's head over to the café and have some coffee while we wait. Deputy Harper, can you tell the marshal that we'll be at the café and when Rachel is ready, could he escort her across the street?"

"Will do, Matt."

Matt took Sarah's hand as she rose, nodded to the deputy marshal, then they left the office, waited for passing traffic to clear, and crossed the street to the café. After Matt and Sarah had seated themselves at the table and the waitress had filled their cups with coffee, Matt took a sip as Sarah asked, "So, what mischief are you up to?"

Matt placed his cup on the saucer and explained, "I've been worried about Rachel since the shooting incident. She was becoming withdrawn and I wanted to bring her out of her stupor. She had finally overcome her past and was becoming a good person when she had to kill a man. A man that deserved a lot worse punishment, I might add, than a single bullet. I've been wondering about what I could do to help her and thought a shopping trip with you might help, but it didn't take long to realize it wouldn't. When I went to see the Marshal Flowers, it hit me rather suddenly what to do."

He took another sip of coffee while Sarah waited impatiently.

"I was talking to Jake. That's his name, by the way, and he's not a grizzled old man. He's actually quite good looking and a little over thirty, I'd guess. I found out that he was unmarried and simply hadn't met the right woman. Kind of like me a few weeks ago."

He smiled at Sarah as he continued.

"I know Jake is a very good man and would be good for Rachel. She needs someone. So, when I told Jake that I was bringing her over to make her statement, I kind of minimized her appearance so he wouldn't be expecting Rachel to be, well, Rachel. I admit, it was funny watching the first meeting. I could have set off a firecracker in the room and they wouldn't have noticed."

Sarah pretended outrage, and exclaimed, "*Mr. Little, you were matchmaking?*"

"I wouldn't call it that. I just set up the circumstances."

Sarah started laughing. Here was this huge man who had been shot, had chased down criminals, leapt from running horses in the dark, and saved her family, and he was matchmaking!

Matt sheepishly smiled and enjoyed her laughter.

When she had stopped, she shook her head and said, "Matt, if this works out, and with your record, I'll be surprised if it doesn't, your legend will be secure."

"Now that you seem to have forgiven me for my social transgression, we need to set you up for this afternoon's shopping. I still think it would be good for Rachel, especially after meeting Jake. And you, my beloved fiancée, need some more clothes to prepare you for the wedding."

With that, he reached across, took her small hand and placed five gold double eagles onto the palm.

"Matt, I don't need any more clothes."

"Sure, you do. When we get back to my ranch, you'll probably need a lot of them."

Sarah paused and looked down at the table.

"Your ranch? Matt, I thought you'd just bring your horses here now that we have all this land. I mean, I can't leave my family. They need me here. You know that."

Her statement stunned Matt as he looked at her downcast eyes, then said, "Sarah, I thought you knew that we'd be living on my ranch. You told me that you'd like to see my horses."

"I do, but why can't you bring your horses here? I can't leave my family, Matt. They need me. You can sell your ranch and move here. We could even build a new house where the old Lazy R is."

Matt just hadn't seen this coming and was struggling to come up with a solution.

"No, I can't do that. It's my ranch. It's my home. I can't describe it any other way. I dreamed about it for years and made it mine. I wanted to bring the one woman to share my life to my ranch. I wanted to bring you, Sarah."

"I'm sorry, Matt. I can't leave my family. I just can't."

She laid the double eagles on the table and started crying and Matt reached over and slid the gold over and put the coins back into his pocket, still trying to come up with some solution that didn't involve giving up his ranch.

"It'll be okay, Sarah. We'll work something out, okay."

She sniffled and nodded but knew that it wasn't possible if he was determined to make her leave her family.

Matt had no idea how they could fix this. The other problems that he had solved seemed like nothing compared to this, so he thought he'd change the subject to make Sarah less distraught.

"Jake offered me a job as a U.S. Deputy Marshal."

She looked up with red eyes and asked, "He did? What did you say?"

"I told him I'd think it over. He seems to think I'm well qualified," then he grinned and added, "Probably because I can take a bullet and get back on the job quickly."

Matt meant it as a joke to lighten the mood, but it was not a good choice.

"Matt, you can't take that job. It's dangerous!" Sarah exclaimed.

Matt knew he was in a danger area, so he said, "I know, Sarah. I just told him I'd think about it."

She looked down at her coffee, feeling incredibly miserable. The closer it had come to Matt's departure, the more uncomfortable she had become about leaving her family. It was all she had ever known. Matt's appearance in her life was so new and so wonderful, but there was that fear of the unknown that still lingered. The warm blanket of family was too much too discard. She had hoped that Matt would be willing to leave his ranch and move his horses to her family's new, larger spread, but now, that didn't sound possible, either.

They may not have been cheerful, but the couple that approached them from the street were. Jake had Rachel on his arm as they reached the café, each of them wearing wide smiles.

Matt looked up and was gratified to see the Rachel he had already considered a good friend.

"You are a cruel man, Mr. Little," Rachel said as she hung onto Jake's arm and still smiled.

Sarah hadn't seen them coming and jerked her head up.

"Matt, I take back all the nice things I said about you," said Jake.

Matt smiled at them and replied, "I just didn't want any preconceived notions. So, Rachel, did you finish your statement?"

"Yes, it's all done. Jake told me about the reward, too. I want you to keep it. I don't want any part of it. I'm pretty well off already, and you could probably add to your herd with it."

Sarah asked, "What reward?"

Matt pulled the bank draft out of his pocket and handed it to her. She handed it back and simply said, "Oh."

Matt replaced it in his pocket without further comment.

Jake asked, "So, are we going to have lunch? It's about the right time."

"Sure," Matt said, as he waved the waitress over.

Jake and Rachel dominated the talk during lunch and neither of them noticed the gloom that had settled over Matt and Sarah as they were concentrated on each other.

After they had finished eating, Rachel asked Sarah, "So, are we going shopping?"

Sarah shook her head and said, "I have to be getting back sooner than expected. You can go ahead though."

For the first time, Rachel could see that something was wrong between them.

"You and Matt can go back. I'll be staying in Fort Worth for a while. Jake can watch over me," she said as she beamed at Jake.

Matt stood and said, "We'd better get going. The train to Denton leaves in an hour. Jake, can you send a telegram to Pat Reed at the Lazy R to let him know we'll be arriving on the next train?"

"Sure, Matt."

Matt took Sarah's hand then they made their farewells to Jake and Rachel and took a carriage back to the depot. The ride home was a long, silent trip even though it was only ninety minutes.

Pat met them at the depot, gave Sarah a hug and shook Matt's hand as Sarah boarded the wagon's seat. Matt sat on the other side of Pat who chattered the entire trip to the ranch about all of the changes that they would be making, which was good because neither Matt nor Sarah were in a talking mood. Pat never noticed.

After they returned to the house, dinner was being served and the family gathered around the dinner table. Jenny could see that something was wrong and even Peggy noticed it, but no one asked. This was a private matter between Matt and Sarah.

After dinner, Matt told Pat and Jenny that he'd be heading back to the Rocking S to pick up his things, told them about the job offer, and that he'd have to think it over. He also mentioned that he'd be leaving soon to check on his ranch. They tried to convince him to stay longer, but he told them that he had neglected his horses too long.

He left the house and walked to the barn, silently saddled Caesar and rode him at a fast trot past the house and down the entrance road.

When he reached the end of the access road, he stopped and turned in the saddle to look at the house, seeing an empty porch. He sighed and turned Caesar onto the road and began riding. He didn't even notice where he was going as he continued to ride.

He passed the Rocking S and continued to Denton. There, he stopped at the general store and purchased some supplies. He wanted to be on the road where he could think.

It was well after dark when he left the streets of Denton heading south. After he had gone another twenty miles, he found a good place to set up for the night but didn't build a fire. He simply stretched out his bedroll and slid inside. He tried to sleep but couldn't. All he could think about was Sarah. He didn't want to admit it, but when she had said she couldn't leave her family, what had hurt most was that she was telling him that despite everything, he was second in her heart and that was why he'd answered as he had.

He liked and enjoyed her family, but when she had said that they mattered more than he did, he felt betrayed somehow. He laid looking up at the stars for another hour or two before he finally drifted off to a dreamless sleep.

CHAPTER 11

He was on the road early the next morning, having breakfasted on jerky and water. He wasn't going through Fort Worth but went east of Fort Worth directly through to Dallas and reached his ranch by noon.

When he spotted the Double M in the distance, he could see the herds of Morgans roaming the pastures, his cabin and the barn. The corrals for the Percherons were done, but other than that, it was the same. It was home, but it already seemed distant.

Twenty minutes later, he trotted Caesar to the cabin and the stallion could already sense the presence of his mares and his nostrils were flared, his ears perked.

"Just a few more minutes, Julius," he said as he patted Caesar on his neck.

He dismounted and shouted, "Rafael!"

From the corral attached to the rear of the cabin he heard the response, "Matt? Is that you?"

"Who else would be screaming your name?"

Rafael stepped around the side of the cabin with a big smile on his face.

"You have been gone a lot longer than we expected. We thought you had been killed or something."

"No, just shot. But I'm okay. How are the Morgans?"

"Shot? You'll have to tell me about that. The horses are all well, including the Percherons. We have another foal, too. A midnight black colt. He has no white on him anywhere. He's very strong, too."

"Let's go see him. His father wants to visit his mother as well, I believe."

Rafael looked at the snorting stallion and said, "And the others, too, I think."

They stripped Caesar of his trappings but didn't brush him down. He was too skittish. Instead they released him to go spend some time with his herd. He took off, racing to the pastures, prancing as he went, announcing his return. Both Rafael and Matt proudly watched him return to his domain.

"He's glad to be home," commented Matt.

"So, what took you so long?" asked Rafael.

"Come into the cabin and I'll tell you."

Matt spent over an hour filling him in on the events of the past weeks, including Sarah and her decision to stay. It ended when Matt showed him the bank draft. Rafael whistled when he saw it.

"What will you do with it?"

"I don't know yet. Tomorrow, I'll ride to Dallas and add it to my account along with the remains of Spike's money."

"Oh, I almost forgot, "said Rafael, "this letter arrived for you yesterday."

Matt accepted the letter, glanced at the return address and knew it was from Mike before he opened it and hoped it wasn't more bad news. After Sarah's decision to stay with her family, he didn't need any more.

He read:

Dear Matt,

I haven't heard from you in a while. I hope your ranch is doing well. Things have gotten bad up here. Sedalia has turned into a virtual sin city. There are seven bordellos and thirteen saloons in town and quite a few gambling houses as well. Maggie and I have sold the farm are heading to Dallas. I hope this letter reaches you in time.

We got a decent price for the farm, but I couldn't sell the Morgans. I know how much they mean to you. The herd isn't as large as yours, I'm sure. There are only sixteen, but we're shipping them and four milk cows a servicing bull, and some of our hogs as well.

We'll be looking for a ranch or farm, hopefully near you. If you can help us find one, I'd appreciate it. It looks like we'll be arriving there in mid-August.

Hope to see you soon. Maggie is excited as well.

Mike

"Now this is a surprise," said Matt. "You don't know of any property for sale around here, do you, Rafael?"

"As a matter of fact, I do. Remember old man Parker?"

"Charlie Parker, with the Diamond P?"

"Yes. Well, he's decided to head up north to Kansas to be with his son and daughter-in-law and he's looking for a buyer."

"That's only four miles down the road. If I remember right, it's about the same size as the Double M and has a ranch house on it as well, too."

"And a big barn."

"I think I'll saddle up and ride that way. Want to come along?"

"No, this is your business."

Matt nodded. Twenty minutes later he was riding a long-legged chocolate mare south toward the Diamond P, then turned at the entrance road and halted about fifty feet from the house.

"Charlie, you in?" he yelled.

A few second later, Charlie Parker appeared at the door.

"Matt, is that you up there? Can hardly see in the glare."

"Yup. Mind if I set?"

"Of course, come on in."

Matt dismounted the mare, named, unsurprisingly, Chocolate.

He walked up to the porch and shook hands with Charlie Parker.

"So, what have you been up to these days?" he asked.

Matt gave him a brief rundown of the events in Denton, leaving out the reward he still had in his pocket, not wanting to ruin any negotiating positions.

Charlie was impressed and asked, "You gonna take that job?"

"I don't think so. I've got my ranch to take care of. Speaking of ranches, Rafael told me that you were leaving."

"True enough. Heading to Kansas and stay with the kid and watch my grandchildren grow. You interested?"

"I got a letter from my brother yesterday. He's leaving Missouri and wants to come down this way. So, when I heard you were looking to sell, I thought I'd see if we could come to an agreement."

"Well, that would work out well for both of us, then. I'm asking a thousand dollars."

"That include the cattle? Last time I knew you were running almost three hundred head."

"Nope. Sold them off already, except for some ornery critters that were hiding in that briar patch in the northwest corner. Hell, if it included the cattle, it'd be five times as much at least."

"I know, Charlie, but this place isn't worth that much. I'll give you a dollar an acre, six hundred and forty dollars. It's what I paid for my place when it was empty."

Charlie pointed out the good water, the nice ranch house and recently painted barn, reminding Matt that there was only a cabin on his place. Matt said his barn was bigger and already had two corrals. Charlie countered that he was leaving all the furniture. They went back and forth for almost an hour, finally settling on eight hundred and twenty dollars, lock, stock and barrel. He even said they could keep the Diamond P brand if they wanted.

They shook on the deal and arranged to meet tomorrow at ten o'clock at the land office in Dallas.

Matt rode back to his ranch and explained the purchase to Rafael.

"Where are the Conger boys?" he finally asked, as he hadn't seen either around.

"We don't have that much work to keep them busy, so they've been doing odd jobs around for other folks."

"Maybe buying Charlie's place will help. We could share the boys and double their salary."

"They'd like that."

After he had eaten, Matt walked out of the cabin and gazed at his ranch. It wasn't as big as others, but it was his. When he first saw the reward money, the first thing he had thought of was using part of it to build that house that he had wanted to share with his wife, now that he had found the right woman. But finding her and keeping her were

235

two different things. He took one last long look at his land, then shook his head and walked back inside.

The next morning, he rode a different horse, a roan gelding named Med because he had a patch of white on his right side that resembled a map of the Mediterranean. He stopped at the bank, deposited the draft and most of his remaining cash into his account, bringing it up to a healthy $5,218.44. Then he walked to the nearby land office where he waited until just before ten, when Charlie Parker walked in. They shook hands and fifteen minutes later had completed the transaction. Matt had the names of Mike and Maggie Little put on the deed.

He could think of no other business in Dallas, but on a whim, he rode to the Western Union office and asked if there were any telegrams for him. He was hoping for one from Sarah, but the one the clerk handed him was from Missouri.

MATT LITTLE DOUBLE M RANCH DALLAS TEXAS

BOARDING TRAIN IN SEDALIA

WILL ARRIVE IN DALLAS ON AUG 10 TRAIN

WILL NEED HELP MOVING STOCK

CAN STORE THEM AT YOUR PLACE UNTIL WE BUY

MIKE LITTLE SEDALIA MISSOURI

That was tomorrow! Talk about cutting it close! Charlie was moving out later today, so they'd have a place to stay and someplace to put their critters.

He boarded Med and rode back to his ranch, and after he arrived, he explained the need to move some stock from the train's stockyards to the ranches. Rafael said he'd get the Conger boys to help and went out to let them know that their services were needed.

He knew he, Rafael and the Congers could handle the Morgan herd, and probably the cows. The hogs would be different. He'd have to ask Mike about the best way to do that. He brought out the wagon and made sure the wheels were greased, then cleaned it up for Maggie and the kids. If only Mike was riding in it, he wouldn't have bothered.

When he was satisfied that everything was good, he relaxed and returned to thinking about Sarah, but still couldn't come up with a solution, so he walked out to the closest corral. He hadn't even seen the new colt, but when he arrived he arrived at the corral, the colt was easy to spot.

As young as he was, he was already showing the spirit of his father. Matt climbed over the fencing and approached the young horse, admiring the correct musculature and lines of the colt as he began talking to him. The colt looked at him for a few seconds and then bolted to the other side of the corral as Matt smiled. He was going to be a good one. He stayed and talked to the colt's mother and the other horses in the corral for a while before returning to the house.

———

The next day, Mike saddled Med again and tied him to the back of the wagon. Rafael joined him, and they set off with the Congers trailing on their own non-Morgan mounts.

The train was on time, and after it had hissed to a stop, people began unloading to the platform. Matt saw Maggie first and wasn't surprised by her appearance one bit. One would think a woman who had borne three, no, check that, four children as he counted, would have gone to fat or lost some of her girlish good looks, but not Maggie. She barely looked twenty. Maggie spied Matt and waved. By then, Mike had bounded from the train with a huge grin on his face and after waving back to Maggie, the brothers embraced in a manly hug, slamming each other's backs while Maggie stood by watching in amusement. Matt turned and picked up Maggie, giving her a big hug and an accompanying smack on the cheek and then Mike introduced his two boys and two girls, the youngest barely a toddler.

Matt told the station master to have their trunks brought back to the wagon while he and Mike discussed moving the animals to the ranch. Matt hadn't told them of their new ranch yet. They finally had the logistics of moving the animals settled. The hogs would be transported in a rented heavy wagon and the other, taller animals would be driven south. Mike paid for the wagon rental and the driver while the Congers and Rafael gathered up the moving stock and soon had them headed south.

After the two large trunks were put on the wagon, there was still enough room for the three older children to find seats. The toddler, little Annie, would ride with her parents. Mike told him that they had six crates of kitchenware, knick-knacks and other family necessities that would be shipped to his ranch, if he didn't mind.

"We may have a problem with that, Mike," Matt said as they started the wagon rolling.

"Room?" asked Mike.

"One of the issues. I'll show you the other when we arrive."

The caravan of heavily loaded wagons followed the horse and cow herd moving south. Thirty minutes later, they passed a ranch with a Double M sign and Rafael and the older Conger boy, Chuck, turned the Morgans into the ranch, after Matt had told Rafael to send the freight wagon on to the Diamond P, the younger Conger brother, James, continued the milk cows moving south.

"Isn't that your ranch?" asked Mike as he turned and watched the Morgans heading east.

"Uh-Uh," was the only answer Matt provided.

Almost an hour later, James turned the milk cows to the left, into a ranch with a large Diamond P sign above the entrance.

"Is this yours, too?" Mike asked over the din of the wagon's creaking.

"Nope."

The caravan continued, the hog wagon bringing up the rear. James Conger reached the barn and drove the cows and lone bull inside.

Matt dismounted in front of the ranch house and waited for the wagon to stop. When it did, he went around to the back and lifted his niece, Margaret, out of the wagon. The boys had already hopped down. Then he went to the front and took little Annie from Mike, before he and Maggie stepped down.

"This is your new home, Mike. I'm not sure of the soil and what would be a good crop, but it'll support upwards of three hundred head of cattle if you want to go that way, or a lot of those hogs, too. Of course, you'll have to build a smoke house."

While Matt was rambling about hogs and smoke houses, Mike and Maggie were slowly walking toward the house. It was a large ranch with three bedrooms, and substantially larger than their house in Missouri.

"What do you mean, Matt?"

"I had spent about a month and a half up around Denton, taking care of some things, and when I came back Rafael gave me your letter. I asked him if he knew of any property available, and he told me about this place. It was owned by a gentleman names Charlie Parker and he wanted to go back to Kansas to live with his family, and I knew you needed a place, so I bought it. The deed is in yours and Maggie's names and so is the brand, if you want to keep it. I was able to get it at a good price."

"So how much do I owe you?" Mike asked.

"I think it was $11.27, or thereabouts," Matt answered.

"At the risk of being rude," Mike said, "you've gone loco."

"Nah. I just threw that number out. It's yours, Mike. Bought and paid for. The furniture is included, so you'll be able to stay here tonight. I'll bring over some horses and tack later, so you can be mobile. I told Raphael to redirect your shipment of crates, but let's get those trunks moved into the house."

"Just a minute, Matt," Mike said as he ran to the hog wagon to tell the driver where to leave the animals, and quickly hustled back.

Maggie had led her brood up the stairs and into the house. The children scattered, exploring their new home as Mike and Matt hauled in the two heavy trunks. Maggie did some exploring on her own, checking out the kitchen and bedrooms. It was more than she could have hoped for.

After they had dropped the second trunk in the main room. They could hear the freight wagon rolling up to the porch. Mike thought it would be better to leave the crates on the porch, and they could take their time emptying them tomorrow. After the crates had been placed on the porch, Mike tipped the two freighters and they mounted their heavy wagon and returned north.

Maggie came to the porch and smiled at Matt as she said, "This is perfect, Matt. I couldn't have dreamed of a finer home for our children," then she walked over and gave him a hug and a kiss on the cheek.

"Do you have food in there, Maggie?" Matt asked.

"Oh, yes. Plenty."

"Good. Well, I've got to get back to the Double M. You folks get settled in. I'll stop by with those horses in the morning."

Matt shook his hand one more time before Matt mounted and turned back north. Seeing Mike and Maggie was wonderful, but it made the loss of Sarah hurt even more, knowing this is what he wanted more than anything.

He returned to his ranch thirty minutes later. When he arrived, he told Raphael that he needed to pick out a pair of nice mares or geldings, as well as three young geldings and tack for all of them to bring to the Diamond P in the morning. He wanted his nieces and nephews to have their own horses.

The next day Matt helped Mike and Maggie settle in to their new home. Of course, Matt had to spend some of the time explaining what had happened when he had gone to Denton.

"You were shot?" Mike exclaimed when he reached that part of the tale.

"Just once," Matt answered as he continued.

Maggie listened to the story, sure that Matt was leaving parts out as he talked about Sarah Reed, because when he had talked of her, she could read his eyes, and saw the misery he was trying to hide.

When he finished, Mike seemed stunned. "My God, Matt! That's almost a lifetime of adventure in one month!"

"Yeah, but it's all behind me now."

Maggie just looked up at him and asked, "Matt, what about Sarah?"

Matt was shaken by her question. He had purposefully left out his deep attachment to Sarah, and thought he'd spoke of her no more or less than her sisters or Rachel. *How had she picked that up?*

"She's staying with her family," Matt answered, trying to sound nonchalant.

"And you're letting that happen?" she asked, her right hand on her hip.

Mike hadn't a clue what Maggie was saying and why Matt appeared so defensive.

"It's what she wants, Maggie," Matt replied quietly.

"And you are going to spend the rest of your life moping around like you couldn't do anything about it? I just don't get you men. Matt, you took a bullet to your chest protecting her and her family. You stopped evil men from breaking into their home, but you won't simply ride up there and steal her back where she belongs. You are all hopeless."

Matt realized that she was right. He had to stop feeling sorry for himself. He loved Sarah. He wanted her to share his life. It's not like he'd be dragging her to Australia. Her family would be just a day's ride away.

"You're right, Maggie," he said and kissed her on the forehead, "We are all idiots. But I'm going to rectify this beginning tomorrow."

"Good. I expect to meet my new sister-in-law soon."

Matt smiled at her, turned and headed for the door, mounted and trotted Med out of the ranch, arrived at his cabin a few minutes later, and found Rafael back with the horses, as usual.

"Rafael, tomorrow morning, I'm heading off to Denton. I'm going to get my wife. Well, she'll be my wife when we get back here. I'll also be having a construction crew arriving in the next few days to start building a house."

Rafael was dumbfounded. *What had gotten into Matt?*

While he may not have known the answer, Matt did and it was surprisingly simple: Maggie.

CHAPTER 12

Early the next morning, Matt had saddled Caesar and packed supplies for the ride north, if it took that long. He rode into Dallas and stopped at the engineering firm of Jefferson & Niles, walked in and after some introductions, told them what he wanted. The draftsman he was talking to showed him some designs they had recently finished, and Matt liked the large ranch with upgraded kitchen and a boiler for making hot water, and he added one other change. He converted one of the four bedrooms to a library, adding a wall of build-in shelves. The construction cost would be eleven hundred dollars, he was told and could be completed in a month, as they had a crew idle at the time. Matt wrote a bank draft and shook hands with the engineer.

Just an hour after walking into the engineering firm, Matt was on his way out of Dallas in a much better frame of mind. His bank account may have been wounded, but he was happy. He was going to get Sarah.

Caesar made good time and by five, he had passed through Denton and was on the familiar road to the Lazy R. His mind was churning with so many different scenarios, he almost rode past the entrance road.

Luckily, Caesar noticed it and automatically turned left, and Matt found that he was more nervous than when he faced Billie's .44. The gun could only kill him. Sarah could break his heart.

But as he rode, he'd already changed one big aspect of his decision to fetch Sarah. He realized after leaving Dallas that even though he was having that house built on his ranch, it didn't matter. Only Sarah mattered, and if she still didn't want to leave her family, he'd do the unthinkable and sell his ranch with the new house and buy one here and move his herd.

As he approached the big house, he saw no one outside on the porch or in the ground nearby, so he was able to pull right up to the house, dismount and tie Caesar to the hitchrail.

His heart was pounding as he stepped up the four stairs to the porch, took five long strides and stood before the heavy door. Matt took in a deep breath, and possible admonishment or not, he knocked, then waited for what seemed like a week.

The door opened, and Peggy stood before him with wide eyes as she looked up him but didn't say anything. She just put her finger to her lips and then waved him in. The great room was empty, so it must be dinner time.

Peggy walked down the hallway as Matt stepped behind her.

Matt heard Jenny ask, "Who was it, Peggy?"

Peggy was almost to the dining room doorway when she replied, "Just some giant of a man on a horse. A big, black stallion."

Matt heard the shatter of a plate and pounding of feet as Peggy stepped aside and Sarah raced around the corner, almost sliding into her sister, but quickly regained her forward momentum, took four long steps and threw herself onto Matt with tears flowing as she held on and just sobbed.

Matt held her close and buried his head in her hair as he hurriedly whispered, "I couldn't stand it any longer, Sarah. If I need to give up my ranch, my Morgans, it doesn't matter. You are my life."

She still held on, although it was unnecessary because Matt had her pressed to him.

She quickly said, "I'm so sorry, Matt. I was being stupid. After all you've done for me and my family and I do something so thoughtless that hurt you so badly. I love you, Matt. I'll go wherever you are. My mother gave me a good scolding, and my father wasn't happy with me either. They were right, too. It's time for me to start a new life with my husband, if you'll still have me."

"It looks like I have you now," Matt said as he smiled at her face just inches from his own, "The question is will I ever let you return to the floor. I'll tell you what. I'll put you down, but then we need to start making plans for the wedding. How about September 15th?"

"I'd marry you right now, if you'd like. But September 15th sounds good, too."

It was an unusual conversation, with one of them suspended a foot off the ground. It was also a well-attended one as the entire Reed clan had left the dining room to watch the pair.

When Matt gently lowered Sarah to the ground, they were startled by a round of clapping by the Reed family.

Sarah turned, wiping the tears from her cheeks as she smiled at them and said, "I guess we're getting married next month."

"It's about time!" said Peggy.

"Matt, would you like to join us for dinner?" Jenny asked.

"Well, I did skip a few meals to come and steal my bride," he answered.

"I don't think she needed stealing. She was getting ready to head your way, anyway," said Pat.

They then all wandered back to the dining room, but Jenny took a detour to fetch Matt's place setting, as well as a replacement plate for Sarah.

Then they all happily returned to the table, Sarah's chair pushed as close as possible to Matt's. Matt could never recall a tastier meal, not that he would ever recall what he was eating.

"Well, Mr. Little," said Sarah, "in case you haven't heard, it appears that your matchmaking skills are excellent. Jake and Rachel have become quite the couple. Except when Jake is working, they are always together. Rachel stopped by to pick up some things and asked me to tell you that she will always be grateful to you for all you did for her, especially the little ploy with Jake."

"I heard about that, Matt," said Peggy. "Can you help me out now?"

Matt laughed, the first time he had since that black day in Fort Worth, then said, "You don't need any help, Peggy. Once I get your beautiful older sister out of the house, I'm sure the beaus will be flocking to the Lazy R to rope one of the prettiest fillies in the state."

"They've already been arriving, Matt. It was bad before we moved to this big house, but now, with all this room, I can't keep track of the rascals," complained Pat.

Matt then said, "And there is one other big change happened in the past week, Sarah."

"You didn't take that job, did you?" she asked, a horrified look on her face.

"No. After I returned to my ranch, Rafael gave me a letter from my brother. The town of Sedalia, Missouri, where they had their farm, had turned into a regular Sodom and Gomorrah. They felt unsafe, so he told me he had sold the farm and was coming to Dallas. He was going to need a place, so I found a ranch close to mine that was up for sale and bought it. He and his family arrived two days later, and we moved them in and spent a few days setting them up."

"Your brother will be our neighbor?"

"Yup. He and Maggie now have four children. Remember when you asked me how many kids they had, and I told you three and maybe four? Well, it's four. Two boys and two girls. The youngest is a toddler named, Annie."

"Matt, that's wonderful."

Matt stared those marvelous green eyes and confessed, "Maggie is one of the reasons I'm here. She saw me moping around like my world had ended, which it had. I was telling Mike and Maggie about coming up to Denton and all that happened. I tried not to talk about you too much, Sarah, because it hurt so much. But Maggie laid into me. She told me that if I loved you so much, I should get up here and marry you and take you home. She woke me up. I realized that she was right. Staying at the ranch and feeling miserable for the rest of my life wasn't very smart. So, I told Raphael I was going to ride to Denton and get my wife. On the way here, I stopped in Dallas and went to an engineering firm and arranged to have them build a new house on the ranch. But as I got closer to the Lazy R, I realized that the new house, my ranch, and even my Morgans didn't matter at all unless you were with me. Nothing mattered to me anymore. Just you."

And despite the crowd around the table, he leaned over and kissed her. She wrapped her hands around his neck and kept her lips pressed on his.

When they finally took a breath, Matt glanced at the smiling faces around the table. Sarah just giggled as she saw the same thing.

"Well, said Matt, "I suppose, now that I've had my sweet dessert, it's time to adjourn to the sitting room."

He stood up amidst the laughter and took Sarah's hand and they walked to the sitting room to discuss their wedding plans.

After they were seated close together on the setee, she asked about the new house and seemed excited about seeing the herds of horses as well as her new home. It was a remarkable shift from the last time that they'd talked about where they would live after they were married.

"You know, Sarah, it's not like we're moving to the other side of the ocean. We're just about forty miles away. We can get a nice carriage. In fact, I may do that more quickly, so Mike can bring his family to the wedding."

"That's a marvelous idea, Matt. Where should we have the wedding?"

"I think the same church in Denton where we had the social is the right choice. Don't you agree?"

"That would be wonderful, Matt," she answered as she snuggled in under his arm.

The wedding plans were handled by the Reeds and Matt took care of the arrangements to have Mike's family at the wedding.

Finally, the 15th of September arrived. Matt was dressed in a new suit he had bought in Denton that had to be tailored to fit his bulk. Even though he and Sarah shared the same house, in keeping with tradition, she stayed out of sight until he had left the house to head to the Rocking S. He talked with John and Mary for a while until it was time to go, then mounted Caesar and rode to Denton.

He arrived at the church and was greeted by many of the guests, including Mike and Maggie. They had their children with them, and Matt was happy to see them all. Jake and Rachel were there, and Rachel, as usual, looked stunning. She came over to Matt and gave him a hug and kiss before Jake shook his hand and thanked him for introducing him to Rachel.

Once all of the preliminary greetings were done, Jake took Matt aside and confessed he was nervous about proposing.

Matt looked at him and asked, "Are you serious, Jake? Why?"

Jake said in a low voice, "Just look at her, Matt. She's too perfect for someone like me."

Matt shook his head in disbelief then told Jake to hang on a minute and walked back across the church where Rachel was talking to Maggie.

He touched Rachel on the elbow, and when she turned, he asked, "Can I talk to you for a second, Rachel?"

"Of course, Matt. What do you need?" she asked as she stepped away from Maggie.

Matt lowered his voice, "You're going to find this hard to believe, but do you know that brave United States Marshall who escorted you to the wedding? The same man who has faced down desperadoes is scared to death to propose to you."

Rachel's face lit up, but she asked, "He is? Did he send you here to ask on his behalf?"

"Not at all. He just mentioned to me that he was afraid to ask because you're so beautiful and such a wonderful person, he doesn't feel good enough. But don't tell him I mentioned it."

"Well, I won't if you'll do me a favor and go back there and tell him to ask me quickly or I'll ask him first and he'll never live it down."

He grinned at her and waved as he walked back to see Jake.

When he got there, Jake as already bright red, and asked, "What did you do?"

"Nothing. I was just talking about this and that and she happened to mention out of the blue that if you didn't propose quickly, she'd ask you first and then you'd never live it down."

"She really said that? You'd better not be pulling my leg, Matt, or I will personally put another slug where that last one was."

Matt almost giggled. Almost.

"Jake for such a smart lawman, you're sure missing this one. Rachel loves you and really wants to be your wife. Now head over that way. I have to prepare for my almost-wife's arrival."

Jake wasted no time in scurrying across the church floor to a smiling Rachel.

As the time for the ceremony approached, guests coalesced toward the pews and Matt and Mike walked to the front of the church. The minister was ready, and now all that was needed was the bride.

The organ began playing and Matt saw Pat escorting Sarah down the aisle. She was gowned in ivory silk and had a white veil covering her face, but it didn't matter. Matt could still see the incredible green eyes and her beautiful face. Remembering how radiant she was at the welcoming dance, he was amazed that she surpassed even that. She was practically glowing, and Matt felt like he was melting inside as she drew closer.

But he didn't. The ceremony was as flawless as the bride. After the ceremonial kiss, Matt and Sarah Little walked down the aisle. All eyes were on them, but theirs were only for each other, as it should be.

They exited the church and went downstairs for a reception in the church basement where the social had been held. There was food and dancing and Matt introduced his brother and his family to his friends. When the reception was over, the newlyweds left the hall and stepped into a rented carriage that took them to the old Lazy R ranch house that had been restored to an almost-new condition. It would be used as a guest house until Mary or Peggy decided to live there when they married, but tonight, it would be a bridal suite.

Matt didn't have to put away any horses or do anything other than to take his new wife into the bedroom and be a husband.

Sarah was surprised when she discovered the almost giant that she married was so gentle when he began to make love to her. She exulted in his kisses and touches as she experienced things she had never imagined.

Matt took every second possible to make Sarah as thrilled as possible, and she responded more passionately than he could have hoped. It was an hour of discovery and love.

The next day, Matt and Sarah returned to the Reed home to say farewell to everyone. They were given a ride on the wagon and dropped off at the Denton train depot then left for a week in San Antonio for their honeymoon.

When they returned, they were met by Pat, who had brought Matt's new carriage. Pat drove as Matt and Sarah enjoyed the smooth ride, still enjoying being newlyweds, even in the limited privacy of the carriage.

They stayed overnight at the temporary bridal suite and continued exploring each other and learning that there seemed to be no end to how much they could learn, but both were willing to spend the rest of their lives in discovery.

Early the next day, they made a quick visit to the big house, had breakfast, made their farewells, and, with the carriage filled with Sarah's personal belongings, they set off toward Dallas. Sarah stayed in the front seat with Matt as the carriage rolled smoothly along.

"Matt, you know, after all of my concerns about leaving, I'm not the least bit upset. I love you so much and I feel like an idiot for ever saying those things."

"Neither one of us were overly smart then, Sarah. But none of it matters now. We have each other and we'll soon be starting our own family and spend the rest of our lives together."

Sarah smiled, and said, "What do you mean *soon*? How do you know we haven't already started? We've sure tried hard enough."

Matt laughed, kissed his bride and replied, "Oh, I think we should still try as much as possible. Practice makes perfect."

Sarah clung to his arm, totally content and happy.

———

Late in the afternoon, the carriage pulled into the Double M ranch. Matt reined in the team and stared. It was the first time either of them had set sight on their new home and both were awed by what they

251

were seeing. Even though Matt had seen the design, he was impressed by the quality of the construction.

"It's beautiful, Matt!" exclaimed Sarah.

"It is that. You deserve nothing less. We'll have to stay in the cabin for a couple of days until we can get it filled with furniture, but it'll be worth the wait. Besides, you'll get to pick out what you like. But let's go look at it first."

Matt drove the carriage to the front of the porch, stepped down and helped Sarah climb down from the lofty perch.

They walked arm-in-arm to the door when Matt, without warning, scooped her into his arms as she let out a squeal. Matt reached for the handle, pulled the screen door open and then swung open the heavier front door, then just stared at the main room. Sarah was still looking at Matt and hadn't looked yet.

He turned sideways to avoid hitting her head, stepped inside and lowered her to the floor as Sarah scanned the furnished main room.

"Matt, I thought you said it was unfurnished."

"It was. I have no idea, but I have my suspicions."

It didn't really matter now, and Matt held Sarah's hand as they inspected their new, furnished home. The furniture was of high quality and even the window dressings were well appointed. Two of the bedrooms had nice beds and chests of drawers. Their bedroom, and it had to be theirs, had a large four-poster with side tables and a large chifforobe in addition to a chest of drawers. The beds even had blankets and quilts. The inside bathroom that Matt noted in the drawings had a large, clawed bathtub with hot and cold running water.

Sarah turned to Matt and said, "Hot and cold water? Matt, that is a luxury. You may never get me out of the tub."

"I could always join you," he replied with a slight smile.

"That's an option," she said before she giggled which was followed by a quick kiss.

The kitchen almost brought tears to Sarah's eyes as she saw the large sink with two spigots, and large cabinets filled with china, glasses and pots and pans. She opened drawers and found two complete sets of silverware, one obviously for everyday use and the other for more formal occasions.

The dining room had a beautiful, dining set with eight chairs and a large, maple table and even a matching sideboard.

Suddenly, Matt said," I haven't checked the library yet."

"The library?"

"The original design called for four bedrooms. I had the engineers add built-in bookshelves in the fourth bedroom, so I could use it as a library."

"That's a wonderful idea."

Matt knew the fourth bedroom was supposed to be at the end of the hallway, so when he opened the door, he saw a solid oak desk and chair and...books. The shelves were filled with books. Matt walked slowly to the shelves and read the titles and immediately recognized them. They were from the Reed's large house.

"Did you know that these would be here?"

"No. I'm as surprised as you are. I see Rachel's hand in this."

"I believe you're right. Let me check something," he said as he walked to the non-fiction and found the volume he sought, *The Wealth of Nations*. He slid the book from the shelf and showed it to Sarah.

"I suppose I should read this someday," he said, then smiled and slid it back into its slot.

"And now, Mrs. Little, I have a suggestion?" he said as he snatched her back into his arms.

"Does it have something to do with that four-poster?" she smiled mischievously.

"Definitely."

EPILOGUE

Billie Bannister was relatively fortunate in that no charges were added to his sentence as the train wreck itself was responsible for his escape, but still had to serve the full thirty years of his original sentence.

Jake and Rachel were married in Fort Worth a month after Matt and Sarah, on the fifteenth of October. Sarah and Matt, as well as all the Reeds attended the wedding. Rachel had used some of her 'dirty money' to buy a large house, but she never did collect the reward money from Matt.

Sarah had been right in her early suggestion that they may have started their family before they left Denton.

She went into labor on the 15th of June, exactly nine months after their wedding day and gave birth that evening to a perfect little girl they named Rachel, after her godmother, who had made the trip down to the ranch for the two weeks before the birth, despite her own advanced pregnancy.

Rachel gave birth to a son just two months and four days after her goddaughter had arrived. She and Jake, with no surprise to anyone, named him Matthew.

Having Mike and Maggie and their children so close made the separation from her sisters and parents much easier to bear for Sarah. She and Maggie became closer than Sarah had even been with her sisters.

Maggie, in keeping with her own timetable, had just one more child two years after the birth of her last, another girl they named Sarah.

But once a year, when the Texas sun was bearing down, the Little family, no matter how many there were, would make the trip to north of Denton and reunite with the families of all the small ranchers, especially with the Sandersons and the Reeds. John and Mary Sanderson had adopted Matt into their hearts as the son they never had.

But the highlight of their annual visit was the dance held in the basement of the church where Matt and Sarah were married.

Each dance would begin the same way.

The dance floor would be empty, with everyone lining around the sides. Matt would lead his still perfect bride onto the floor and put his right hand on her waist as she put her left on his shoulder. He would look down and smile, gaze into those incredible green eyes and his wife would smile up at him.

They would stay frozen for just a few moments, as if time itself seemed to pause, then they would start to glide across the floor as the first notes of *The Blue Danube* floated through the hall.

1	Rock Creek	12/26/2016
2	North of Denton	01/02/2017
3	Fort Selden	01/07/2017
4	Scotts Bluff	01/14/2017
5	South of Denver	01/22/2017
6	Miles City	01/28/2017
7	Hopewell	02/04/2017
8	Nueva Luz	02/12/2017
9	The Witch of Dakota	02/19/2017
10	Baker City	03/13/2017
11	The Gun Smith	03/21/2017
12	Gus	03/24/2017
13	Wilmore	04/06/2017
14	Mister Thor	04/20/2017
15	Nora	04/26/2017
16	Max	05/09/2017
17	Hunting Pearl	05/14/2017
18	Bessie	05/25/2017
19	The Last Four	05/29/2017
20	Zack	06/12/2017
21	Finding Bucky	06/21/2017
22	The Debt	06/30/2017
23	The Scalawags	07/11/2017
24	The Stampede	07/20/2017
25	The Wake of the Bertrand	07/31/2017
26	Cole	08/09/2017
27	Luke	09/05/2017
28	The Eclipse	09/21/2017
29	A.J. Smith	10/03/2017
30	Slow John	11/05/2017
31	The Second Star	11/15/2017
32	Tate	12/03/2017
33	Virgil's Herd	12/14/2017
34	Marsh's Valley	01/01/2018
35	Alex Paine	01/18/2018

36	Ben Gray	02/05/2018
37	War Adams	03/05/2018
38	Mac's Cabin	03/21/2018
39	Will Scott	04/13/2018
40	Sheriff Joe	04/22/2018
41	Chance	05/17/2018
42	Doc Holt	06/17/2018
43	Ted Shepard	07/13/2018
44	Haven	07/30/2018
45	Sam's County	08/15/2018
46	Matt Dunne	09/10/2018
47	Conn Jackson	10/05/2018
48	Gabe Owens	10/27/2018
49	Abandoned	11/19/2018
50	Retribution	12/21/2018
51	Inevitable	02/04/2019
52	Scandal in Topeka	03/18/2019
53	Return to Hardeman County	04/10/2019

Made in the USA
Columbia, SC
24 April 2019